CW00869187

REVENGE OF THE DEMON

WARRIORS OF THE MYSTIC MOONS BOOK 3

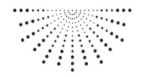

S.A. LAUGHLIN

Copyright (C) 2021 S.A. Laughlin

Layout design and Copyright (C) 2021 by Next Chapter

Published 2021 by Shadow City– A Next Chapter Imprint

Edited by Sandra Laughlin

Cover art by CoverMint

This book is a work of fiction. Names, characters, places, and incidents are the product of the author's imagination or are used fictitiously. Any resemblance to actual events, locales, or persons, living or dead, is purely coincidental.

All rights reserved. No part of this book may be reproduced or transmitted in any form or by any means, electronic or mechanical, including photocopying, recording, or by any information storage and retrieval system, without the author's permission.

BOOKS BY S. A. LAUGHLIN

Science Fantasy Series

Book 1: *Mystic Moon Warriors*
Book 2: *Uncharted Land Between*
Book 3: *Revenge of the Demon*
Book 4: *Sands of Dragon Fire*

Romance/Adventure

Hidden Between the Lines

Historical Novel

Fly Toward Death

My lovely daughters and granddaughter

ACKNOWLEDGMENTS

Thank you to one of my readers (who has become a dear friend), Ronald Dyer, Retired USAF Master Sergeant, Security Police/Forces and First Sergeant for giving me the great suggestions about the Rukkhas. FYI Mr. Dyer is a fantastic up and coming Fantasy writer.

CHAPTER ONE

A strong wind reached the crescent-shaped sails of the flying ship causing it to move further away from the portal to Mystovia. Etheria brushed a tear away. "I cannot see her anymore. They have entered the portal to Mystovia. I miss Kess so much already. To have found my daughter after all these years." She shook her head slowly, "And to lose her again."

"No. You haven't lost her," Jhondar patted her shoulder. "We shall see them soon. This has been a difficult time for all of us," his voice faltered for a moment. "Mac, my son. Mac," his voice softened.

"Stop it you two," Saaz snapped. "You have not lost them. You will join them in Mystovia as quickly as you can. I mean, look at you two. You are covered in what did they call it?"

"Silvery stuff," Etheria gave a short laugh.

"Yes, that was what they called it." Saaz moved to the side of the ship and looked down at the passing landscape below. "There has to be a way to get there quickly. The Zetch will become extremely powerful by possessing the Skull of Semetter."

"Yes," Jhondar replied. "Enough power that he may destroy all of Mystovia."

Etheria sighed. "We have to wait two weeks before the ectoplasm wears off."

"Maybe the Plexias can help you with your...," Saaz was interrupted by a shout from one of the crew.

"Look there!" A warrior yelled and pointed to a massive swarm of huge insect-like creatures flying directly toward them. "Rukkhars!"

Jhondar grabbed his shield and sword that were on deck and ordered the sails furled. "They are coming in fast."

Etheria and Saaz pulled arrows from their sheaf and waited until the dangerous creatures got close enough to hit.

The Rukkhars wings were beating so fast they could barely be seen against their plump, dark purple and yellow bodies

"Their stingers are readied for fighting," Etheria observed. "There so many this time."

Jhondar signaled for the warriors to be ready to fight.

"Wait," Etheria yelled. "It was something one of the teens mentioned. In their world to keep insects away, they would use smoke." She thought for a moment, "Yes. The ship's machines create a very foul and thick smoke."

"We usually vent them out through the bottom vents. We can try to open the top vents," Jhondar shouted. "If it doesn't work the smoke may work anyway to our advantage, because the Rukkhars will have to fly in low to try and find us."

"I hope it works," Saaz's grimaced at the foul-smelling, smoke that quickly filled the deck.

They watched in stunned silence as the swarm of Rukkhars suddenly veered away from their ship and headed back toward the mountains.

"I don't know if the smoke or the smell," Etheria laughed and choked.

"Or, something else," Jhondar said stoically.

———

Kess stood quietly near the open portal to Mystovia. Her heart was heavy, and her brown eyes filled with tears at having to leave her mother after just finding her in the Land Between. She waved one last time as her mother's flying ship pulled away and headed back to their domed city of Kelador. "Well, I only hope the next two weeks go quickly," Kess spoke solemnly.

"It will, cousin," Mac said looking down at Kess. "But I'd like to go back to the Land Between and get to know more about what happens in there when technology mixes with magic. And to check up on our friends."

"Yes, they were so excited to stay. They loved the Land Between." Kess nodded slightly.

"And, add the fact they were each given their own apartments" Mac smiled.

Kess's smiled faded. "But I am afraid they don't know all the dangers that our roaming around in there."

"They will be advised of any dangers," Mac said trying to reassure Kess.

"Yes, Jhondar said we are not to worry about them. And as for Brody, he is still trying to accept all of the weird and strange things that had happened." Doc chuckled.

"Okay, change of subject: What is taking them so long?" Mac asked staring hard at the open portal in front of him.

"Mac they are checking things out to make sure it is safe for us to enter Mystovia," Kess reached over and touched his forearm. "Kybil and Sirel are seasoned warriors, and they have Maaleah one of the most powerful Sabbot witches with them. Not to mention Rakmor who is a clever and knowledgeable Sorcerer."

"Mac is right," Doc shook his head and crossed his arms. "They have been gone a long time."

"*You not worry. I stayed back because I am a powerful dragon.*" Drago sent a telepathic message for everyone to hear. "*I stay and protect my friends until we go through the portal.*" His long, spiked, red tail switched about but did not touch anyone.

"Dat's right," Yaneth agreed. The Dwarger patted the hilt of his sword with his hand. "We stayed back wid da little dragon. We tought dis be a good idea." He wiped his large bulbous nose with the cuff of his sleeve. The yellow feather on his Peter Pan hat began to move from the wind filtering into the tunnel. His deep-set lavender eyes focused on Nordaal standing next to him, "Right?"

"Yep, we tought dis be a good idea," Nordaal replied happily. He looked at his friend Yaneth for a moment then broke into a huge grin showing his large, unevenly spaced teeth.

Mac stopped and looked at the two Dwarger for a minute. He shrugged slightly. "I have to ask. Does everyone resemble you two where you come from?" His frame towered over the shorter Dwargers. "Just curious cause you two look so much alike."

"Nope, da females, dey looks different," Nordaal said.

"Good come back," Doc's dark-brown face broke into a grin.

Mac laughed and then his attention turned back to the portal that his friends had gone through. He narrowed his blue-gray eyes and leaned forward, straining to see any movement. "Why can't we see clearly through the opening?"

After a couple more unnerving moments, Kybil appeared in front of the portal door and motioned for everyone to come through.

Kess was the first one through the portal and was immediately greeted by the cold biting winds. "Are we sure this is Mystovia?" She asked brushing her light-brown hair from her eyes.

Kybil smiled, "Yes. I am positive." The hood to his cape blew down as the cold wind whipped his shoulder-length blond hair around his face.

Doc stepped through the portal joining Kess. "Say this is really cold. How long were we gone? What happened to Summer? Where are we?" Doc worked feverishly to try and pull his cape from being blown around by the fierce winds.

"We are back in Mystovia," Maaleah's dark-blue face lit up as she sighed with relief.

Drago and Mac were the next ones through the portal.

4

"Well, we're all here safe and sound," Mac looked around him at the frozen terrain, as the sleet and cold wind beat at his face. "Whoa, did we cross over into Siberia?"

Nordaal and Yaneth came through last. They took a deep breath of air and broke into huge grins as they looked around them. "We be back," Yaneth said happily.

The closing of the portal made a loud shushing sound before it snapped shut. They turned around just as the portal between the Land Between and Mystovia disappeared completely.

Kess grabbed the hood of her cape to keep it from blowing off. "Say, what's up with this weather?"

"Yeah, no wonder we couldn't see too clearly through the portal," Mac hollered against the wind.

"Unfortunately, this is what the weather should be," Kybil stood somberly next to Kess. "We have to go that way." He pointed beyond the giant trees surrounding them. "I can just make out the faint outline of the mountains."

"I can't see my hands in front of my face, let alone the faint outline of a mountain," Doc grumbled.

"Well, you can't miss these trees; that's for sure," Mac said looking at the massive trees all around them.

"I'll say. Those are the biggest, fattest trees I have ever seen," Doc exclaimed. His short, thin frame struggled to walk against the high winds.

Kybil saw the difficulty Doc was having against the ferocious wind and nodded toward Nordaal and Yaneth. "Would you two, please help Doc?"

Without missing a step, the two muscular Dwargers took Doc's arms and began to walk with Doc safely between them. "We hold on ta ya little doctor," Yaneth's arm tightened around Doc's thin arm.

"I'm getting squished with every step," Doc mumbled.

Kybil linked his arm with Kess to keep her from being blown away as well, while Rakmor linked his arm with Maaleah. Each step was becoming more laborious as they traveled through the forest.

"I know somebody knows where we're going, but how much longer?" Doc's teeth chattered uncontrollably.

"We have quite a way to go. You can see the peak of the mountain where Castle Remat sits from here," Rakmor's hand came out from his cape and pointed toward the barely visible mountain range.

"I can't see anything. I think my eyeballs are frozen." Doc quipped as the two Dwargers guided him through the biting winds.

"Say, Rakmor. Can't you just plop us in the castle with some of your magic?" Kess asked.

"No. I don't have any of that potion left," he shrugged.

"Darn it," Kess's head whipped around as she looked at the surrounding terrain. "Say, we're not in Evoos territory, are we? I'd rather not run into those hairy, cannibalistic creatures."

"No. We are closer to the Xelrils Mountains," Kybil said.

"That help ya any, Kess?" Mac laughed and smiled down at her. "Being that you're so familiar with all of Mystovia," he said sarcastically.

"You have no fear of being lost," Sirel said matter of fact. "We are all familiar with this territory," she stated, easily keeping in step with Mac's long stride.

"Okay. Fair enough," Kess said. She peered around Kybil to speak with Rakmor walking next to him. "Why didn't the portal open near the Evoos this time?"

"I was wondering the same thing," Rakmor said and shrugged.

The two Dwargers left Doc alone as they moved to stand next to Kybil. "Yep, dat be da way ta go." Yaneth pointed to the mountain range.

"Yep," Nordaal repeated, "Dat be da way ta go."

Kess smiled at the two Dwargers, who were half-ogre and half-dwarf. The only way she could tell them apart when she first met them was the feather on top of their Peter Pan-type hats; Yaneth's was yellow and Nordaal's was red.

"Not that I'm complaining or anything," Doc grabbed the edge of his cape and tried to yank it closed. "However, if I don't get warm soon, my face is going to be blue instead of dark brown." He looked at the little red dragon next to him. "Say, Drago, you wouldn't happen to be able to control that fire-breathing of yours and get a fire going, could ya?"

"*I could try*," Drago's telepathic thoughts were sent to everyone.

Maaleah's brow furrowed slightly. "Wait, Drago. Even if you started a regular fire the winds and rain would dampen it for sure. And it may even let those we do not want to find us, find us."

Rakmor broke into a big smile as he pointed toward a group of trees. "Look! I believe we are in luck. It is a Dak tree. Hurry."

"That tree? Which tree?" Kess wiped the sleet out of her eyes.

"Yep," Nordaal.

"Yep, what?" She asked the Dwarger walking behind her.

"Dak be right dere," Nordaal pointed to a huge tree off to their right.

"Everyone, quick to the Dak tree," Kybil grabbed Kess's arm and raced toward the tree.

"Now, I know how you feel, Nordaal," Kess said being ushered toward a group of trees. "That tree? There are a whole bunch of them ahead." She was grateful that Kybil was leading her to the tree in question.

Rakmor held Maaleah's elbow as they followed behind. "Maaleah, do you have the Dak stones with you?"

"Are you serious? A Sabbot witch without a Dak stone is like an Evoos without hair." She replied stopping in front of a large tree. "This Dak will do nicely."

Rakmor called out to everyone in front of him, "We're stopping here for a while to warm up."

"What are we going to do - cuddle?" Kess asked looking at the open space with no shelter.

"Even this or that huge tree can't stop the wind from finding us," Mac stated confused.

Maaleah stopped in front of the massive tree. Quickly, she reached inside her cape and pulled out a pouch. Carefully, she dropped three little stones into the palm of her hand. After a few incantations, a thin golden line began to form on the tree. Swiftly, lines raced over the trunk of the tree to form the outline of a large door. A loud groan could be heard, as the door began to open at the base of the tree. Inside the entrance was a small platform, and a set of steps leading downward.

"I'll light the pathway down," Rakmor said brandishing a small stone in his hand. He said a few words and then blew on the stone. Rays of light filtered out lighting the small lanterns lining the walls of the passageway. Rakmor motioned for everyone to follow Maaleah. "I will come last because the doorway must be erased of all magic."

Wooden steps had been carved out that only one person at a time could traverse. The short steps twisted and turned down inside of the tree.

"No like steps," Drago mumbled to no one in particular.

Mac was surprised that the steps ended abruptly into a large, enclosed space. A soft, golden glow lit up the room.

"Wow!" Kess marveled at the girth of the room. It was large with wooden benches carved out of the tree roots. There were chair-like fixtures next to a roughly hewn table off to the side of a small fireplace. "Well, I'm certainly glad it was this tree."

"Nope." Nordaal shook his head and smiled. "Dis not dis. Dis be Dak."

"Huh?" Kess blinked several times as she stared at the Dwarger's toothy grin. "Are you getting this, Mac?"

"Nope," he shrugged. "They lost me with this and that a long time ago." He stood with his hands on his hips. "But hey, this is some hideout."

"How's about getting a fire started." Doc's teeth chattered, as he looked longingly at the little fireplace. "And I don't give a puppy's puddle if it's this tree or that tree."

Kybil laughed as he pushed one side of his cape away, "It is spelled D-A-K. It is a Dak tree."

"Ohh," said Mac and Kess simultaneously as they nodded in understanding.

"Maaleah," Rakmor eased toward her. "How about starting a warm fire?"

"Wait!" Mac looked anxiously toward Rakmor, "Won't the tree catch fire?"

"No." Maaleah's blue face broke into a wide grin. She walked over to the open hearth and threw in a few crystals that immediately erupted into a glowing, warm fire.

"Won't the smoke or magic send a signal to whoever might be out there? You know demons and such." Kess moved closer to the fire, holding her hands out to catch its warmth.

"They would have to have extremely strong magic to find us down here." Rakmor sat on one of the cutout chairs, "besides, I put a spell blocker on this place." He folded his arms across his chest and smiled, looking pleased with himself.

"I know you are a great sorcerer, but can't they see and smell the smoke from the fireplace?" Mac sat down next to Sirel on one of the benches.

"Well, they could have, except this is the Fire of Night," Maaleah said.

"Remember the cave?" Doc looked at Mac. "You know, where we met the Wereshadows."

Mac nodded. "Yeah, now I remember."

Maaleah squatted down next to the blazing fire. "No smoke, no smell, but lots of warmth. Having a Sabbot Witch traveling with you is a smart thing. Not to mention having a great sorcerer like Rakmor," she smiled smugly. The light from the fire cast shadows around the room, almost making Maaleah's deep-blue skin appear black.

"Magic," Kess and Mac said at the same time.

"Did you two speak the same thing at the same when you were partners as police officers, too," Doc asked. "Yep," they said. "Geesh," Doc rolled his eyes, shook his head, and chuckled. The room quickly became warm and comfortable for the frozen group. They sat there quietly soaking up the heat.

Sirel broke the silence. "I wonder why we weren't greeted by other warriors to escort us." Sirel leaned around Mac to address Rakmor. "The sorcerers and the others would have sensed our coming through and sent us help, in case we would have need."

"Oh, no!" Maaleah spoke solemnly. "I sense trouble heading our way."

"Yes, I feel something, too," Rakmor got up and walked to the fire.

"I dun't feel someding," Nordaal looked quizzically at Maaleah.

Rakmor pushed his hands nearer to the heat of the fire. Deep in thought, he turned to Maaleah. "I am going to need your help." He walked back to the small table and stood in front of her. "Spell of View?"

"Yes. Do you have it?" Maaleah asked.

He nodded.

"Okay, you use the spell to see what is out there, and I will use a spell to make sure they do not sense your magic."

Mac listened to Maaleah and Rakmor and shook his head. "Do you understand them, Kess?" Mac whispered to her.

"Are you kidding me? Even with our mind-meld with the sorcerers, I'm as lost as a pigeon in a chicken coop," she whispered back.

"We have to time this perfectly." Rakmor pulled a pouch from under his cape and poured the silvery contents on the table. He closed his eyes and began the incantation.

Maaleah pulled out two glistening stones. She muttered a few words and squeezed the stones tightly in her hands before dropping them in the middle of the silvery sand on the table.

Slowly, a misty glow began to form on the table. It began to weave a kaleidoscope of colors until they blended to form images from above. "Well, it looks like the wind and sleet have let up," Kybil said. He studied the images forming on the table. "And that may be the trouble you are sensing. It looks like there are people headed our way."

"Who are they? Friend or foe?" Mac asked leaning closer to the blurry vision on the table.

"I can barely make out their forms," Sirel stared intently at the images.

"Let's go out and see," Mac said.

"No, we must stay here and wait to see if they are human or demons. It could be a trap." Sirel stated.

"Not just another pretty face, eh!" Mac glanced over at her. He thought the word pretty was such a gross understatement for this Ankhourian warrior. He never tired of looking at her beautiful face, her golden hair and blue eyes, and her lithe, well-proportioned body. It still amazed him that she was almost as tall as his six-foot-four frame.

Everyone at the table watched in fascination as the scene unfolded in front of them. Demons were chasing a small group of humans. The fleeing humans were headed straight toward them. The small group inside the tree watched helplessly as the demons closed in.

"Anybody want to join the party outside?" Mac moved toward the steps of the Dak tree.

Rakmor called out to him. "Mac! Wait! I see horses."

"Horses?" Mac questioned ambling back to the table.

"Yes. Horses that would have come up behind us," Kess pointed to another vision coming into view on the tabletop.

"Well," Mac asked restlessly. "Are they the good guys or the bad guys?"

"Ah," Rakmor smiled. "Those on horseback are the good guys. Wait until they pass us, then we can join them. And, before you ask me ..."

"Yep, go it." Mac snapped his fingers toward Rakmor. "Don't want to be trampled."

"Yes," Rakmor smile.

CHAPTER TWO

$\mathcal{T}$he woods came alive with Indian and Ankhourian warriors on horseback. They came in at a fast pace, swords drawn, and the sound of war cries filled the frigid air. They did not slow down as they raced past the small group of humans being chased and charged into the demon horde.

"Okay," Kybil said. "Let's go."

The door to the Dak tree opened automatically. "*No steps!*" Drago said as he flew up the steps and out the door.

Mac and Sirel were right behind him as they raced outside. Mac was not surprised to see that everyone had followed him to join in the fracas. His amulet was bright and hot against his skin.

"Doc! Maaleah!" Kybil turned and shouted at them. "Get back inside!" They started to protest when he yelled again, "Now!"

Reluctantly, Doc, and Maaleah turned and headed back down the tree stairs. The door groaned as it shut.

Swords held high and blood-curdling screams pouring from their lips, Mac and the others charged toward the attacking demons. Quickly, they reached the warriors on horseback who were already in heavy combat.

The demons were grotesque creatures of various sizes and shapes. Most of them had large fangs that dripped white foam, and their long, bony arms ended in sharp claws that almost touched the ground. Their foul smell of decay and rotting flesh permeated the air.

Several demons advanced toward Kess: the hilt of their swords alive with writhing snakeheads. Drago saw the demons charge toward Kess and immediately sent out a burst of fire that destroyed them on contact. He spotted a group headed for Mac: They met with the same fate. Drago flew into the air and created a fiery path that engulfed all demons in its wake. Several times he dove down letting his claws and teeth tear at the demons.

Kess's sword the 'Protector' worked feverishly to dispatch the advancing demons. Her sword never missed its mark bringing down those that came too close. A demon charged at Kess. She turned to see another demon coming at her from behind. In one swift movement, she jumped out of their path, as the two startled demons impaled each other.

Kybil stepped over a fallen demon to place himself nearer to Kess. His sword stopped a blow aimed at her and with lightning speed, took out an arrow from the quiver on his back and impaled a demon advancing on his flank.

The fighting was too close for Rakmor to use his magic. He took up a position on the other side of Kess, dispatching demons with a long sword in one hand and a smaller sword in his other hand.

Sirel and Mac fought side-by-side hacking their way through the throng of demons. As they fought, they managed to keep a protective eye on each other, moving to strike down a demon not seen by the other.

An Ankhourian warrior's arrow killed a demon who had managed to sneak up behind Mac and Sirel. Just then, another demon jumped up behind the warrior on horseback. In one swift movement, she clasped her sword in both hands thrust it up and over her head impaling the demon seated behind her. It howled and fell lifelessly to the ground.

Yaneth and Nordaal cut through the demon horde like angry bulls, leaving a path of slain demons.

Suddenly, the demons, even though they greatly outnumbered the opposing fighters, began to retreat into the sparse trees of the forest.

Stunned, yet, relieved by the quick retreat, they watched until the demons were no longer visible. However, Mac's amulet continued to glow brightly.

"Why hasn't your talisman or my sword stopped glowing?" Kess asked confused.

"It may be that some of the demons are still alive," Rakmor shrugged. "So, be careful everyone."

"We'll check the perimeters for any surprise attacks," A Captain of the Ankhourian warriors said. She signaled to the other warriors on horseback to ride out and check for demons.

A fast check to make sure everyone was okay in their group brought a sigh of relief to Mac. "All accounted for on our side," he said.

A small group of humans came from around the trees and joined Mac and the others.

"You came as quite a surprise, and just in time." A tall, lanky male gasped. He bent over the hilt of his sword trying to regain his breath and eyed the little dragon warily.

"Is everyone all right?" Sirel's golden hair whipped about her face.

After catching his breath, the male stood up straight, sighed, and spoke calmly. "Thanks to all of you we are all well. I am called Olo. We are woodsmen and were in search of game. We have been forced to travel in large numbers to hunt because of the increased attacks of the demons. Unfortunately, we were attacked by the demons at the base of Wolf Mountain and have been fighting them ever since. Many of our friends were slaughtered."

"That is a long way from here," Sirel said. Mac watched her as she stood back and studied Olo's men.

Mac picked up on their uneasiness. "It's okay for now. Your men can relax. They won't be back for a while." Mac thought they were a mismatched group of men. Most of them were much shorter than Olo and kept looking around anxiously.

"You must be very tired and hungry. Would you like some food and warmth from a fire?" Kess addressed the men standing around fidgeting nervously with their swords. "It has been well protected from demons."

"No," Olo spoke quickly. "We have to get back to our families. We have been gone for a couple of days. I am sure they are worried. But thank you for the offer. I didn't catch your names."

"Oh, sorry, I am called Kess and this is Mac," she gestured toward Mac and continued with the names of the others in her group.

"If you like we can travel together," Rakmor wiped off the black blood from his sword on the cloak of a dead demon. "We are headed toward Castle Remat."

"We are not going that far," Olo said.

"Where are you headed?" Mac asked, wiping his bloodied sword on a cloak of another dead demon.

"Our homes are near Port Zanadur," Olo responded, nodding in its direction.

"That is in the opposite direction we are headed," Rakmor shook his head, looked to the others in his party, and continued. "But we can go with you as an escort if you like."

Everyone in Rakmor's group nodded in affirmation. "Nordaal. Yaneth," Rakmor motioned to the two Dwargers," please get Doc and Maaleah. We are ready to move out."

"Yep," Yaneth said as Nordaal followed him to the Dak tree.

"There are more in your party?" Olo inquired.

"Yes," Kess said. "As you can see, we can protect you quite well from the demons. There is a lot of powerful magic in this group. In fact, you haven't even met our friend, Maaleah, a very powerful Sabbot witch."

"And let us not forget about Drago. He is an Arega dragon. He may be small, right now, but he is extremely dangerous. He helped us dispatch a powerful master demon. I believe it was called a Zetche." Mac interjected.

Olo, let out an involuntary gasp. "A Zetche?" It took him a moment to regain his composure. "They have not been in Mystovia for many years." He looked at Drago and smiled, "This little dragon killed a Zetche? That is very impressive. How could such a little dragon kill such a powerful demon?"

"Well, let's just say that this Zetche tried to possess Drago from the inside, and everything got reversed. Anyway, with him and the Ankhourian and Indian warriors, whom you just saw in action, you will be quite safe." Mac said.

"We didn't even use our talismans. If the fighting had continued we could have destroyed those demons instantly." Kess looked at Mac's amulet and her sword. "Strange, why are they still glowing?"

"Strange? Why is it glowing?" Mac asked rubbing his chin.

"Even stranger. I keep waiting for Bilbo or Frodo to show up and claim the sword," Kess shook her head and sighed.

"Who?" Mac turned to look at Kess.

"They're characters in a . . . never mind I'll explain later," she laughed.

"Yes, they are both still glowing," Rakmor said ignoring the conversation between Kess and Mac. "Olo, I think you and your men had better get away from here. I don't think all the demons are quite dead."

Olo quickly looked around at the demons on the ground. "That is a possibility." He took one last look at the bodies of the demons and shrugged. "The other demons left in quite a hurry. They must have figured out they would need reinforcements to attack such a powerful group."

"I sure hope they don't return with reinforcements," Kess said. "But if they do it may prove to be too dangerous for you and your men to travel without support."

"Again, we offer our assistance," Kybil replied sincerely.

"You may need all of your protective powers for you and your friends on your journey. Besides, we have learned a few tricks to keep from being detected by demons or anyone." Olo's hand went up and the others in his group sheathed their swords and gave a slight bow. "We must leave immediately before they return. Thank you again, and we shall never forget what you have done. We shall be ready to repay it."

Olo and his men turned and hurried through the woods toward Port Zanadur.

"Well," Kess watched in amazement as the men disappeared at a fast clip. "At that pace, they'll get there before Doc, and Maaleah gets here."

"It's still cold. Brrr," Doc rubbed his hands together as he walked toward Mac.

"Wait!" Maaleah hushed everyone. "Ah-ha!"

"Wait? Ah-ha?" Doc shook his head. "For crying-out-loud woman, what are you ah-ha-ing about."

"Look," Kess moved to stand next to Kybil. "It's the Ankhourian and Tahotay warriors returning."

"Oh, boy," Doc reached behind and rub his backside. "This is gonna hurt." He watched with interest as the other warriors rode their horses among the dead demons. "What are they doing?" Doc asked.

"We are checking to make sure the demons have been dispatched and will not get up in a surprise attack behind us." The Captain halted her horse in front of them.

"Whew, they are all dead now," Kess said looking at her sword and the talisman around Mac's neck. "Your amulet and my sword aren't glowing or whatever they do."

"We saw humans being chased by the demons." The Captain's red-orange hair was tightly braided and held by a coronet. "We came as quickly as we could. I hope there are no injuries." She raised her clenched, right fist and snapped it quickly against her chest in an Ankhourian warrior salute to Kybil.

"We are all fine." Kybil returned her salute. "It is good to see you Captain Glynna. How did your warriors fare?"

"We only had a few minor injuries. And it is good to see you again as well Prince Kybil." Then, Captain Glynna spotted Sirel and dismounted from her horse greeting Sirel with a grin and a hug. "Sister, it is good to see you again."

"And you as well," Sirel said warmly.

Kess sighed and smiled. "Glad you came to help rescue them."

"Them? We were traveling to meet up with you." Glynna said. "We thought it was all of you being chased. Who were they?"

"Don't know, except they were woodsmen and humans," Kybil said.

"Humans? Other than you?" Glynna queried.

"Yes, they were the ones the demons were chasing, and you rushed in to help," Kybil stepped back to make more room for the rest of the warriors to join the group.

"They must have just blended with the group." Captain Glynna's deep green eyes scanned the bodies of the slain demons. "I certainly hope we did not dispatch one of them by mistake."

"They are hunters, not fighters. Maybe they stayed away from the fighting," Kess said.

"That would be a good assessment," Kybil stated.

Mac paused and looked at the dead demons strewn on the ground. "I don't see any human forms. Well, it appears you all did well."

"Did well? That is an understatement," Kess eyed the weary warriors. "You all look exhausted, and in need of some food and drink."

"It is a great distance we had to cover to try to meet you at this opening," Glynna said. "We were waiting in an area along the Evoos border of Mystovia when the Imperial Sorceress Cedwynna sent a message that they sensed the portal had opened up near here." Glynna shivered slightly.

"Mercy," Maaleah gestured toward the Dak tree. "You are

freezing and . . ." Her sentence was cut short by the sound of horses racing toward them.

"The scouts have returned." Glynna pointed toward the approaching riders.

Four riders rode in fast, each from a different direction. An Indian rider reached them first and dismounted his horse quickly. "They are advancing, hundreds, maybe thousands, of them from the North," he reported. The three other scouts confirmed the same thing from their assigned direction. Masses of demons were heading for them from all four sides.

"So, I take it; we're surrounded," Kess said.

"Yes, they are converging now, as we speak," an Ankhourian rider said as she slid off her horse.

"Even all your magic could not stop them," another Indian rider spoke out.

"Did you happen to pass some hunters on your way here?" Kess looked at the faces of each rider.

"There must have been ten men headed that way," Mac pointed to his left.

"I saw no signs of anyone," an Elven warrior said. "That's the way I came."

"Maybe they switched directions. Did any of you see human hunters?" Kess asked the other riders.

They all shook their heads and said they had not seen anyone.

"That man, Olo, said they had become very good at hiding from the demons. Let's hope they are clever enough to avoid them." Mac rubbed his chin absent-mindedly.

Maaleah and Rakmor exchanged a knowing look of concern and turned toward Kybil, who was watching them.

Kybil nodded, "We will have to take our chances down in the Dak trees."

"Umm," Doc reached over and quickly grabbed Maaleah's arm. "There are about fifty warriors, and us. How in blue blazes do you think we are all going to fit in that little space? And, what about the horses? There's no space for them in that little room, let alone all these warriors."

"No, there is not." She replied stoically.

"So, the horses are supposed to stay out here to freeze or be killed. And, I may not be great in battle strategy, but wouldn't that be a dead giveaway in letting the demons know where we are?" He shook his head in confusion.

"You are worried about the horses. That is a good trait. You know you are really very sweet," Maaleah laughed as she pulled a pouch from her cape pocket and looked over at Rakmor. "We have to do something so we can get out of harm's way up here. Unfortunately, there is much to be afraid of down there."

"Huh?" Doc said startled by her comment. "Down where?"

Maaleah did not hear Doc's question as she visually began to scan the area. She smiled and pointed to a huge open area between the trees. "That will be perfect." She paused for a moment in deep thought. "Don't you find it rather strange that this is one of the potions Etheria kept for so many years in the Land Between and thought to give it to us before we left?"

"She may have sensed something. I mean she was very insistent that we take this potion and a couple of other ones." Rakmor pushed his cape to the back so it would not encumber his next movements. "Maaleah and I have some work to do," Rakmor pulled out another pouch from his cape. "There will be sufficient room for all of us to enter." No one heard him mutter, "I only hope we can escape the deadly creatures down there."

CHAPTER THREE

"*B*ring your horses and stand behind Rakmor and me," Maaleah ordered.

Everyone moved away from the small clearing, as Maaleah and Rakmor began to work their magic.

A hazy mist appeared in front of them hovering for a moment and then shot through the trees disappearing into the forest.

"Okay, that's done." Maaleah's shoulders heaved as she moved to the large open space and began to spread sparkling sand onto the ground in front of them.

After she was done Rakmor threw several small, glowing stones up in the air. The stones landed with an exceptionally loud thud on the ground in the middle of the sparkling sand. Immediately lights exploded all around the area, sizzling and popping until they finally stopped.

Suddenly, the earth began to shake under their feet, and a loud groaning sound seemed to come from all around them.

At first, a small crack appeared in the solid earth in front of them. It began rapidly to expand as the ground began to shift and lift at the same time.

One final great heave and the earth opened and began to roll itself up like a rug on either side of the opening. Massive roots moved and undulated like giant snakes. They intertwined until they formed a network that braced the sides of the opening. After everything stopped moving, a large earth-ramp appeared leading down, deep underground, with just barely enough room for a horse to walk under.

"Lead the horses down first and you will find some water for them." Maaleah pointed to the path leading underground. "The entrances to the Dak trees are all interconnected. You will find an open area large enough for your horses."

"Well, I'll be," Doc walked down the wide ramp into a vast arena-type opening.

"Will the demons find us down here?" Kess ducked under a large hanging root.

"No, they will not." Kybil stepped aside as a rider led his horse to drink from one of the small pools of water sprinkled throughout the underground refuge.

"Wow," Kess could not believe her eyes at the sight of the huge cavern. Enormous roots of all sizes twisted down into the earth creating support columns throughout the entire expanse.

"This is something you would have to see to believe," Mac strolled next to Sirel as they entered the underground shelter.

Once the last warrior and horse entered the chambers, Maaleah and Rakmor produce a shiny, bright stone, said a few words, and the earth began to groan again. The roots twisted and turned to pull the earth ramp back into its folds until the large opening was sealed, and all evidence of it ever being there had disappeared.

Rakmor used his powers to illuminate their surroundings, and a spell so that no one would be able to detect his magic or any other magical signatures. "Thank you, Etheria," he said softly referring to Kess's mother who had furnished him with the potions.

"Maaleah," Rakmor walked toward the Sabbot witch. "I have

taken care of the lighting, and disabled the ability to detect magic, but I don't have anything to quiet the horses, just in case."

She took out another pouch and smiled while she whispered a soothing incantation. "Done," she said.

Everyone gathered in a large area of the cavern to talk and catch up on what had just happened when Kybil jumped up startling everyone. "Listen," he said.

There was complete silence as the ground above them reverberated loudly. Loose dirt fell on everyone in small and large clumps. Quickly, Maaleah took out the stones that enabled them to see what was happening above.

The warrior scouts were right; the demons came back and in great force. Skinny looking creatures with four legs, black hairy bodies, and long, narrow noses were sniffing the ground overhead. They almost resemble a canine, except for the large sharp fangs jutting out from their lower jaws, and one eye centered in the middle of their forehead.

Maaleah let out a little gasp and ended the sight. "My magic has sensed very powerful magic up there," she whispered. "I do not think it could detect us, but I did not want to take any unnecessary chances."

The earth shook overhead for a short while and then there was silence.

"It worked, Rakmor. They're gone," Maaleah chuckled.

"What worked?" Kess asked.

"We created a false trail of scent to mislead them, just in case they brought the Taarcers." Rakmor shook his head. "Good thing we did."

"Taarcers? What are Taarcers?" Doc queried.

"They are demons who can follow someone's trail by their scent," Sirel answered.

"Won't they smell us down here?" Kess asked worriedly.

"No, because we made a false trail that leads right into the Evoos and Snagar territories," Maaleah smiled mischievously.

"Captain Glynna," Kybil called over the din created by the warriors talking to each other. "Distant Runner, if you two would join us and tell us what has been happening."

"The demons have not been very active, until just recently," Distant Runner said. The leader of the Indian warriors stood in front of the group rubbing his hands to try to warm them up.

"It seems the demons are on the rise again," Mac said trying not to stare at Sirel standing next to him.

"I wonder why?" Kess asked leaning up against a thick, sturdy root.

"Actually, we have not encountered any demons until today," Captain Glynna placed one leg on a short, wooden stump.

"That woodsman, Olo, said the demons attacked him and his men at the base of Wolf Mountain. And, that they have been attacking them in the mountains for a while. What have you heard about it?" Mac asked.

"Hmm," Glynna tilted her head. "This is the first I have heard about demons attacking anyone since we fought the Jomkobi, and that Smyith creature."

"What about you, Distant Runner? Have you encountered any demons or heard of any attacks?" Kybil asked the Indian brave.

"No, I have not heard of any attacks, but if it happened in Wolf Mountain, we would not have heard, especially if it has just begun," he shrugged.

"Yes, he is right about that," Glynna dropped her leg off the log stump onto the soft, damp earth. "If something were going on in Wolf Mountain we wouldn't know."

Mac scratched his head absent-mindedly. He leaned forward perplexed.

"It's just all of sudden there are all these demons on the prowl again."

Kess sighed and slumped back against the root lazily. "Why don't we try to figure it out later? Suddenly, I'm getting sleepy. Can we find a comfy Dak tree and get some sleep?"

"Umm, actually, no," Kybil winced and looked at everyone around him. "We have to get moving and quickly. We have escaped the demons from above, but there are a lot of nasty things down here we have to avoid."

"What kind of nasty things?" Kess pulled away from the root and glanced over at Mac. He rolled his eyes and gave her a quirky smile.

"Groglemytes for one," Rakmor spoke hurriedly.

"I can relate. I've had some really groggy nights myself," Doc yawned and placed his hand over his mouth.

"It is Grog-le-mytes," Maaleah pronounced it very slowly for Doc.

"Oh," Doc shrugged. "Whatever, as Kess would say."

"It has been told that there are creatures down here that devour anyone who comes in contact with them," Rakmor said matter-of-factly.

"What?" Kess and Mac blurted out in total shock.

"It is just folklore," Maaleah looked at them and added, "At least we think it is folklore. Although it is said that people who come down here never return. Of course, it could also be the trolls."

"Well," Kybil said, "we had to figure out, which was the lesser of the evils; hundreds of demons, Groglemytes, or Trolls."

"Sabbots have been using the Dak trees for hundreds of years and have never had any problem with the Groglemytes. I have on occasion opened a door to the underground chambers myself. I always had a bright light, of course. I would walk around a little, usually looking for water. Sometimes I thought I heard little scuffling sounds around me, but I was never confronted by anything."

"Demons or Groglemytes? How did you two decide we would be better fighting the Groglemytes over the demons?" Mac crossed his arms and stared hard at Rakmor and Kybil.

"I suppose it was easier to fight the Grogle's because basically, no one has ever seen one, and hopefully with this large party, they will not attack us," Rakmor said with little confidence in his voice.

"Maaleah and I have attempted to put protective spells around all of us."

"Unfortunately," Maaleah gestured toward her cape pockets. "We're running out of magical potions. Etheria was kind enough to give us some potions. However, these capes can only hold so many, and we have had to use up a lot of it just in the few minutes we've been back in Mystovia."

"Do not worry, not need magic." Drago waddled next to Mac. *"They not bother any of us. Drago will be a big surprise."*

"That is wonderful, Drago, but just the same we must all be very careful and as quiet as we can be," Maaleah said softly. "We have a long journey, and the quicker we get started the better. Come along, Doc." She grabbed his arm and began walking around and through the enormous, twisted, roots of the Dak trees.

"Okay, I guess we're walking," Doc mumbled and went along with no resistance.

"For some reason, I like being in your company," Maaleah said to Doc but did not look over at him.

"Well," he tried to hide the smile creeping across his face. "I guess it's mutual." He patted her hand as they walked among the roots.

"Okay everybody let's clear this place as fast as we can." Kybil gave the signal to move out. "And stay as close together as possible."

"So, how far do we have to travel to get out of this place?" Mac walked next to Sirel and Kess.

"I think a couple of miles should do it," Rakmor said from behind. "Hopefully, that will get us far enough away that the demons will be gone."

"You didn't have to add the 'hopefully'," Kess looked over her shoulder at him. He just shrugged. She dropped back to walk with Kybil and Rakmor.

"Watch out." Kybil gently grabbed Kess's arm pulling her toward him, and away from the large, hanging tree root next to her head.

"The Sorceress Cedwynna may have heard more about the

attacks. It will be interesting to hear what she has to say about all of this." Sirel moved in closer to Mac.

"Dat's right," Nordaal adjusted his battered feathered cap that sat askew on top of his head.

"What be right?" Yaneth looked over at his friend.

"Everyding," Nordaal rolled his big lavender eyes and snorted through his large bulbous nose. "Everyding she said. I dink."

"Drago," Mac looked down at the little dragon walking next to him. "I want you to stay close to my side. I mean, I might need protection."

"*No, you mean you worry about Drago,*" he looked up at Mac. "*You do not have to worry. I will be okay. But I must remain alert, so I can see if Groglemytes are near.*" He turned his head around and spoke telepathically to Rakmor. "*I worry some because I could not read minds from demons aboveground.*"

"You don't have to worry about that, because we blocked magic going in or out so they wouldn't sense our magic from above," Rakmor smiled at the little dragon.

"*Oh, that is right. Drago forgot . . . I mean . . . I forgot.*" His waddle was a little more confident as he kept pace with Mac's long stride.

"I just love these adventures." Kess's voice dripped with sarcasm. "I can either be killed by demons, eaten by Trolls or Gargoyles or the whatever's."

"Look at the bright side," Mac called back to her. "If you get eaten by the Grogle's, at least you'll get your revenge by giving them a good case of indigestion."

Kess laughed and shook her head. "Gotta love him, no matter how annoying."

Everyone froze in place as the sound of an anguished scream directly above them reverberated loudly underground.

———

The Taarcers followed the scent of the humans at an incredible speed until the shrill voice of their Master caused them to halt.

"Stop!" Their Master screamed. "Stop!" All the demons froze as if one. They cringed low and turned to look at him.

"They have tricked me!" He shouted hysterically. The hood on his long, flowing black cape covered his face. "Magic," he spat. "My Taarcers have been led down the wrong path. Very clever with their magic. But they are not as clever as I, the Master. They must be hiding close to where we last saw them. Those puny humans with all their magic cannot escape me. Back!" He screamed.

"Yesss. Massster," his demon scouts bowed with a grand gesture.

"Back. Follow the path back. Divide yourselves into four groups again. I want you to search everything and everywhere as we head back. If they have tried to use a cloak of magic to hide them, I will sense it." His voice filled with anger. "When you find them leave no one alive."

They arrived close to the spot where Mac and the others had been. His demons and the Taarcers poured over the area, but their search came up empty. There was no sign of them anywhere.

A loud, piercing scream erupted from the tall creature in the black cape. "I will find you and hunt you down." Hatred spewed from his lips and a bright, red light glowed eerily from under the dark hood that shrouded his face. "You think you are so clever. You are not a match for me." Slowly, the red glow faded.

A cruel laugh escaped from his unseen face. "Not finding you right now is much better, for it would have been too easy, too fast. Not enough fun for me. One-by-one I shall destroy you and enjoy every moment of your pain and suffering."

Slowly, he raised his head and the hood on his cape flew back to expose the gray skin and piercing black eyes of a Zetche.

CHAPTER FOUR

*T*he blood-curdling scream echoed throughout the cavern. It almost broke the magic that was keeping the horses' calm. Quickly, the warriors steadied their anxious steeds.

"What was that?" Doc grabbed at his chest. "That scared the bageebees out of me."

"The demons have returned looking for us," Rakmor heaved a deep sigh of relief. "Perfect. Our magic blocked all signs of us and any of our magic. He probably roared because he thought he could sense our magic. He greatly underestimated us."

"Too bad you didn't have one to block its screams," Doc brushed off some dirt that fell from above. "I almost had to change my pants."

"How on earth did that scream reach us down here?" Kess asked catching her breath from the fright.

"I can't even imagine how earsplitting it must have sounded up there. Hey, Maaleah, does the Zetche know about the Dak trees?" Mac asked.

"Apparently not," Maaleah picked up her skirt and began walking faster through the maze of massive roots. "Good thing for us. Come on little man; let us travel at a faster pace. And everyone stay close and do not attempt to go around one of these trees unless you see Rakmor or me doing so. We do not want our magic to encompass the Groglemytes."

"You don't have to ask me twice," Doc hurried next to Maaleah. He looked nervously around him. "These Groggynites . . ."

"Groglemytes," Maaleah gently corrected him.

"Yeah, those things," he stumbled over a root protruding from the ground. "Oops, I'm okay," he said to no one in particular. "Do you have to worry about these underground creatures pulling you under when you're on top just walking along minding your own business?"

"No, I don't think so. There are myths and stories that they can, but I have never known or heard of anyone who has been pulled down." Rakmor said.

"Why would anyone want to come down here?" Kess walked swiftly next to Kybil.

"Well, it is an excellent place to rest and get out of any inclement weather or other dangers lurking about," Rakmor looked down at Kess. "And the one good thing about the root rooms that we stay in, the Groglemytes cannot penetrate the wood. So, you can sleep peacefully and not have to worry about them coming in and carrying you off. At least it has never happened."

"What do they look like?' Mac asked dodging a root that hung down too close to his head.

"Actually," Maaleah shrugged. "I cannot say. I have never seen one. I don't think anyone has ever seen a Groglemyte and lived to talk about it."

The magical light that Rakmor created kept flickering above their heads casting dark and eerie shadows between the twisted roots. The hollow footsteps of the warriors, and the clopping sound of their horses, added to the ominous atmosphere that surrounded them as they ventured deeper into the cavern. No one spoke as they guided their horses quietly through the damp, musky smelling tree roots. Occasionally, the light from the magical force field would travel across a mummified figure, some looked human, and some bore no resemblance to humans at all.

Suddenly, Kybil stopped and turned. He tried to peer into a group of large, twisted roots off to his right. "I hear something," his voice was barely audible, except to the warriors.

Silently, they pulled out their sword. Their horses, still under the magical spell, showed no signs of nervousness. A strange whining sound began to filter through the group.

"It sounds like a puppy crying," Kess looked into the shadowed spaces.

The farther they walked into the cavern the more the whining sounds increased. Something shadowy darted among the roots.

"Stay close so the magic encompasses you and your horses. Keep moving and watch for any breaches in the protective barrier," Kybil ordered.

Everyone picked up their pace as they cautiously moved through the roots. The warriors were on high alert: their swords readied for action. The whining became louder and faster.

"Oh, my goodness!" Kess turned to Kybil, her eyes wide with wonder. "Now it sounds like a baby crying. Is that possible?"

"No," Rakmor said walking behind her. "It might be a trick to lure unsuspecting victims into their trap."

More movements could be seen darting in and around the outlying roots, only to disappear into the darkness of its shadows. A strange gurgling sound began to reverberate through the cavern, along with the sound of a child crying. Just as quickly as the sounds had begun, they stopped.

The warriors kept moving. From out of the dark corners of the cavern, a rock about the size of a baseball was thrown at the travelers. The magic Maaleah and Rakmor placed on the group repelled it.

Soon, the air was filled with hundreds of rocks of all sizes hitting the magical force field. A pinging sound and a small flash of light appeared wherever the stones hit the shield. Some fell harmlessly to the ground while others ricocheted back at their unseen throwers.

"Rakmor," Kybil spoke barely above a whisper. "I'm hoping that these creatures can't understand us. But to be on the safe side we should communicate telepathically through Drago. We must let him know how long this magic will hold."

"*Rakmor already tells me 'not very long' maybe another half-hour, if we are lucky. Not sure how long half-hour be, but it does not sound like a long time.*" Drago moved out of the way of a horse's hoof. He continued. "*I can make trouble, great trouble for them if they try to attack. They do not like their roots being burnt.*"

"I am counting on that, my friend," Kybil looked down at the little, red, and gold dragon behind him and smiled. "*Drago, ask Rakmor when is it safe to go up-top?*" He asked.

There was a short pause and then Drago answered. "*Rakmor says maybe another hour or more to be sure that all the demons are gone from above,*" Drago waddled in quickstep next to Mac. "*I like to fly and see what I can see down here.*"

Kybil shook his head. "Thanks, Drago, but it would be too dangerous for you to do that alone and especially with no magic to protect you."

Mac instinctively ducked at a large stone thrown his way, only to have it reflected away from him. "Okay," he whispered, "seeing as we are going to be running out of magical stuff, what's the next plan?"

"I am working on it," Kybil murmured.

Just then several large stalagmites fell from above and landed on the top of the force field, and immediately began to sizzle and burn on the protective shield. The warriors jumped and held their swords ready for a possible breach. But the magical shield of protection was still holding up.

Kess looked down and saw a thin, hairy arm trying to get through the protective shield from underneath them. A strange humming sound began to form, and she could see sharp-pointed objects of the Groglemytes as they tried to burrow up. A few howls and the burrowing stopped from underneath them. "That should hold them for a while," Maaleah spoke quietly and placed another pouch back under her cloak. "But they are draining our power with every rock they throw."

"I know. The magic is starting to lose its power," Rakmor looked about him nervously.

"And no one knows we are down here, so the Calvary won't be charging in to help us either." Kess moved closer to Kybil.

"Who be Cal Vary?" Nordaal quickly lost interest in the shadowy figures stalking them in the dark shadows of the cavern.

"He must be some big warrior," Yaneth said.

"No, it's a whole bunch of warriors coming to the rescue," Kess smiled despite the situation.

"Dey must get confused a lot," Nordaal scratched his head. "Everybody has da same name of Cal."

"How dey know who be calling dem if dey is all named Cal Vary?" Yaneth asked.

"Oh, boy!" She looked over and smiled at the two brave men. "It is the name of a group of warriors who come to rescue you just in time. They could be like the Ankhourian or Indian warriors, or the Dwarger warriors and they all have individual names."

"Oh, dat makes more sense," Yaneth nodded in understanding.

"Yep, dat Cal be dere leader," Nordaal said as his face disappeared into a huge grin. "How we get dis Cal ta come down here wid his warriors?"

"I wish I knew, my friend. I wish I knew," Kess said glumly.

Mac glanced at more movements among the roots' shadows. "The light from the protective shield appears to be keeping them at a distance,"

"Yes," Maaleah cocked her head toward the direction of the Dak roots. "That would make sense as supposedly they have never seen the light of day."

Rakmor hurried forward, "Maaleah? Do you have any more of the Dak stones left?"

She pulled out a pouch and opened it up to drop the contents into her hand. "Yes, but they are very weak."

"We have passed many Dak trees to house and protect us, but not enough to get all the horses out of harms' way." Rakmor sighed.

"We probably could get the horses up through some of them, but we are not sure if the demons are still following our path of travel." Maaleah reached over and patted his arm. "We will be okay. It's not far now."

No sooner had she spoken those words when the force field began to falter. It hissed and spit, glowed for a second, and then was gone. Darkness enveloped them and the scurrying sound of hundreds of creatures could be heard coming toward them.

Suddenly, the large cavern room was filled with light. Rakmor and Maaleah had quickly produced lights from their meager supply of magical stones and just in time, as hundreds of Groglemytes were converging toward the small group of warriors.

As soon as the light appeared it caused the Groglemytes to scurry back into the darkness of the roots. But not before everyone got to see what they were up against.

The creatures had rodent-like heads and a long oval, brownish, flat body that hugged the ground. Those that charged at them had the top half of their flattened body upward. Four large hairy arms held rocks of all sizes. Several white circles could be seen on the top of their gelatinous bodies with another six legs on each side.

"Oh my," Kess exclaimed. "They look like giant spiders."

"Wow," Mac held his sword high, ready for action. "They look more like a spider ran into the rear end of a rat and got stuck."

Kess wrinkled her nose. "And they don't smell too good either."

"Okay?" Mac looked back at Rakmor. "So, how long will these lights last?"

A sound of resignation escaped Rakmor's lips. "About another ten minutes at best."

"Then what?" Kess asked. "We won't be able to see down here when the lights go out."

"We will just have to trust our senses to fight them," Sirel said.

"All of us have been taught to fight in the dark. We will give them a fight they will remember."

"Yes," Captain Glynna spoke up. "We are not afraid of the dark. But they should be." The cavern became filled with the sounds of the warriors agreeing.

Suddenly, hundreds of creatures began to circle the group with ear-piercing screams. They did not charge, instead, they kept placing themselves in front of the group jumping up and down and charging the small group, but never near enough to be struck by a sword. At the end of their twelve hairy, thin legs were sharp claws that dug into the ground. Dirt flew all around the Groglemytes as their claws tore at the ground.

"Why aren't they charging us? They outnumber us a hundred to one." Mac asked.

"I don't know," Kybil studied the strange behavior within the group. "With those claws of theirs, they could rip us apart in one charge."

"Thanks," Kess gulped. "That makes me feel so much better."

"I wonder why they keep putting themselves in front of us," Sirel studied the creatures' every move. "They keep screaming, is that part of their attack plan?"

"I don't know, but I think we are about ready to find out." Rakmor looked down at the stone in his hand. "The power is almost gone."

"My stone is also starting to dim," Maaleah picked a small, sheathed sword out of an inside cape pocket. "We will all be fighting them in a short time." She leaned over and whispered in Doc's ear. "I will try to protect you best I can."

"I will do the same for you," he gave her a big smile. "You're okay, you know that?"

"You, too!" She smiled back and patted his arm gently.

"What about using my ring to fight them?" Kess held up her hand with the ring on it, although no one could see it in the dark.

"We can fight them with the ring and my amulet," Mac grabbed the amulet hanging on his chest.

"That might bring the dirt and trees down on top of us," Kybil shook his head in thought.

"Yeah," Mac said. "You're probably right. We don't need that."

"You know I'm not trained to fight in the dark," Kess spoke loudly. "I don't want to be sticking one of the good guys."

"Hey," Mac exclaimed. "That goes for me, too."

"Then I suggest you two stay inside the group and not fight until you feel yourselves being attacked." Kybil pulled Kess to him. "Stay close to me and cover my back."

Sirel grabbed Mac's arm. "Do as Kybil instructed Kess. You must stay close to me and cover my back."

Mac looked at the beautiful face fading before him in the dimming light. "I will always cover your back and be there for you."

"I know," she whispered and leaned toward him just as the last light went out.

The sound of hundreds of creatures began to charge the small group when suddenly they heard Drago's thoughts scream out. "*Wait!*"

All sound in the cavern stopped. The darkness enveloped the group as they stood swords readied.

"*I have read their minds,*" Drago said.

"These spider-thingies have minds?" Kess whispered to Kybil.

"It appears, they do," he whispered back.

"*We are headed toward their main place of dwelling. It is where they live and house their young ones. They are just trying to stop us.*" Drago continued, "*They will kill us to protect their homes.*"

"Can you explain to them that we are not here to harm their dwelling or their young, only to escape the demons from above, and try to find a way out?" Mac spoke out loud to the little dragon.

Drago let everyone hear him as he spoke telepathically to the Groglemytes, "*We came down here to escape the demons. We mean your home or your young no harm. We are just looking for a way out of here.*"

There was a long silence before Drago spoke to the anxious group again. *"They will show us the way out. They mean us no harm."*

"Can we trust them?" Rakmor asked Drago somewhat apprehensively.

"I can read their minds, and I am talking with their leaders," he said. *"I have not found any false words."*

Maaleah spoke up, "Then why is it when people come down here and go outside of the Dak tree they never come back?

"And we have seen a lot of what looked like dead things down here," Doc chimed in.

"I will ask," Drago said. There was a long pause before he spoke again. *"They said those that go in search of the shiny stones in the earth lose their way."* Drago stopped and then continued. *"The whimpering sound we heard was the pain of the light striking their eyes."*

"Why is it that no one has ever seen them before?" Maaleah asked.

"I can answer that," Drago said. *"They hide from travelers when they come down here because the light hurts their eyes. The only time they interfere with a strange being is if it tries to capture them or their young."*

"You mentioned some people tried to capture them, why? And, if they are never seen, how the heck does anyone know they even exist?" Kess asked staring into the darkness.

"Oh, Kess," Maaleah said. "We have always known about their existence. A Sabbot, hundreds of years ago, found a tablet etched with the words 'Groglemytes live in the underworld of the Dak trees.' The tablet told us to use only the Fire of Night, and it would be safe to enter their realm only for water."

After a moment, Drago spoke, *"You asked why people try to capture them. It is believed that the Groglemytes can make jewels and gold out of the earth, so many have come down here to try to capture them. It is then that they must protect themselves."*

"Okay," After a few attempts in the dark, Mac placed a protective arm around Sirel's waist. "I'll bite. Can they make jewels and gold out of the earth?"

"Who Mac gonna bite?" Nordaal asked.

"I dun't know, but in da dark stay away from Mac, just in case he mistook ya fer dem big bugs," Yaneth whispered to Nordaal.

"Okay," Nordaal whispered and edged closer to Yaneth.

"They say they do not make anything from the earth around them," Drago relayed to the group.

Doc groped for Maaleah in the dark and ended up getting his hand slapped. "Easy little man," Maaleah said firmly.

"Just … just trying to find you," he stuttered. "Noth...nothing personal."

"It may not be personal to you, but it is to me," she snapped.

"I am so sorry," Doc's voice was an octave higher.

"I was just kidding with you," Maaleah laughed softly.

"You are an annoying woman sometimes," Doc huffed.

"I know," Maaleah grabbed him and pulled him into the folds of her cape. "You will get used to it."

"If you two are done," Rakmor chided, "we can try to get out of here. Drago ask them how we can see to get out of here, and if they know of any demons that may be around."

"They say they can light a little to show the way, and evil demons are not down here."

"How do they keep the demons from coming down here?" Mac questioned.

"They have a special magic to protect them from demons knowing about them. It is special magic they have had for hundreds of years."

"Can they tell if the demons are above or not?" Kess asked as she moved forward and stepped on Kybil's toe.

He grabbed her and pulled her back to his side, "Stay put, please."

"Okay, but it's so dark down here," she winced with embarrassment.

"Exactly," he whispered into her ear.

"They say wait and they will have a Seerer check it out," Drago's tail could be heard thumping quietly on the ground.

The horses neighed and fidgeted in the dark, while their riders tried to comfort and control them. "We have to get these horses out of here before the magic wears off completely." Distant Runner said as he stroked his horse's neck and whispered soothing words to calm it.

"Yes," Kybil said reassuringly. "We are working on that, and hopefully we will be able to get out of here soon."

"They say their Seerer is one that can see above and around their world without actually going there. And the Seerer can look at the light for a short period with little pain." Drago said quickly.

"Drago ask them if there is anything we can do for them. How do they live down here? What do they live on? What can we give them in return?" Rakmor raised his hand to his face and could not even see an outline of it in the dark. He added, "And, can they help get a little light in here?"

The horses were becoming more agitated with each passing moment. Sounds of neighing, hooves stomping on the ground, and riders patting and talking to their mounts could be heard throughout the cavern. Slowly, a small glimmer of light could be seen coming from the backs of the Groglemytes. It was a very dim light, but it was enough to make out the person next to you, and it seemed to quiet the horses at the same time.

"I will speak fast because their Seerers are returning. The Groglemytes get their magic from the roots of a Dak tree and their nourishment from the sap of the Dak trees. They are careful not to take too much, or they would kill the trees. They cannot stray far from the roots because they would lose their magic." Drago looked at the hundreds of Groglemytes and the faint light that they were emitting. *"They are giving us light so that we can see, although it is a little uncomfortable for them, it is not painful."* Drago's outline could be seen surrounded by the Groglemytes.

"Did you get all that?" Mac laughed quietly with burgeoning pride. "That's some dragon!"

"*Yep,*" Drago turned his head toward Mac. "*That be me!*"

"Yes, little buddy," Mac smiled warmly, "that be you!"

"*Okay,*" Drago turned toward the small group of warriors. "*Seerers say could not see any demons moving around up there. But we must go quickly before they come back.*"

"You will get no arguments from any of us, but how do we get out of here?" Kybil released his tight hold on Kess.

"Before we go, please, tell them that we, Sabbot witches, will provide them with more magic if they need it."

"*They say you are good for Dak trees and never hurt them. You make no fires to burn, and the only time witches leave Dak trees is to get a little water. Maybe powerful witches can put a strong protective spell around the young ones and their homes?*"

"Tell them it will be done. I will be back to put a spell of protection on them." Maaleah said.

After a moment, Drago spoke again, "*They say they are pleased. We must follow them now.*"

They followed the Groglemytes away from their homes and nursery. "*We are being taken to the largest Dak tree they have. They say it will be large enough for the great four-legged beasts to move through.*"

"Other than Maaleah helping them, how can we repay them?" Kess asked.

"*Friends do not have to repay friends. They have gathered all our scents and everyone in this group will always be welcome. It is a special magic they have to remember the scent of those that mean them harm and those that do not.*" Drago continued to follow the small lit path the Groglemytes had formed.

"I am glad they think of us as friends," Kess clutched Kybil's arm and followed Drago through the labyrinth path to the Dak tree. "I wish there was a way for us to speak to them. It would certainly make it easier."

"*You can talk with them.*" Drago chuckled a little. "*All you need to do is take a little, a very little taste of the Dak trees sap. If you take too much, it has strong poison, but a tiny drop of it will not hurt you or*" *make you sick. It will just give you the ability to communicate with them."*

"You could have told us that before," Rakmor said startled by the information.

"I did not know until I mentally asked them that question just now."

They traveled for what seemed like miles to Kess until they came to the root of a Dak tree the size of a house. "That's huge!" She exclaimed.

"This is all well and good, but I do not have any more magic to open the door to get in. Do you Rakmor?" Maaleah busied herself looking through pockets in her cape.

"Not that I know of," Rakmor shook his head. "Now what?"

"Woman, you have more layers of clothing than an onion." Doc pulled back her cape. "Are you sure you don't have something in one of those layers hidden away."

Maaleah thought for a while and then her face lit up. "You wonderful little man. I have just the thing." She took off her cape and handed it to Doc. Quickly, she peeled off a layer of clothing and pulled out a stone that glistened brightly in the dim light. A few incantations and a doorway appeared in the middle of the huge Dak tree. A small light began to glow illuminating the steps inside. Maaleah turned back to thank the Groglemytes for their help, but they had disappeared back into the safety of the shadows and were gone.

"Okay everyone let's get out of here," Kybil gave a chirping order, and everyone filed into the large Dak tree one-by-one. They led their horses through a doorway with wide, dimly lit steps leading up.

It was slow going to get all the warriors and horses topside. The magic that surrounded the horses to keep them calm had worn off. Now the horses became jittery and agitated as they climbed the long set of winding steps.

Warriors scrambled to keep their horses from panicking and injuring themselves in the crowded stairwell. They also had to be careful the horses did not step on them or crush them in the enclosed area. The expertise of the warriors in handling them enabled everyone to walk safely out of the Dak tree and into the frigid air.

The freezing sleet greeted them as they exited the giant Dak tree. Everyone grabbed at their blowing capes and pulled them closed against the brutal winds. The stinging, slanted sleet made it almost impossible to see in front of them, or around them. Winds whipped and howled through the trees, causing branches to break and fall dangerously closer to them on the ground.

A shrill, chirping sound broke through the howling wind. It was Kybil telling the warriors what they had to do. Each warrior took a rope from their saddlebag and then attached it to the horse directly behind them and the horse next to them. After everything was done they rode off toward Castle of Remat two-by-two.

It was becoming difficult for the horses and riders as they pushed against the fierce winds. No one could speak, as their voices were drowned out by the screeching winds.

Kess, Mac, and the others were each seated behind a warrior. Much to Drago's dismay; he was forced to ride on a horse's back. It was a new experience for him, and he was not sure he liked it, but the winds were too strong even for him.

They rode for a while until the winds and stinging sleet finally eased off and let them see around them. Off, in the distance, was Castle of Remat. Almost in unison, a sigh of relief escaped from the riders at the sight of the castle.

The warriors quickly jumped down from their steeds and untied the ropes connecting the horses. Now, they could ride at a faster pace and get to the warmth and safety of the castle. As they traveled into the valley, the snow and sleet became less, and it was easier to traverse. The freezing winds died down so that their visibility was no longer hindered.

Suddenly, without warning, a shrill scream erupted from behind them. They turned to see a horde of demons in hot pursuit. The warriors kicked their horses into high speed and set off in the direction of the castle.

Drago flew off his horse and sailed high into the sky. Dark shadows were there to greet him as he dodged an attack by one of the Drakluf dragons. Another charged at him from behind, shooting out a fiery burst. Drago moved swiftly out of its path. The Drakluf dragon missed his mark and incinerated another Drakluf dragon, causing it to fall like a burning torch to the ground.

Mac saw a Drakluf dragon heading straight for Drago, who was busy fighting with another demon. They were too far up in the sky for the arrows of the warriors to hit any of them. Mac screamed to warn Drago and was relieved when Drago heard him and moved out of harm's way. But there were too many for Drago to fight alone.

Mac took off his amulet and raised it to help his friend, but his horse stumbled and threw him to the ground.

Instantly, all riders reigned in their steeds and surrounded Mac. They drew their swords and readied themselves for the battle. Mac came to his feet, bruised and angry. He had to wait for a moment when Drago was clear to use his powerful magic. But the Drakluf dragons and their riders were moving so fast he could not take a chance on hitting Drago.

The shrieking sound of demons caused everyone to whirl around. Pouring out of the woods were hundreds of demons racing toward Mac and the others.

CHAPTER FIVE

*K*ess aimed her ring at the advancing demons on the ground, while Mac concentrated on protecting Drago from the myriad of Drakluf dragons. But it was impossible because Drago kept moving through the sky at such a high speed.

The demon riders filled the sky with their arrows. But Drago had one major advantage; he was a small target and incredibly fast. Drago darted and flew between them, causing many a rider to kill one of their own by mistake.

Mac did not see some of the demon dragons breaking off and heading for the warriors on the ground. His attention was drawn to shadows of more dragons flying among the thick clouds and heading straight for Drago. "No! No!" Mac screamed. He raised his ring and waited until they cleared the clouds before destroying them.

Suddenly, the shadowy forms of the dragons in the clouds burst though. The sky became alive with the color red. It was the Arega dragons.

"Yes! Yes!" Mac screamed jubilantly.

The red and gold dragons burst on the scene with a ferocity that startled the demon dragons.

Now the dragon riders aimed their poisonous arrows at the Arega dragons only to have their arrows bounce off their scales. The tide had turned, and the demons were outnumbered and destroyed before they could escape.

A few of the Arega dragons left the attack and headed for the dragons who were flying toward the warriors. The Drakluf dragons and their riders never made it. They fell like bright, sizzling torches to the ground where they sputtered and spewed until there was nothing left but a glob of smoldering gray.

Other Arega dragons had sized up the situation and headed straight for the demons that had been chasing Mac and the others on the ground. A fiery path of destruction was all that was left of the demons who could not get out of the way fast enough. The others ran screaming back into the forest and out of sight.

Mac searched the sky for Drago. He was nowhere to be seen. His breathing became labored at the thought that something had happened to Drago. Telepathically he called his name over and over. There was no response.

Kess saw the worried look on Mac's face and ran to his side. Sirel was already there, her hand on his arm. "Mac? Is it Drago?"

"*Drago is here,*" he said hobbling toward Mac.

"Drago!" Mac's face lit up as he moved toward his friend. "When you didn't answer me, I thought . . . I thought . . ."

"*I did not hear you call my name. My father and I were busy chasing the last of the bad dragons.*"

"You're injured," Mac's voice filled with concern.

"*An arrow hit my foot. I hurried up and breathed fire on my foot to kill the poison. I will be good again, real soon.*" He picked up the injured foot and shook it gently. "*See no arrow anymore, just a little hole.*"

"I think I can help you with that," Doc moved past everyone and took out a small container. He opened it up and sat down next to Drago. Carefully, he picked up the injured foot and put the soothing salve onto the puncture wound. Immediately, the salve turned into a hardened substance closing the puncture wound completely.

"*That is good stuff,*" Drago picked up his foot and carefully placed it on the ground and then began to jump up and down on it. "*My foot is fixed. Thank you, Doc.*"

"You are quite welcome, my brave little friend." Doc looked up at everyone staring down at him. "Umm . . . If someone doesn't mind could they help these old bones get up?" He was swiftly lifted to his feet by two warriors who were standing the closest. He put the lid back on the small container and placed it into one of the pockets hidden inside of his cape. "It's something the Healers in the Land Between gave me. They used it to fix one of his spikes. I thought it might come in handy at some point."

"*I trust all are unharmed,*" a deep, booming voice resonated through the warriors.

Doc jumped and placed his hand over his heart. "Don't sneak up on an old man like that."

"*I am glad to see there are no injuries.*" It was the deep, rich baritone voice of King Zaatyr of the Arega Dragons that had startled Doc.

"How did you get here so fast?" Mac asked.

"*We have been at Castle Remat,*" he spoke telepathically so that all could hear him. "*Our Oracle spoke of a resurgence of demons, and that we must leave immediately for Castle Remat. The Imperial Sorceress Cedwynna told us they had received a signal of your arrival, but you had disappeared. She said they had become aware of a massing of demons. So, I thought it might be a good idea to stay at the castle until we knew where you were.*"

"How did you see us so far away?" Kess looked toward the castle far off in the distance.

"*One of our scouts spotted a large contingent of Drakluf dragons, so we all headed out to see what was going on. We knew it would not be good, no matter what they were doing.*"

"That is one brave son you have there," Mac looked down at

Drago, smiled, and then more sternly. "He just about scared me to death with worry for him."

The large dragon looked down at his son. *"We were prepared for a fight. I had no idea my son would be caught up in the middle of everything. If we had not stayed, I fear great harm would have come to Drago."* The king's voice trailed off.

"Trust me," Mac looked up into the face of the giant dragon. "I would have done everything in my power to try to protect him. If I could only fly."

"Yes," his large, golden head nodded, and Mac could have sworn he heard a chuckle. *"I truly believe that, or Drago would not be with you now."* Zaatyr changed the subject abruptly. *"For now, I think we should get to the castle before they send others and come back in full force. The Sorceress made sure that the castle had a special, powerful protective barrier surrounding it. You will all be much safer there."*

"That is a very good idea," Kybil gave a chirping sound, and the warriors mounted their horses.

King Zaatyr turned to Maaleah and began speaking to her alone. Maaleah nodded and gave a faint smile to the giant dragon. Zaatyr began speaking to the group again.

"We will follow you to the castle and keep watch for any demons who may resurface, then, after you are safely at the castle, we shall fly to our home with Drago. He has been missed."

Maaleah turned to Doc and grabbed his arm, "I cannot go with you right now. There is a great change going on, and I must be there."

King Zaatyr spoke directly to Maaleah, *"I will have a couple of my warriors' escort you back to your home, just in case there may be trouble."*

Maaleah was helped onto the back of a large dragon and waved good-bye as they took off into the sky.

Soon, the air became filled with gold and red as the dragons took flight.

"We will follow you to Castle Remat," Zaatyr's voice boomed telepathically to them all from high above.

In less than an hour, they reached the base of Castle Remat.

"*Bye, Mac,*" Drago's thoughts reached out to Mac. "*I be back...I mean, I will be back as soon as I can.*"

"*I will look forward to seeing you soon, my friend,*" Mac waved good-bye to the little dragon and watched as they spread out and flew in a large diamond formation and disappeared into the white, thick clouds.

"I should have asked him to warm me up before he left," Doc's teeth chattered as the cold winds picked up again.

They stood at the base of the castle when Kess remembered the winding, staircase that led up to the entrance. "Oh, no!" She exclaimed, "We aren't going to take these horses up that winding staircase. Are we?"

"Huh?" Nordaal looked over at Kess. "Dey never make it up dem little, itty-bitty steps."

"Not to worry," Rakmor leaned around to look at Kess. "We have another alternative."

As they reached the base of the castle, a large outline of a door began to form on the outside. It grew and grew until it was four times the size of a normal doorway. The sound of scraping could be heard as two large doors swung open.

"So, why didn't you use this door before, instead of making us walk up the winding flight of steps?" Kess quipped sliding off the horse she had been riding.

"Because we weren't riding horses," he nodded in her direction.

Kess rolled her eyes, "Really?"

"No," he shrugged. "I didn't have the right stones to open this section," he smiled sheepishly at Kess.

Mac and the others in their group climbed off the back of their horses. Except for Doc who had to be helped down.

"Can we go inside?" Doc shouted from behind and then much softer. "I'm freezing and my bottom still hurts from the last time I was on a horse's back."

A sorcerer motioned for Mac and the others to enter first and then signaled for the warriors and their horses. Without hesitation, the warriors two abreast rode their horses directly into the doorway, where they were immediately embraced by the warmth of the castle. Sorcerers and servants alike rushed to aid the cold and weary riders. As each rider dismounted, their horse was taken from them and led to a manger where other horses and animals were bedded down.

Stationed nearby were baskets, with cushioned seats inside, large enough for six people to sit in. As each basket filled up with occupants, it would start to move forward on a rail. The baskets glided around the pristine corridors along the inside walls. The amethyst and marble floors and columns glistened and sparkled as they passed one level after another.

The baskets came to a stop down the hall from the conference room they all were familiar with. A young male and female in green robes opened the two massive doors for the warriors. As soon as the last warrior was inside the doors closed.

Already seated at the table was the Sorceress Cedwynna, who was getting up to greet the warriors as they came into the room. As she moved toward them her purple robe flowed gracefully around her. Her silver-gray hair was pulled up and fastened with a gold-net. Her large blue eyes sparkled with joy, as her face broke into a huge smile at the sight of Kess and Mac.

"Grandmother," Kess ran into her opened arms.

"Kess," she hugged her tightly. "My dearest Kess. It is so good to have you back safely." Cedwynna pulled away and gently stroked Kess's face. She looked over and saw Mac standing there waiting for his turn and cried out. "Come here, Mac."

In two steps, he was in front of her. She opened her arms and pulled him to her. "You are both safe. I am beyond happy. You must tell me what has happened. Did you find Prince Nordaal and Captain Sirel?" She tried searching through the mass of warriors standing before her.

"Yes," Mac smiled and motioned for Sirel and Nordaal to come forward from the throng of warriors. "Here they are, and in good condition."

Kess pulled away and stared into her grandmother's eyes brimming with tears. "We have so much to tell you, and what we have to tell you will amaze and stun you. But it will bring much joy. Please sit down."

"Now, first tell me where you found them?" Cedwynna said, as Rakmor and Kybil gently escorted her to her cushioned chair. Cedwynna sat down and quickly looked around the room at the standing warriors. "Please all of you be seated."

Chairs scraped against the marble floor as the warriors sat down at the long thirty-foot table in the room. "But wait, before you start I will have them bring food and drink for everyone." Cedwynna nodded in the direction of the two young people in their green robes. They returned the nod and left the room.

It was not more than two minutes before the doors opened again, and servants began filling the table with food and drinks, hot and cold. Plates, silverware, and cups were brought in and the warriors dove into the food.

"Kess. Mac. You are not eating," she motioned for them to eat and drink before they spoke of their adventure.

"I am too excited to eat right now," Kess said.

"Okay, I'll eat now," Mac walked over to the table and picked up a plate, and quickly began helping himself to the food on the table. "I'll take over telling what happened while you eat."

"Where do I start?" Kess asked herself. "I think I'll start with the Silver people."

"Silver people?" Cedwynna questioned. "You found Sirel and Yaneth with silver people?"

"Umm, hold onto that thought. Mac and I were separated when we used our powers against that powerful demon. Mac was thrown into Earth's dimension. Oh, and that is where he found Sirel and Yaneth. But I'll let him tell you all about that."

"Mmm," Mac nodded while chewing on a piece of meat.

"Kybil, Rakmor, Maaleah, Doc, and I were thrown into the Land Between."

"Oh, my," Cedwynna gasped in horror and stood up and began to move toward Kess.

Kess got up and walked over to the Sorceress. "Grandmother, please sit down. What I have to tell you is going to be a shock to you."

A quizzical look came across Cedwynna's face, but she let Kess escort her back to her chair. After she was settled Kess pulled a chair up next to her. Now, everyone in the room stopped eating and drinking as they wanted to hear what was so important.

Kess took a deep breath and began, "Grandmother, remember years ago when my mother and uncle were trying to take Mac and me to a safe place, and they encountered the Zetches."

"Of course, I will never forget it." Her voice was filled with sadness.

"The silver-coated people I just mentioned. Well, some of them are from Mystovia."

"What are you saying, my dear?" Her brows furrowed in confusion.

"My mother and Mac's father are alive. That's what I am saying." Kess collapsed back in her chair. She had no idea how she was going to break the news to her grandmother, and now it was done.

"What? I do not understand," Cedwynna's hands trembled as they rose to her lips.

"Etheria and Jhondar are alive and coming home to Mystovia in a couple of weeks."

It took the Sorceress a moment to register what she was being told and when it finally did her hands covered her face as she cried softly.

After the startled whispers and cries from the warriors had subsided there was total quiet in the room.

Finally, Cedwynna pulled a handkerchief from a pocket in her dress and dabbed her eyes and nose. After she had regained her composure, she anxiously began to question Kess. "Did Etheria look well? Jhondar? Why did they not come back with you?"

"Well, it was hard to tell what they looked like because they were all silvery," Mac said and shrugged as he continued to eat.

"Silvery? I do not understand," Cedwynna's voice trembled as she looked at Mac and then back at Kess.

"Well, you see they have to be coated in this silvery, glowing stuff, because they need protection to travel throughout the Land Between. This coating enables them to see the invisible creatures that live there," Kess said.

"Silvery stuff?" Cedwynna's eyes widened. "Invisible beings?"

Kess continued, "Yes, anyway, they wanted desperately to come with us, but they didn't know what kind of effect this silvery coating would have on Mystovia. They did not want to take any chances of causing any problems. Oh, trust me, grandmother, they wanted to come home very badly, but it takes about two weeks for this stuff to dissipate, you know, go away."

"But how will we know when they are ready to come back? We sensed the Orb and knew you were ready." Her face was filled with worry.

"Remember the Stone of Islet?" Kess asked.

"Oh, yes! Yes! The Stone of Islet will let us sense them. She clasped her hands together. "How clever of you. This is all too wonderful to absorb." She dropped her hands onto the arms of the chair and gripped it tightly. "When will they come home? Oh, yes in a couple of weeks. Is there a possibility they will come sooner?" Cedwynna asked.

"They told us it would be a couple of weeks, and they are so looking forward to seeing you again." Kess smiled and wiped away a tear trying to find a path down her cheek.

"I am so excited about the news of Etheria and Jhondar; I can barely breathe," Cedwynna leaned back in her chair and after a moment looked at Kess.

"Well, as I said we ended up in the Land Between and encountered bizarre and frightening creatures," Kess began to fill her grandmother in on the events and strange creatures they had encountered.

Gasps could be heard coming from the warriors who were listening to the whole story.

After Kess was finished telling about her journey into the Land Between Cedwynna lowered her head for a moment and then raised it slowly. "Etheria. Jhondar alive," she sighed deeply.

Kess patted her hand gently. "I left out the Zetches for Mac to tell you about."

Cedwynna grabbed at her throat. "Did you say 'Zetches'?" She got up and began to pace the floor behind her chair. "Zetches were in the Land Between? How did they get there?"

Mac pushed away from the table, brushing a crumb off of the side of his mouth, "I think I can take over from here."

Kess got up and walked to the table. She took a glass handed to her by Kybil and took a long drink from her cup. Her stomach rumbled as she began to put food on her plate.

Mac thought for a moment. "Here's what we were told. The Zetches were thrown by a blast of magic into the Land Between at the same time as Jhondar, Etheria, and the rest of the warriors."

"Why are they back? How? What happened?" Questions poured out of Cedwynna.

"When Kess met the Jomkobi in the tunnels, he pushed both Nordaal and Kess into the portal. But before it closed Nordaal pushed Kess back through the portal. I believe at that point one of the Zetches grabbed a hold of Kess and came through with her."

"But there are two of them. Did both get through the portal?" She motioned with her hand for him to continue.

Mac rubbed his chin with his hand and continued. "Here's what we think happened. One Zetche grabbed hold of Kess and ended up here and the other grabbed hold of Sirel. Both thinking they were going to the same place."

"Yes, the Zetches would never part from one another," Cedwynna said.

"Right," Mac said.

"I think I understand now," Cedwynna sat back in her chair with a deep sigh. "Oh, my goodness." She realized what he had just said, "Your dimension? The people there will have no way to protect themselves from that creature."

"No, they wouldn't have. But the good thing about that is there is no magic in our world. The Zetche did not have any magical powers to feed off of. We think every time he used his powers; he became weaker. He was about to possess Drago but was in for a big surprise."

"I can imagine," the Sorceress nodded and smiled.

"Drago fought with him and then consumed him," Mac blinked his eyes involuntarily at the thought of the smelly aftermath. "Oh, and we had some help from some kids from my dimension."

"Kids?" Cedwynna's eyes widened in disbelief. "How the stars could young goats help you?"

"No," Mac threw back his head and laughed. "I am sorry. I should have said we had some help from some young people. They decided to join our group and come with us to Mystovia."

"Where are they?" Cedwynna peered around the warriors seating at the table.

Well," Mac continued, "Jhondar and Etheria were so impressed with them that they offered them a home in Kelador."

"I hope these . . . kids," Cedwynna smiled for the first time, "come over to Mystovia. I would love to meet them. But Mac, what did Jhondar and Etheria do in the Land Between?" Cedwynna asked.

"They live in a magnificent city called Kelador. They are kind of in command or co-leaders. I'm not quite sure about that." He shrugged. "I mean they probably share the responsibilities with others but again, I am not quite sure on that point."

"This city called Kelador is that where they have been staying all these years?" Cedwynna questioned.

"I believe that is where they have been staying. As to what do they do; they are still warriors and fighting the nasty little creatures that keep attacking them." Mac shrugged slightly.

"All these years and they have been within reach," Cedwynna said sadly.

"How would you know where to look in there?" Kess put down the bread she was eating. "It is a vast place and extremely dangerous if you don't know what lies below or above you. You once said you thought you felt something in the Land Between, but thought it was Mac's or my magical signature. It could well have been Etheria's or any of the others. You tried, grandmother. You tried. You did not know. How could you possibly have known?"

"I could have brought them home years ago," her hand rose to her forehead.

"Maybe not," Mac spoke up. "You see the city of Kelador, and the flying ships are protected and covered by magic and technology. Together these forces could have blocked all of their signatures. Anyway, they did try to find a way home for years, and finally gave up."

"That would explain a lot of the strange readings we got from the Land Between," Cedwynna said.

"Aunt," Mac's voice softened as he looked at her sitting anxiously in her chair. "They have made a home for themselves in Kelador and have done well in an unforgiving land. Not that they did not miss you or Mystovia, but their lives are now attached to the Land Between."

"But this is their home. When they come back, they must stay here," Cedwynna's was speaking more to herself than anyone in the room.

"Grandmother," Kess rose from the table and walked to the side of her chair. "It has been over twenty-five years. They have found a new life and a new home. You must always remember this; the love for you and Mystovia has never wavered in them ever. Hopefully, Mac and I are all wrong on this because they may wish to stay here in Mystovia. We want to prepare you just in case they choose to go back to the Land Between."

Cedwynna sat very still in her chair. After a while, she reached down and patted Kess's hand which rested on the arm of her chair.

"Yes. You and Mac are right. I will have time to deal with their returning to the Land Between. It will not come as such a shock to me. "Mac it is now your turn to tell me about your visit to the Out World, and the Zetch."

Mac regaled the whole adventure to her, although parts of his story brought much-needed laughter to everyone who was listening. "And, Drago . . ."

"Drago? Oh, my," Cedwynna's said with some urgency. "The Arega dragons may require our help."

"Whatever it is - they have it!" Mac said emphatically.

"I will be back shortly," Cedwynna got up from her chair and left the room.

Everyone had finished eating, and the table cleared before Cedwynna came back into the room carrying a large rolled-up piece of paper.

Rakmor took the rolled-up paper from her and escorted her to a chair at the table. A couple of warriors helped him unroll and spread out the paper, exposing a large map of mountains.

"This is a detailed map of the Mountains of Arega and where the Arega dragons have their lairs. The Oracles said their visions can sometimes come true or can be altered. They have had a vision that one of their own may be in danger. Unfortunately, the vision of which one is in danger was not clear enough to see. However, they did see help coming in the form of beings of great power."

Mac stood up and walked toward his Aunt. "What can we do?"

"We will help them in whatever way we can," Kess interjected.

Cedwynna smiled. "The mere presence of all of you would be a good deterrent to stop anyone who plans on using their magic against the Aregas or their Oracles. At least, I will not be sending any of you into danger this time. You would be there to keep watch for any signs of someone trying to use their magic to harm any Oracles." She sighed deeply and smiled.

"That's a good thing," Kess said settling back in her chair. "How long will we be gone this time? I mean, if we're gone for long we won't be able to make sure everyone from the Land Between gets here safely," Kess turned her chair toward her grandmother.

"Oh," Cedwynna smiled and nodded to Kess. "That was one of the reasons I left so quickly. I have informed the other Sorcerers and Sorceresses to keep a vigil for any signs of them trying to crossover using the Stone of Iszel. And, I do not foresee you to be gone for long."

"Good," Kess sat up straight and smiled. "After a good night's sleep, I'll be ready."

"One other thing," Cedwynna stood up. "Just before the Oracles lost their vision, they saw the wizard Baalizar. Somehow he has to help or is vital in some way and must be found immediately. He is a hermit, and I have not seen him in many years. They say he lives in the Xelrils Mountains, but no one knows exactly where." As she headed toward the door, she turned and said, "Some of you must head to the Arega Mountains, and another group must find the wizard Baalizar. Kess. Mac. Please choose those you will travel with." She gave a short laugh, "I think I know already.

CHAPTER SIX

*T*here was quiet in the room after the door shut behind Cedwynna. Kess was the first to break the silence. "Mac," she said firmly. "I think you and your team should go to the Arega dragons. It only seems fitting as Drago is so close to you. But if you prefer to go and find this wizard that is okay, too."

"I would like to go to the Aregas if that is alright with everyone."

"How are we breaking up into teams this time?" Kess asked reluctantly.

"I think the way we have been teamed up works best," Rakmor stated to the agreement of everyone else. "As mentioned before, no one knows where the wizard Baalizar lives exactly, but we may be able to trace his magical signature through the mountains – unless he has blocked it."

"Wizard? Sorcerer? What's the difference between them?" Doc asked.

"This particular sorcerer calls himself a wizard," he shrugged. "I really don't have any great explanation of the differences, because here in Mystovia there is none."

"I think that explained it very well," Doc crossed his arms and smiled.

"I dun't get it," Nordaal shook his head.

"It's okay," Kess patted his muscular forearm. "I don't either."

A big grin escaped across Nordaal's face as he pulled himself up from his chair.

"Kess," Mac moved to her side. "I almost forgot to tell you I mailed the letters when I was in our dimension, Earth, home . . . whatever you want to call it. I bought stamps from the girl at the hotel's front desk and asked her to mail them for me."

"Oh, my gosh!" Kess exclaimed. "I forgot all about them."

"Ya can turn letters into males? Why dey do dat anyway?" Nordaal asked looking at Yaneth.

"Ya got me der, Nor," Yaneth said.

"What letters?" Kybil asked.

"We had written letters to our police department submitting our resignations effective immediately, and two personal letters," Mac said. "It is a good thing I was carrying them and not you," he turned and looked at Kess. "Think about that. How ironic is it that I was carrying the letters and ended up in our dimension? Hmm," he thought pensively for a moment. "Anyway, it's a done deal."

"The personal letters were for our personal belongings," Kess interjected. "I turned my condo and everything in it over to a friend of mine, and Mac did the same to one of his buddies. In return, we asked if they would turn in our police equipment, resignations, and there were just a few other requests. I don't feel guilty about quitting without giving notice, because our department was overstaffed, and they were trying to get a couple of the older officers to retire and they really didn't want to have to retire." She turned to Mac and gave an audible sigh, "Well, that's done. We are here permanently, and I couldn't be happier about that."

"That makes two of us," Kybil smiled.

"Make that three," Sirel spoke up.

"I think we are all glad you two have decided to be with us," Rakmor agreed.

"Yep," Nordaal said. "Me be glad, too."

"I dink we got dat covered," Yaneth took off his hat and scratched his head.

"No ya dun't," Nordaal looked at his friend. "Ya just took off yer hat. Nuttin's coverin' yer head."

"Before we go any further with this electrifying dialog between you two," Doc smiled at the two Dwargers and then turned to Kess and Mac. "I just want to say I am beyond happy that you two are going to stay."

"We will spend the night here, but we have to leave very early in the morning," Rakmor said. "I have things I have to do before we leave, so I will bid you all a good-night."

Just then the doors burst open and a young man in a green robe rushed to Rakmor's side with a large envelope in his hand. "This just got to us, Master Rakmor."

"Thank you," Rakmor took the envelope from the small hand. The envelope had the seal of the Sabbot Witches on it. He broke the seal, opened the letter, and began to read it to himself. After a moment, he folded the letter and looked up at the expectant faces all around him. "It is from Maaleah. She has finished what she needed to do, and all went well. Shortly after she returned to her village they discovered that the demons were going to attack it. Everyone left for safer havens. Maaleah is safely ensconced in a Dak tree and will wait for us." He folded the letter. His face etched with worry. "We will leave first thing in the morning."

"How do we know which Dak tree she is in?" Kess asked perplexed.

"She will signal us," Rakmor said. "Doc, you are going with us this time."

"I go where I'm needed," Doc smiled and shrugged.

Kybil stood next to Kess and touched her arm, "I would like to spend a quiet evening just talking about absolutely nothing, but unfortunately, I too, have many things to do before we leave in the morning."

"We'll have plenty of time to talk later," she smiled up into his Elven face.

"Yes. Yes we will," he looked into her eyes for a moment, smiled, and left.

———

Kess was awakened by a young girl in a green robe. "Mistress," she called softly. "Mistress it is time to leave."

Kess pulled the warm comforter off her and sat on the edge of the bed. "Geez," she peered over at the French doors to her room. "It's still dark out. What time is it anyway?"

"I was given the message to awaken you for your journey," she said. She gave a slight nod of respect and quickly left the room.

"What? Is this Wizard Baalizar a sleepwalker?" She grumbled as she made her way to the bathroom.

A short while later Kess met up with the others who were already waiting for her at the main dining room. Still groggy from getting up so early she yawned, sat down, folded her arms on the table, and rested her head on them.

"Good morning," Kybil said with more energy than Kess could even think about.

"Are you sure this is morning?" Kess still did not lift her head from resting on her arms.

"I communicated with the Gralcons to see if it was safe for them to take us to the Sabbot village, but it is still overrun by demons," Kybil said. "So, the closest they can take us is to the base of the Xelrils Mountains."

"That will do fine," Rakmor stood up and shoved his chair under the table. "We are headed to the Xelrils Mountains anyway to find the Wizard Baalizar."

"Get something to eat. We are moving out soon," Kybil nudged Kess's elbow. "Rise and shine."

"I'll rise, but I don't feel like shining," Kess lifted her head and slowly drew a plate in front of her. "What time is it anyway?"

"What difference does it make? We're up and moving out," Kybil pushed a cup of hot coffee toward her. "We have about three hours before the sun comes up."

"That puts us at about three o'clock in the morning," she said blinking her eyes and trying to focus on the plate in front of her. "Geez, I'm gonna get Mac for this. He felt like talking last night, so we talked until about midnight."

"He's wasn't very happy this morning either," Rakmor said. "They left about a half-hour ago."

Kess perked up after hearing that, "Okay, I'll be fine now." She finished breakfast, pulled her cape around her warm jacket, picked up her sword and knapsack, and headed for the door with everyone else.

A cold wind drifted over the veranda stirring the black, white, and gold feathers on the giant, eagle-like heads, and wings of the Gralcons. Their huge, black panther-like bodies were fitted with ropes for everyone to hold on to during their flight.

Everyone began to situate themselves on top of the mammoth beasts, and this time Kess sat between Kybil and another warrior. She was quick to learn that being the first rider was a cold, bug-eating affair.

The Gralcons spread their wings and gave a firm push with their front legs that ended in black, razor-sharp talons. A final thrust from their powerful back legs gave them the momentum they needed to fly into the dark sky.

One-by-one they flew into the cold morning air gliding effortlessly through the wispy clouds. All Kess could see below was total darkness, not even a speck of light broke through the blackness. It was an uneventful trip as they were deposited at the base of the Xelrils Mountains.

"Where are we going now?" Doc asked.

"We are heading west toward the Dak trees to find Maaleah," Rakmor pointed the way and began walking at a brisk pace. Suddenly, he stopped. "Listen," he whispered.

At first, Kess could hear nothing, and then the dreadful sound of demons could be heard coming their way. "Now, what?" She asked in a whisper.

"Back toward the mountains," Rakmor said anxiously.

Kess listened as Kybil gave orders in the now-familiar bird-chirping sounds to his warriors, and they turned and headed toward the mountain at a fast clip.

They began scrambling up the mountain until they reached a large plateau. Rakmor began running along the ledge saying strange words until he stopped in front of a large boulder nestled in the mountainside. He pulled a small stone from a pocket in his cape and said a few words. "Stand back," Rakmor ordered.

Kess watched as he poured what looked like glittery sand into his hand and then threw it at a large boulder in front of them.

The ground began to shake, and a loud rumbling sound appeared to be coming from the massive boulder embedded in the side of the mountain. The boulder pulled free and rolled to one side leaving a large gaping hole in its place. "Quickly," Rakmor ordered firmly. "Everyone. Get inside."

"I hope this has a tunnel or something with a lot of room for us, or we are all going to be a lot flatter looking," Doc gulped as he ran toward the opening. He sighed with relief at the sight of a passageway behind the gaping hole.

After everyone was safely beyond the cave entrance, Rakmor chanted a few more words, and the huge boulder rolled swiftly back into place, closing off the entrance.

"Are we safe in here?" Kess asked.

"Only temporarily," Rakmor shook his head. "They will have picked up our scent and will easily find another way in here. Now we have to find a way out."

"Just make another big boulder move out of the way," Doc shrugged.

"That was a special boulder with markings on it that show up when you say the proper incantation." Rakmor pulled a wand from his pocket, said a few more words, and the top part of his wand began to glow.

"Wow," Kess exclaimed. "I saw that happen in a movie once."

"I hear ya say moo vee long time ago. What be moo vee?" Nordaal asked.

"It is where they capture things on film." She looked up into his barely lit face but still could see the confusion on it. "Nordaal, I will explain later, okay?"

"Yep, dat be okay." He turned toward Yaneth. "Moo vee? Why dey want ta capture cow sounds?" He shook his head and his brow furrowed slightly.

"Alrighty then," Kess blinked a couple of times at the wonderful, but slightly dense Dwarger. "Okay, where are we now and what are we going to do?"

"Let's get away from this opening as fast as possible." He led the way with the light from his wand that cast weird shadows along the uneven, craggy stone tunnel walls.

They walked down the tunnel taking different paths looking for a way out of the mountain until they came to a large cave opening. "This is huge and smelly," Kess brought her hand to her nose. "Look at all the openings that lead into here. Which one do we take? Whew, what is that smell?"

"From the looks of it," Kybil's eyes narrowed as he scanned the area. "This has been used as a feeding ground."

"For what?" Doc gasped.

"I don't think you want to know," Kybil replied.

"Enough said," Doc said as he looked nervously around.

Kybil quickly gave orders for his warriors to search for another way out. Warriors broke into teams and headed down the openings in the cave. Soon, they all returned and reported back to Kybil. He stood there and shook his head solemnly. "There is not much good news here. Each of the passageways has demons coming down them. I am afraid there is no way out of here. All the avenues of escape are blocked."

At first, the sounds were barely audible, but slowly as demons drew nearer the sound of their shrieking began to reverberate throughout the massive cavern walls.

"Here. Move in here," Rakmor pointed to an opening in the stone wall.

Kess moved toward the small opening behind them. "What is this place?"

"It is just another cave, only smaller," Rakmor said. "But it would give us protection from being attacked from behind."

"What was that?" Doc asked looking toward the small cave.

"What was what?" Kybil asked.

"I thought I saw something move in there," Doc stared at the opening.

Kybil and a couple of his warriors immediately turned and entered the opening with their weapons drawn. After only a few moments they gave an all-clear and motioned for the others to enter.

"I could have sworn I saw something move in here," Doc scratched his head.

"It could have been the light from Rakmor's wand casting shadows in here," Kess said looking around at the stone walls all around them.

"I knew it wouldn't be long before I lost my mind," Doc shook his head.

"I don't think you have lost your mind, Doc, because I thought I saw something in here, too," Rakmor said.

"Well, if the demons get too close couldn't I just use the Ring of Remat to get rid of them?" Kess asked.

"Kess, your magic in here could bring the mountain down on us." Kybil pushed on the sides of the crumbling wall. Pieces of stone flaked off and fell noisily to the floor.

"You're right," Kess moved against the wall causing a small cascade of stones to fall.

Look," Rakmor pointed behind her on the wall. "You loosened those stones around something."

Everyone turned to see a smooth, shiny, diamond-shaped object embedded in the rock wall. The metal plate glowed softly in the darkness. "Geez, it's only about a couple of inches in size. I mean who would put such a tiny thing in the wall, and better yet what does it do?" Kess said as she gingerly felt around it.

The sounds of the demons grew louder as they got closer. Their shrieking filled the tiny alcove where Kess and the others waited, helplessly trapped.

"Well, should I press this little thing and see what happens?" Kess asked the warriors.

"Why not?" Rakmor shrugged.

"Do. I'd rather not be eaten at this point," Doc said nervously.

Kess looked around at the others in her party and saw their heads all nod in agreement. She reached out and quickly pressed the small diamond metal plate. Nothing happened. She pressed it again more firmly, still nothing.

Rakmor gently moved her aside as he studied the small markings etched in the center of the plate. "Hmm," he rubbed his chin, and then his face registered recognition. "We need a powerful stone or something to hit this plate.

Nordaal walked over and looked at the small plate, raised his fist, and punched it. A large rumbling began, and the whole cave began to tremble. Stones began to fall everywhere, but mainly outside of the alcove.

Kybil gave a chirping order to his warriors, and they all moved back away from the opening.

Just then, a mass of demons came from around the corner and began to charge. Their voices were trilling with excitement at the sight of their trapped quarry.

The trembling in the cave increased as Kess watched the ceiling on the outside of the cave fall on top of the approaching demons. It kept falling until the entrance to their alcove was blocked with stones and rocks from floor to ceiling. Their tiny area filled with a cloud of dust, as small rocks and debris fell from above.

Kybil pulled Kess to him covering her best he could from the falling debris.

Suddenly, the wall they all were leaning against began to move. Everyone jumped away from the vibrating wall, only to feel the top of the cave start to crumble.

"It looks like we're going to be next," Kess reached her arms around Kybil's waist and felt his arms tightened around her.

"At least we weren't eaten by those nasty things," Doc said with a forced smile.

"Ohh," Nordaal took off his feathered cap and beat it against his muscular thigh. "I make big mistake." Frustration filled his voice.

"No, buddy," Rakmor coughed and patted the sad Dwarger's arm. "You probably saved our lives. "Look", he said and pointed to a small beam of light that traveled down the edge of the back wall.

"What is that?" Kess asked trying to peer through the billowing dust.

She watched in fascination as the dust from the room was being sucked out through the widening crack in the wall.

"It appears to be an opening of some kind. Stay here," Kybil said to Kess as he and Rakmor walked toward the opening. It only took them a couple of steps to reach the wall and in that space of time, the wall stopped moving. They ran their hands over the hard-flat rock.

"I am not finding any kind of lever or handle," Rakmor's hands traveled the entire length of the opening.

"Me either," Kybil searched for hinges or anything that would open the crack further.

"Maybe if we pull on it," Rakmor and Kybil tried to pull it with their weight. Nothing happened.

"Nordaal and Yaneth could you help us out here?" Rakmor yelled back to them.

The two Dwargers moved toward the stone wall, "Okay, stand back." Yaneth said, motioning for Kybil and Rakmor to step aside. Their broad hands were just able to grasp the side of the stone door, and they began to pull.

Slowly, the wall began to swing back toward them. The rest of the warriors rushed to help the two dwargers pull on the stone wall. Soon, there was enough room for a couple of warriors to squeeze through the door and push. The door opened to reveal stone steps that only led upward.

Kybil entered first, testing the strength of the steps. "It is safe, at least on these few steps. Well, we have no choice. Let's go." He motioned for the rest to follow him.

The walls were coarse and lined with rough, sharp edges protruding from them. Everyone was careful not to brush up against the it as they climbed the steep, winding steps. Finally, they reached a long, wide hallway with strangely marked tiles on the walls.

"So?" Kybil said, rubbing his chin absent-mindedly. "Where the heck are we?"

"Well, I'll be," Rakmor said studying the markings on the walls. "These are markings of magic." Carefully he began to run his finger over some of the symbols on the wall with his fingers. "They have been carved into these walls."

"Can you make them out?" Kess asked.

"Some," he continued to look curiously at the markings. "It appears there has been a magic spell to keep demons away or destroy them." He shook his head. "The carvings aren't that good or easy to read. However, they were definitely put there by someone quite familiar with magic."

"Keep alert everyone," Kybil said as they started to walk down the long, wide passageway. After a while, Kybil raised his hand, and everyone stopped. "Tiles on a cave floor? Look at the strange markings on these tiles. What do you make of them, Rakky?"

Rakmor studied the symbols and then laughed softly, "Yep.

These are signs that tell you which stones to step on to get through this part of the hallway. Everyone step exactly where I do."

Everyone followed one another through the intricate maze of steps as Rakmor carefully guided them. They leaped, jumped, and stepped exactly as Rakmor indicated until they came to the very last set of stone tiles when he called for everyone to stop.

He studied the marking on the wall and nodded. "These markings indicate that these are the last tiles to traverse." He ran his finger over the strange markings. "This seems to indicate," Rakmor pointed beyond the tiles on the ground, "that safe ground is just past this last set of tiles, but I can't make them out." He squatted down to try to get a better view. "These are unknown markings to me."

"Okay," Kess moved closer to Kybil to try to see the strange markings on the last few large stones that led to the safety of the solid ground. "Am I going crazy, but does that look like the top of two wooden doors over there?"

Just then the ground beneath them began to shake and tremble.

"Everyone! Stand your ground," Kybil ordered.

"Can we jump over them?" Kess peered around Kybil at the twenty feet of tiles in front of them.

"No, they are too far," Kybil tapped his chin in thought with a finger.

"Maybe dis be ta far to jump, but maybe we could swing ya over der," Yaneth shrugged.

"If we could get to the other side of these tiles, I am pretty sure we will be safe over there." Rakmor shook his head.

"Look at this," Doc pointed to what looked like a large, metal hook high up the wall next to him.

"Don't touch it," Kybil and Rakmor yelled at the same time.

"Don't touch it?" Doc said sarcastically. "The only way I'd be able to reach it is if I had arms that could expand about five feet."

"Everyone brace yourself and be ready for anything." Kybil motioned for Nordaal to turn around and pulled a thick, long rope from his backpack. Again, the ground rumbled beneath their feet.

"If we could get someone across there maybe they could find something to attach this to," Rakmor said.

"Look," Kybil spotted something across the wide expanse. "It looks like another hook just like this one, only not as high."

"No one can jump this," Kess said eyeing the wide separation.

"Hmm," Kybil thought for a moment and then said. "I'll bet we could get someone who was lightweight across. The hook isn't as high as this one."

"I can do it," Kess said. "Nordaal and Yaneth can get me across safely."

"No. It's too dangerous," Kybil looked down solemnly. "You could hit your head or hurt yourself being thrown over there. We could try one of the warriors."

He looked up to see all of them with their hands in the air volunteering.

Kess laughed softly, "No. I am the lightest one, and if I hit my head, no problem. Okay," she heaved a sigh, "let's try it." The floor beneath began to heave and shake more violently than the last time. "No time for discussion, let's do it."

"If Drago were here it would be no problem, but he isn't. She's right." Rakmor said and motioned for the two Dwargers to come forward.

"Are we sure they can throw me that far without putting me in the ceiling?" Kess had just got the words out when Nordaal grabbed her under her arms and Yaneth grabbed her feet.

"Hold on," Kybil tied the other end of the rope around her waist. He lingered for one moment and looked into her face. "Try to land safely on the other side," he said softly, his voice filled with concern as he stepped away.

"Well, here I go," Kess gulped as the two Dwargers began to swing her back and forth, and then she was airborne sailing across to the other side of the tiles. Kess turned slightly in mid-air and landed on her backside on the other side of the expanse. The floor was at an incline, and Kess slid up and over the slanting tile floor and out of sight.

"Kess!" Kybil screamed.

At that instant, Nordaal and Yaneth grabbed the rope that was anchored around Kess's waist and held on tightly. The rope yanked her to an abrupt stop. The ground beneath began to shake heavily as she jumped to her feet. Kess quickly untied the rope around her waist and grabbed the loop made at the end of it.

She climbed back up the heaving floor toward the hook on the wall. The floors were still heaving and bucking violently as she pulled the noose over the hook and pulled it tight. "Hurry," she yelled to the group. "It's getting worse." No one moved. "What are you waiting for?" She tried to keep her balance on the wavering floor and gasped in terror when she saw Nordaal slip and fall onto an unmarked tile on the floor.

Everyone froze and waited for whatever was to come. After a while, realizing that nothing happened, Kybil gave the order to get to the other side where Kess was standing. No one hesitated as they charged across the heaving floor tiles. It took only seconds for everyone to cross the floor and stand safely next to Kess.

"You mean we were playing 'Simon Says' the whole length of that hallway and all we had to do was run?" Kess rolled her eyes and laughed.

"And just think," Doc patted her arm gently, "you got here first. Of course, it wasn't exactly a very dignified approach, but rather entertaining." He laughed and gave her a big hug.

Everyone began to move toward the two large doors when loud popping sounds erupted behind them. They turned to see the tiles explode and smash into the stone ceiling causing large chunks of the ceiling to fall where they had just stood. They watched amazed at the destruction: No one would have survived that eruption. After a moment, everything was quiet; the dust began to settle.

Suddenly, a loud bang behind them caused them all to whirl around. The two large doors at the end of the hallway flew open and a tall man in a long, purple sorcerer's gown appeared. He stopped abruptly and stared at the group in front of him. His small eyes widened in total surprise. His face broke into a huge grin, and just as quickly it disappeared. "Are you real?" He asked suspiciously.

"Yes," Kybil said in a relief filled voice. "We were trapped in here by the demons."

"Yes. Yes," the tall man walked away motioning for them to follow him through the two large doors.

"Who are you?" Rakmor asked as they moved toward the old man in the sorcerer's gown.

"Who am I?" He asked incredulously. "Who are you? How did you get this far? That's impossible?"

"Guess not," Kess said as she looked around at the incredibly messy room.

Apothecary jars still boiling, papers and books were strewn about everywhere in the large dust-filled room. A couple of tables and chairs placed haphazardly throughout the room were covered with papers and books. A large fireplace had been hewn out of the stone and glowed brightly into the room. The only other source of light was from the oil lamp placed by an uncluttered chair by the fireplace.

"But I went into the cave and set the destruct button," he said, shaking his head.

"That was what I saw in that little cave," Doc said.

"Yes. Yes," he muttered. "I saw a glimpse of you and thought it was the demons. My eyes are not as good as they used to be." His finger came up and began tapping the side of his face. "Now, where was I? Oh, yes," he began scurrying around the room picking up some papers and throwing them down, only to repeat the same actions over and over.

"Excuse me," Rakmor finally spoke up. "We seem to have a problem here and wondered if you could help us out."

The old man stopped for a moment and looked at Rakmor as if seeing him for the first time, "What are you doing here? How did you get in here?"

"Oh, boy," Kess shook her head. "This is going to be a long day."

"What do you want?" The old man looked from one face to another.

"We seem to have demons chasing us, and we need to get out of here," Kybil spoke up.

"Oh, yes! Yes, I see," he resumed picking up papers, keeping some in his hand, and throwing down the others. "We must leave. It is no longer safe here."

"Yes, we are thinking the same . . ." Rakmor stopped in mid-sentence as he picked up a sheet of paper with strange writings on it from the table. He moved a book that was partially covering another piece of paper and began to study it. "This is amazing."

"Of course," the tall man hurried over to Rakmor and snatched the paper from his hand. "I have been working on this for years."

"And does it work?" Rakmor asked.

"Yes. Yes, of course," he said indignantly. "I told you I have been working on it for years. Does it work? Humph!" He snorted.

"Are you two going to let us in on this or are we going to have to guess?" Doc said somewhat annoyed.

"In on what?" The old man grabbed more papers from the table and put them into a box on the floor.

"My guess is that you are Baalizar, the Grand Wizard." Rakmor folded his arms and stared at the bustling old man.

"Well, of course," he stopped abruptly. "Wait. How did you know my name?"

"The Imperial Sorceress Cedwynna charged us to find you," Rakmor said.

The name of Cedwynna brought him to an abrupt halt. "Did you say Cedwynna?"

"Yes," Rakmor nodded. "She asked that we seek you out, but we did not expect to find you here so quickly."

"Cedwynna," he said her name as if caressing every syllable. "I have not heard her name in a long, long time."

"She said you were one of the greatest Sorcerers of all time,"

Rakmor studied the lined face and his tall, lanky body with curiosity. "What brought you here?"

"What brought me here? Did you say what brought me here?" He snapped unexpectedly, "Ask Cedwynna."

"I will, but right now we have to get out of here," Rakmor shook his head. "If you can't help us, we'll figure something out."

"I must leave now," the wizard began to move about the room as if no one were there.

Kybil stepped in front of him. "Fine, but we're going with you."

Rakmor pushed a book on the table away that was slightly covering a sheet of paper and pulled it out. "Well, I'll be. This will get us out of here very nicely."

"Not sure," Baalizar rudely grabbed the paper from Rakmor's hand. "Very powerful demon. Not sure it will work against it. Against lesser demons, yes. Definitely. But powerful demon I am not sure." He began to argue with himself. "Of course, it will work. Maybe not. Yes, it will."

"Let's go with the one who says it will work," Kess piped up. "Which one thinks it will work?"

"I think it will work," the wizard's voice changed into a higher pitch. "But then again, may not work."

"Could you argue with yourself later?" Doc asked impatiently.

"I am Baalizar, the Grand Wizard of Mystovia," the voice said indignantly. "It will work."

"I like the one with the positive attitude. Let's go with that one." Doc said.

"Can you get all of us out of here?" Kess inquired warily.

"Actually, I think I can get you out of here." The wizard said, his deep voice echoed in the small room.

"Okay, then," Doc smiled up into the face of the wizard. "Let's just get out of here."

"I have been packing only the important papers to go," he gestured toward the small box on the table. "I do not want the demons to get a hold of this information, because they might be able to figure out what it is that I have discovered. The rest of this stuff I figure is of no importance."

The faint sound of demons in the distance could be heard throughout the room. "They are coming," Baalizar said.

"You have a very powerful spell here," Rakmor grabbed the box on the table. "You could use it on us as well."

"Yes," he said. "But I do not wish to."

"That's because it doesn't work," Kess' eyes narrowed. She had to try to trick him into helping them. "It doesn't work at all, does it?"

"No, that is not true," his deep voice screamed. "It is not that I do not want to help you, but I am not sure it will work on so many."

"I think you are brilliant, and it will work on all of us," Kess motioned for everyone to agree. The room was quickly filled with agreement from everyone.

"First, I must save my work," He reached over and quickly grabbed the box that held his formulas and pulled it close to his body. He said an incantation and the box he held disappeared. "There it is safe until I can get to it."

"Wow, is that what you have planned for us?" Kess asked amazed at how he made the box disappear.

"No, I cannot do that on all of us. I will use my new formula, but if it doesn't work we are all going to die." Baalizar quickly pulled a boiling apothecary from its burner. He said a few words that Rakmor listened to intently. The boiling liquid disappeared and was replaced by an orange sandy substance.

Baalizar poured the sand into his hand and then blew on it. The grains of sand began to twirl and twist, rising upward above the heads of the small group in front of him. The sand expanded until it was completely above everyone's head, and then it began to drift down slowly until it covered the entire warrior party, as well as Baalizar.

They all watched as the particles began to glow a bright orange that quickly turned into a brilliant silver flash, and then it was gone.

Baalizar brushed his hands and smiled. "Now we shall see. This has been years and years of work on nothing but this. I have perfected it." Baalizar said in a high squeaky voice.

"Oh, boy," Doc said nervously. "Why do I feel like a human guinea pig?"

"Because we are," Kess said.

"Listen," Kybil began turning around in the room. "The demons have stopped screaming."

"Of course," Baalizar quipped. "They no longer sense you. Come we must leave here. The potion does not last for long. It is something I am working on."

"So, exactly how long does this potion last?" Rakmor asked curiously.

"Not sure," Baalizar moved toward a wall with several markings on it. He raised his hand, and the outline of a door appeared. "We must go this way." The door outline shimmered for a moment, and then an actual door appeared. He pulled on the door handle and opened it, and immediately they could feel the cold air pouring through it. Baalizar grabbed his staff, turned, and looked at everyone just standing there. "What are you waiting for? We must leave now."

He had no sooner spoken those words when the room began to shake. Baalizar led the way up the steep winding stairs. It was a difficult climb up the stairs as they dodged the falling debris and tried to keep their balance while the mountain continued its sporadic shaking. At the next twist on the winding steps, a bright light came filtering down. Everyone ran in earnest to reach the door that led outside of the mountain.

"Finally. Oops!" Doc tripped and fell to his knees just outside the doorway.

Nordaal was right behind him. He reached down and scooped Doc up in one arm. "Hey der little guy," he carried him further away from the doorway. "Dis be better. Nobody fall on ya."

Doc's arms and legs hung down as he was gently deposited away from the exiting warriors. "I feel like a rag doll, only a lot more exhausted."

The last warrior came through the door, followed by billowing clouds of dust. There were more rumbling sounds and then the mountain shook so violently it caused several warriors to lose their balance and fall to the ground. Kess knew the reason she did not hit the ground was the firm grip Kybil had on her.

Doc looked up and spotted hundreds of demons running toward the top of the mountain where they stood. "I guess this stuff didn't work. Look!" He pointed at the demons racing toward them.

"There are way too many for us to fight," Kess pulled away from Kybil and looked down at the Ring of Remat. "I would rather die having the mountain come down on us, then becoming a dinner for them." She turned and raised her ring toward the demons rushing at them.

"No!" Baalizar screamed. "No!"

CHAPTER SEVEN

*D*rago flew with the other dragons toward their lairs in the North Arega mountains. The mood of the dragons was sullen as they approached their dwellings. They knew they had to stay on high alert because recently they were being attacked by the Spree dragons from the forests, and the Haquada dragons of the sea.

King Zaatyr told Drago about the blue Haquada dragons. They did not have the power to breathe fire, but they spewed a deadly poison when they got close enough to use it on their intended victims. The poison, deadly to any other species, only stunned the Arega dragons. But it was long enough for the Haquadas to coil around them and plunge them down into the depths of the water where their victim would drown.

The Haquadas had an advantage in the skies as they moved at incredibly fast speeds. Their disadvantage was they could only breathe air for a short period making it impossible for them to stay airborne for any great length of time.

The green and purple Spree dragons were just as big and powerful as the Arega dragons. They lived in the Rils and Myam forests and feasted on the Evoos, but preferred the Snagars, and occasionally a farmer would find a cow or one of his sheep missing.

King Zaatyr passed over the foothills of their mountain when the familiar shapes of the Haquadas broke the still, cold air. Their forms were almost a blue blur as they charged the cluster of Arega dragons.

Instantly, they assumed their battle stances. King Zaatyr sent a message for reinforcements to his clan and then one to his son. *"Drago, head for the mountains. We will try to hold them off,"* he ordered.

The Haquadas attacked in vast numbers. They dove in and around the outnumbered Aregas spewing their poison. The sky was on fire with flames bursting from their mouths causing the poison to disintegrate before it reached them. Some Aregas managed to maneuver above them and came down on the Haquadas grasping them by the head and killing them.

But more Haquadas were rising from the sea, and to Drago's dismay, he saw they were not alone: The Spree dragons were now joining in the fight.

Drago saw a Haquada about to attack one of his clan from behind. He swooped down and did a backflip and came up behind the enemy grabbing it by the back of the head and killing it instantly.

Two more of the Haquada dragons charged at Drago. He tucked in his wings, and like a projectile climbed above them and out of reach of their deadly spray. The two snake-dragons hissed and immediately followed him higher into the sky. They were gaining on him when he reached the thick cover of the clouds.

Drago stopped for a moment to assess the situation. His ability to be able to see through the denseness of the clouds gave him the advantage as he dove straight down at one of them. Drago's claws grasped the startled snake-dragon's head and killed him. Quickly, he flew back into the dense clouds to hide.

The shriek from the dying Haquada caused the other snake-dragon to spew its deadly poison in the direction of the scream. It could not see into the murky clouds, but it knew his enemy was in there somewhere. Drago saw the poison coming his way and flew out of its reach.

The body of the dead snake-dragon fell from the clouds almost striking the other Haquada as it fell. The second snake-dragon hissed in anger and charged toward the clouds, but this time he was followed closely by a large Spree dragon.

High winds had torn through Drago's cloud cover and he could no longer hide or attack unseen. He watched nervously as the two dragons raced toward him. The Haquada was coming in from his left and the Spree dragon was coming in from below.

Instead of flying away from them, Drago held his position. He hoped his plan would work as the snake-dragon closed in. Racing toward him from beneath was the Spree. Drago waited. The Spree dragon was almost on him when it sent out a blast of fire; Drago felt it on his tail but held fast to his position. The Haquada was closing in rapidly. Drago knew the Haquada was going to try to stun him with its poison and the Spree dragon would kill him.

It all happened within seconds. Just as the Haquada released its spray, Drago zoomed upward out of its reach and that of the charging Spree dragon. The poison meant for Drago struck the Spree dragon causing him to fall silently down into the sea.

The Haquada shrieked and began to chase Drago again as he burst through the now wispy clouds. The angry snake-dragon was so intent on destroying Drago, it did not see the two other Arega dragons behind him, and when he finally did: It was too late.

Drago was relieved to see that the Aregas were no longer outnumbered. The message they had sent brought a huge contingent of Arega dragon warriors to the battle. The battle was fast and fierce as the Aregas fought the Spree and Haquadas. Soon, the remaining Haquadas returned to the sea, and the Spree dragons turned and fled back to their forests.

"Were any warriors killed?" Zaatyr asked solemnly.

"Sire, only a couple of our warriors were wounded. No one was killed today," A female warrior reported stoically.

"*That is good news. Thank you. Return with the others.*" Zaatyr ordered.

"*Father,*" Drago caught up with Zaatyr.

"*Drago. You should have fled when I gave you the order.*" Zaatyr greeted him sternly.

"*That was an order? I thought you were just telling me to get out of the way because I am so little. But I knew I could help.*"

"*I was so busy fighting I did not know you were still here. I thought you had gone,*" Zaatyr said.

"*You were busy. I saw you fighting three of them. I would have come to help, but I was a little busy myself.*" Drago flew next to his father as they headed back to the Arega Mountains.

King Zaatyr looked over at his son. "*You are a very clever young dragon.*"

"*Yes, father,*" he said looking over at the giant dragon next to him. "*I come from a great line of dragons. But all our clan fought bravely. I can learn much from you and them.*"

Zaatyr looked at his youngest son with pride. "*We had no idea that they would try to ambush us. We will not be surprised again like that.*"

As Drago approached the Arega Mountains, he saw sentries guarding its perimeter. The sentries greeted the returning dragon warriors and sent a telepathic message that all was safe for now.

The warmth of the caves and sulfur from the brewing lava beneath the mountain filled the air in their caves; the dragons welcomed and enjoyed the acrid aroma.

Each dragon had a cave they shared with their mate and the treasures they had accrued over the years. There were a few dragons who were loners, some by choice; others because their mate was killed in battle.

Drago's heritage was that of dragons who mated for life and stayed true and faithful to their mate until the end. The dragons had a predestined mate they had no control over. Once they met there was an immediate bonding, and from that point on they were a mated pair, never interested in any other. They shared all their wealth with their mate and helped to raise the little dragonets. If one mate would perish, then, and only then, were they free to select another mate.

Drago shared a lair with his father. Until a dragon was full-grown, they were expected to live with their parents.

They landed together and entered the cave opening. It was a huge cavern with gold, and jewels heaped in mammoth bunches along the perimeter of the walls.

An opening in the floor of the cave against the farthest end was the only source of light. The never-ending stream of lava below kept all the caves warm while emitting soft lighting around the walls which were encrusted with gold nuggets that sparkled and twinkled continually. It was as if they were vying for attention against the hoard of gold and jewels piled in the room.

King Zaatyr paced back and forth in the huge cave, while Drago curled up against a pile of jewels and closed his eyes.

Soon, a bellowing noise interrupted Drago's sleep, and his father nudged him. "*It is time for the meeting with the new Oracle.*"

"*Hmm,*" Drago stood up and stretched his tired body. "*Okay.*"

"*What is 'okay'?*" Zaatyr asked.

"*It means . . .*" Drago looked up and tilted his head. "*I do not know, except it must mean 'yes' or 'alright.*"

"*Yes, I see,*" he shook his large head. "*It is a strange language they speak at times. Come we must attend the ritual.*"

"*What ritual is that?*" Drago asked.

"*We must welcome our new Oracle,*" Zaatyr moved toward an opening off to the side of the cave. It was large enough for him to go through easily and led to a labyrinth of connecting hallways. The ground began to slant downward as they moved slowly through the wide corridors.

Finally, the passageway opened up into a mammoth cavern inside the mountain. There were thousands of dragons perched on ledges adjacent to their private dwellings. King Zaatyr moved to the center of the cave with Drago at his side.

A rustling noise was heard as the old and new Oracles entered the cavern. Drago peered around his father and watched in fascination as the two approached them.

The old Oracle was in her human form. Her long hair was as black as cooled lava. A few strands fell gracefully over her shoulder, and the rest hung down to her waist. Her skin was the color of dark golden sand, and her eyes were large and brown. The wings on her back were sturdy, silvery, and opaque. The bottom part of her dress was made up of multi-shades of white that swirled softly around her bare feet. The cloth across her bodice and breasts was covered in jewels of deep shimmering gold and silver.

But Drago's attention was riveted on the Oracle who was in her dragon form. He blinked several times as he stared at the small dragoness. She was the most beautiful dragon he had ever seen.

Her wings glistened like frost on a window in the sunlight. Her body, covered in blue and silver scales, shimmered iridescently. Her regal head had two slim horns, which held brilliant red rubies in them. Drago's mouth dropped as he began to study her wings. They were transparent, shimmering, gossamer-like wings with only a trace of the bones showing through. Her eyes were the color of a calm sea.

"I have come to introduce your new Oracle," the old Oracle, Byla, said and stepped away from the dragoness. Her hand flowed gracefully as she gestured toward her replacement. *"Her blood-line is impeccable and has given us one of the greatest Oracles of our time. As you know, my fifty years are up, and a new replacement has been found. I have well enjoyed my connection with you and will miss you greatly. I hope our paths cross in other aspects, and if you ever require two Oracles, hesitate not, for I will always be there for you."*

At once, Byla's body began to shake, and a hazy mist began to form around her. The thick mist grew and grew until it reached the size of a full-grown dragon. Slowly, the mist dissipated and before them stood a silver dragon with a gold and silver chest. Golden horns and bronze scales adorned the face of the dragon, and black scales formed the rest of her head. The body of the dragon was silver except for the bronze claws and talons at the end of her wings. Her eyes changed from a deep brown to deep gold.

She was a beautiful dragon by any standards. She was a Dragling: a dragon changeling. *"Introduce yourself to this wondrous gathering of powerful and wise dragons."* She looked down at the small dragon standing next to her.

"My name is Xen," the dragoness raised her head proudly and looked around the room. *"My father is a Dragling, and my mother is a Sabbot witch. I will serve you well, for I have great magical powers, and I possess the ability to perform as your Oracle."*

A question from one of the dragons came forth. *"But you are not a full-blooded Dragling. Can you mingle with the others to find out things we would not be able to know otherwise?"*

"Yes, I can change into other forms. I have just recently been shown how to change into my dragon form, as I was in an entirely different form than you see me now. And, yes, it is true; I am not a full-blooded Dragling." Xen thrust back her shoulders and held her head high, *"so, if you wish for another Oracle we will search until one is found."*

"No!" Drago heard his voice loud and alone in the cavern of dragons. *"I mean we need a good Oracle. What does it matter if she is not a full-blooded Dragling?"*

Xen turned and looked at Drago. *"Thank you,"* she said just to him.

Drago heard her thoughts. They felt like gentle kisses from the wind, as he nodded ever so slightly toward her. There seemed to be something familiar about the sound of her voice.

"Please," Byla's voice was gentle and reassuring to the myriad dragons surrounding the great hall. *"She is worthy of this place of honor. Trust in her. You will not be sorry. She is not only a gifted Oracle but possesses very powerful magic."*

"Are we now to challenge the selection of our Oracles?" King Zaatyr began to walk around the room looking up at the dragons he

ruled. *"We shall go with the counsels' choice of this Oracle and question this no further."*

An affirmative reply was sent by all dragons. Drago sighed with deep relief.

Byla spoke again, *"I must depart now, and listen well, as Xen has much to tell you."* She turned, bowed to Xen, and walked from the hall, but just before she left the hall she sent a message to Zaatyr alone. *"You, my lord, have not seen the last of me. I shall be back to win your heart."*

For the first time in his life, Zaatyr was speechless. He watched as the beautiful dragon, Byla, disappeared from his view.

"Father?" Drago nudged his father with a wingtip. *"Father? Are you listening?"*

"What?" He bristled slightly. *"Ahem, yes, of course. What insights do you have for us?"* He asked the new oracle.

"I am afraid it is not good," Xen lowered her head for a moment and then raised it slowly. *"A powerful evil being has been set loose among the demons, and it will affect you directly."*

"What being?" Zaatyr questioned.

"The being is an evil, ancient one. It has great powers and is extremely dangerous. There are many visions of this ancient one. It is a thing of change. It is a deceptive, cunning beast. We do not think we have seen its true form. All we know is that it commands great magical powers."

"We are very powerful and dangerous as well," Drago spoke angrily.

Xen turned to Drago, tilted her head, and stared at him for a moment. *"Yes, you all are indeed powerful and dangerous."* She did not take her eyes off Drago, as if studying him. When she spoke to him, she was firm. *"Drago I see you helping your friends. You must warn your friends that danger lurks everywhere for them. They are sought by the deceptive being. It has brought dark evil to this land. It knows its enemy's powers. And, through this knowledge, it will try to* destroy them one-by-one. I feel this evil growing stronger. Tell your friends to trust their instincts."

"We will help Drago keep them safe," Zaatyr said.

"My Lord, you will have much to do for our kind," she looked at the tall dragon before her. "The dragons of the sea and forest are being influenced by this dark evil. They will soon attack. You must prepare for a great war. It is coming. And Drago you must go and warn your friends before it is too late."

King Zaatyr nodded and then added, "Can this deceptive being be detected?"

After a while, the young dragoness lifted her head, "Yes. Our Chan-Draa can warn us if it has changed its form."

"Then, we will be able to find this deceptive being and destroy it," Zaatyr said.

Again, the dragoness was quiet in thought. "We do not foresee the Aregas destroying this evil presence. But for now, you and the others must fight to protect your homes and loved ones. Be warned that when the Chan-Draa returns from the council of Oracles she will go out for her usual morning mind-cleansing; it is at this time she may be in danger. Guards must accompany her at all times when she chooses to leave the protection of our mountain."

"Done," Zaatyr said.

"Well," Drago said. "Is that all?"

"No, I see a vast land of sand," her large blue eyes looked at Drago with sadness. "This evil being will try to destroy all. Before the vision faded there was another being who possesses great magic and who shall become his ally. This shall come to pass in the future. There is much danger headed our way."

"We can protect our own." A dragon said indignantly perched on the edge of his cave.

"Yes. You can protect your own." Xen's thoughts traveled to all the dragons. "But for now, this demon has great magical powers; greater than we possess. We have sent for the two humans who possess powerful talismans to help protect us from an attack by this being."

"But no human has ever been allowed to enter our mountains." A dragon spoke out defiantly.

Drago's foot tapped against the stone floor, the sound of his claws hitting the floor echoed in the silence. His tapping stopped, and he said, *"I know the two humans who possess the powerful talismans. They are my friends, and I trust them with my life."*

"Yes, I too, have met them. They will be most welcome, as Drago has said they are great friends to not only Drago but all Aregas as well." Zaatyr said for all to hear.

Xen continued speaking with the dragons. *"This evil being has much power and controls the underworld of demons and wraiths without fear of retaliation. It can and does possess the minds of the lesser forms. It has powers we Oracles cannot detect at this time. Even worse, this demon creature fears nothing or no one."* She moved her head back and forth trying visually to engage the dragons perched high above her.

"It does not fear us?" Zaatyr's question brought complete silence in the room.

"No, it fears nothing," Xen looked up at the King, and then to Drago. *"Its arrogance may be the cause of its destruction, and that may be the greatest advantage we have against this rising menace."*

"We shall all meet back here when the . . ." Zaatyr was interrupted by one of the sentries posted outside the mountain.

The dragon flew to the grand opening of the cave. *"The Haquada dragons are approaching."* His thoughts were loud in the minds of the other dragons as they quickly flew toward the sentry and the large opening.

"Drago, you must stay here and guard Xen," Zaatyr said firmly. *"And when I return there are some things you must know about yourself."*

"Okay," Drago replied somewhat puzzled by the unexpected comment from his father.

"We will help guard them," a red-gold dragon, said and bowed to

Zaatyr. The two dragons had flown down from above and stood next to Drago.

Zaatyr nodded in acceptance. *"You must take her down to the nursery, as that is the most protected and safe place for her to be."*

"But I am a great fighter," Even though Drago wanted to protect her, he also wanted to help fight the Haquada dragons.

"That is precisely why I want you to stay and protect her and the dragonets." His wing brushed ever so slightly over Drago's wings before he stepped away to make room for his lift-off. *"Several dragons are guarding the young ones, so she will be safe there. The young ones are our future, as is the Oracle who will help to ensure it. Now, go! Quickly!"* King Zaatyr nodded toward an opening at the farthest part of the cave. *"You must hurry!"*

Drago watched as his father flew out of the cave and out of sight. His heart was heavy as he thought of the fighting that his clan was about to encounter.

"Drago," Xen's thoughts were gentle and reassuring. *"They will come back victorious. Please trust me on this."*

"Then, I am not needed here to protect you," he turned and looked into her beautiful face. *"I mean it is not that I do not want to protect you."*

"There is something about this that I feel is not right," Xen cocked her head to one side and spoke only to Drago. *"I feel a betrayal is imminent. I fear for you and me. I do not see it, but I feel it, and it is real."*

The urgency in her thoughts surprised Drago. He spoke to her alone, *"I will stay and protect you with my life."*

They hurried toward the opening and began to walk down the wide tunnel. Suddenly, Xen sent Drago an urgent message. *"Drago,"* she spoke quickly to him. *"We must not lead them to the nursery. When we turned the corner, I picked up the thoughts of one of the dragons. He is a traitor. But I know not which one, or if it is both. What should we do?"*

"I will lead them away from the nursery," He stopped and looked at the two passageways that were just a few feet into the main tunnel.

"What are you doing?" One of the large red dragons stood over him glowing down at him.

"I am trying to think," Drago let his thoughts sound sincere.

"What are you trying to think about?" The second dragon behind him asked with great annoyance.

"Well, how do we get to the nursery from here." Drago's shrugged. *"I have only been there once. I am trying to remember."*

"You," the large dragon looked at Xen and ordered. *"You lead the way."*

"I am afraid I have never been to the nursery," she looked over at Drago and was relieved when he gave her a quick wink of the eye.

"We have to be careful which way we go because after this split in the tunnel, there are a whole bunch of twists and turns up ahead, and if you make a wrong turn you could be lost forever," Drago said with asserted knowledge. He noticed the exchanged look between the two massive dragons. *"Oh, wait, I think there were markings on the different pathways to show the correct way."*

"Move," the dragon from behind brushed past Drago and walked to the two paths leading down into the depths of the cave. *"What kind of markings are we looking for?"*

"I think the markings on this passageway are . . ." He stopped as if in thought and instantly sent a private message to Xen.

"Are what?" The second dragon whipped his head toward Drago.

"Oh, yes, they are circles. Yes, circle. That is what is etched into the stone to show the correct way."

"I see strange markings, but I do not see any circles on this side," the largest of the red dragons said with exasperation.

"Nor do I. Wait I found them," the other dragon nodded toward the tunnel splitting to the left.

"How many of these signs are there?" The larger dragon asked.

"Oh, each tunnel has a different marking to show the way," Drago fell behind with Xen as they moved farther into the cave tunnel.

"*Look for a star-shaped sign next*," Drago suggested to the two anxious dragons when they came to another split in the tunnel.

"*We have been walking for a long time to get to this nursery*," grumbled the smaller of the two dragons.

"*How long have you been Arega dragons?*" Drago chided. "*Of course, it is. It would be pretty stupid to have the nursery so close to the great cave. It would make the younglings too easy of a prey for the enemy.*"

"*Well*," the red-gold dragon snapped. "*We have never guarded the nursery before, so, logically, we would not know the way.*"

"*Of course*," Drago's thoughts were masked by his carefree attitude. He knew that these two large, powerful dragons were dangerous. He had to keep them off guard. "*Look at me. I have been there once, and I still do not know the way, unless I read the markings.*"

"*Keep moving*," the lead dragon said as he turned to Xen who had stopped.

"*I am sorry*," she said dropping her head down. "*I am very tired from my long journey here.*"

"*I will stay here with her*," said one of the two larger dragons, as they exchanged knowing glances.

"*If she stays, I stay. Father ordered me to stay with her. I do not want the wrath of my father for disobeying him. And neither do you.*" Drago said trying hard to keep his voice from betraying the angry emotions building inside of him. He caught another conspiratorial exchange between them. "*And I do believe we are almost there.*" He lied.

"*I can keep up.*" Xen lifted her head and walked quickly behind Drago.

"*I will stay behind her and watch her*," The mammoth body of the dragon brushed past Drago and Xen.

"*He plans to kill me*," Xen sent a message to Drago. "*They will keep you alive until you have led them to the nursery.*"

"*What about you? Why not kill you now?*" Drago asked.

"*They won't kill me now because they know you would not show them the way to the nursery.*" She looked back at one of the dragons. "*They are so big.*"

"*I know,*" Drago said.

Drago knew the tunnels could hold two large dragons walking abreast very easily, but these two dragons made a point of bumping into both him and Xen every time they walked past them.

They were completely trapped. There were solid stone walls on both sides with a large dragon in front and one behind them. His mind was racing. He had to think of something. They were far too large and powerful for him to fight alone, and he could not take a chance of fighting them in these cramped quarters for fear that Xen would be hurt.

"*They are getting suspicious,*" her voice showed no signs of fear to Drago. "*I am new at this Oracle thing, and it is very frustrating for me because I know not what will happen to us.*"

"*In your vision, you saw me helping my friends. That is enough for me to know we are going to get out of this somehow.*" He moved closer to her letting his wings brush up against her ever so slightly.

"*What I see can be changed,*" she lowered her gaze to try to hide the fact she was communicating with Drago.

It took everything in Drago's power to stop from blurting out 'huh?' After he gained his composure, he questioned her. "*What do you mean it can be changed?*"

"*What I see is the future at that moment, without any complications. I cannot foretell any instances in the future that may alter or influence the prediction to go in another direction. It is not always true, due to unforeseen problems. Although, it is usually accurate. You see everyone can choose to follow their chosen path, or they may veer from it and choose another by their choice or others.*"

"*Great!*" He turned his head away from her and glanced back at the looming dragon behind them. "*So, what you are saying is my path was chosen for me, but these two traitors may end my life, thereby, canceling my choices.*"

"*Yes, that would be a brief and concise way of looking at it.*"

"*Okay! I do not like 'looking' at it that way,*" He turned very slightly again to glance back at the dragon behind him and knew the raw power he contained. There had to be away out of this. He had to think and think fast. Then he saw it. Up ahead there was a small opening, just big enough for the two of them to escape into. He had no idea where it went, but he had no idea where he was going anyway. They had to be quick. He shot a message to Xen.

"*But we do not know where it leads or ends. And it may be just a small cut in the walls and not go anywhere.*"

"*You are the Oracle, you tell me,*" He looked away from her as if he were studying the stone walls surrounding them. "*Can you create a distraction so that we can slip in there? You have done wonderfully with the fake images on the walls so far.*"

"*I will make a distraction for them but be ready to move very quickly. I am very tired of using my powers, as this is all very new to me. This may take much from me. Walk closer to me so that I may use your body to lead me through the tunnel. I have to close my eyes and concentrate.*" She closed her eyes and moved closer to Drago who was already grabbing her wing from underneath to guide her. She lowered her head and began to chant so quietly that even Drago could not hear her. Slowly, she reached underneath her body and pulled out a small stone concealed behind one of her scales.

"*We are almost upon it,*" Drago said.

Suddenly, a wailing sound pierced the quiet. It built into ear-splitting cries coming from both ends of the tunnel.

"*Demons!*" The large dragon shouted behind them.

"*We will take care of them. You two stay here,*" ordered the larger dragon in front of them. "*I will handle those coming this way. You go the other* way."

Drago watched as the two dragons headed down the tunnel in different directions at a fast clip. "*Quickly,*" he said.

The opening was smaller than it looked, but they managed to squeeze inside of it. A narrow path led downward. In some places, their scales scraped against the stone walls causing little sparks to occur.

They had traveled quite a bit when they heard the roar of the two dragons. *"I think they figured out they have been tricked,"* Drago said hurrying down the narrow pathway. They could hear the sound of the two dragons beating on the stone wall as it reverberated down the pathway.

Drago and Xen kept walking until they came to an opening with a small ledge perched almost a hundred feet above the churning, moving lava. The path led out to a small half wall of stone on one side and a sheer rock wall on the other. The pounding of the two dragons became more and more muted.

"I think they found the hole in the wall that we came through and are trying to make it big enough for them." Drago stepped cautiously onto the ledge that gradually widened from four feet to seven feet. "Let me see if it's stable or not first." Drago went a short distance and motioned for her to come forward.

"They certainly would not be able to use that pathway. It was almost too narrow for us." She looked down at the bubbling, churning lava.

"Right now, I am more concerned about this ledge." Drago looked ahead and smiled. *"Look, after this overhang, there is a wide opening. We can fly out of here."*

"Drago," Xen's voice rang with fear. *"The pounding has stopped."*

"It just may mean the walls are too thick to breakthrough. Even if they knocked a big hole in the entrance, as you said, they would never fit down the pathway. Come on, let's get out of here."

Drago and Xen followed the path around a corner and were pleasantly surprised at the enormous size of the cavern. Steep stone cliffs rose high up the inside of the mountain, giving them more than enough room to fly. Below, the glow from the red lava cast eerie shadows along the jagged rocks. Drago motioned for Xen to come forward so they could fly upwards to see if there was a way out.

"Well. Well. Well," One of the large red dragons flew toward

them. They heard his thoughts as he sent a message to his comrade. "*I have found our little friends.*"

Drago quickly communicated with Xen to get back to safety via the passageway. He watched as the menacing dragon took his eyes off him and looked toward Xen. In that, instant Drago took off and flew straight at him. If he could reach the vulnerable spot on his stomach, they may have a chance.

Xen yelled an insult at the dragon in hopes that he had not noticed Drago, but the second dragon approaching them saw Drago and warned his partner.

The large dragon moved away and reached for Drago with his powerful claws. Drago dodged out of the way, flying under the dragon and around to the back of it. Drago turned and was horrified to find the two dragons were now concentrating on Xen. Drago dove down and smacked the back of the head of the largest dragon, and quickly flew up into the highest part of the cavern to try to draw the two dragons away from her.

Drago looked back and saw that the large red dragon kept his attention only on Xen. He had hoped she had moved to safety but was startled to see that she had not moved.

He heard her hurl more insults at the two dragons below and watched in horror as they began to approach her. They would perish together. Drago spread his wings and was about to fly back to her when Xen sent him a message to stay where he was. No sooner did he receive that message than Xen burst into a brilliant white light, blinding him for a moment.

It didn't take the two dragons long to get their sight back and snorted at her feeble attempt to ward them off. "*She is not a very clever thing, is she? This is much easier than we thought.*" One said to the other.

"*She cannot even move she is so afraid,*" the other chortled. He turned to his partner, "*should we make her suffer for a while?*"

"*No one will ever find us down here,*" he replied with a throaty sound of laughter. "*We can just take our time with her.*"

He turned smugly to face his partner and noticed the terror registering in his partner's eyes. Confused he swung around and came face-to-face with a massive dragon formed out of lava hovering over them.

The face of the creature was brimming and dripping with lava, and its eye sockets were a piercing glow of white. The mouth of the lava dragon opened wide to expose huge silver fangs. The two dragons bumped into each other as they moved out of striking distance and headed back toward the large opening they had come through. They were startled to see several of the Imperial Guards of the Royal Court. They turned around to fly away and were faced again with the massive lava Dragon. The encounter lasted only seconds, and the two dragons were led away by the Royal Guard.

Drago had watched in awe at the powerful actions of his father's Royal Guard, and with a sigh of relief looked back at Xen. She had pulled a small box from under one of her scales and placed it to her forehead and carefully put it back. Then she slumped to the ground as the massive lava dragon disappeared back into the churning molten river. One of the Royal Guards reached her just before Drago and gently picked her up in her large claws. *"We were in battle when we got her message. King Zaatyr ordered us to leave."*

"But how did you find us in this maze of tunnels so quickly?" Drago asked.

"We followed the signs left by our Oracle. While she was leaving false trails to the nursery, she also left signs for us to follow." She carried Xen swiftly to a large opening that led into the cavern. *"While the two traitors were looking for you, they found this opening. Fortunately, we heard their thoughts once we entered the passageways and followed them."* She was greeted by the dragon healers who quickly took Xen from her gentle grasp.

Drago nodded to the dragon healers. They were tall, thin, scaly, black lizards who walked erect. Gently, they laid her on a long, board that floated aboveground and guided it down the long passageway.

The healers had formed an alliance with the dragons of Arega centuries ago when the dragons first appeared. The Aregas provided the healers with protection, shelter, and food, and in return, the lizards took care of the sick and wounded dragons. The saliva of the lizards is poisonous to everyone else but proved to be a great healing tool for the dragons.

Drago followed behind them until they came to the entrance to the main chamber hall. He paused and watched as Xen was taken to the healing rooms.

The Royal Guard escorted Drago into the main chamber where his father, Zaatyr was waiting.

"There is not much we can do for her now. They will let us know her condition as soon as possible," Zaatyr spoke softly to Drago. *"Stay here while I find out who sent these two dragons."*

Time passed slower than Drago had ever known before. He paced back and forth with worry for Xen. Finally, a dragon healer appeared at the entrance to the main chamber hall. *"She will be fine. All she needs is a little rest for now."* The black lizard turned and walked away.

A short while later his father appeared. *"How is she?"* He asked.

"They said all she needs is rest for now," Drago shook his head. *"You should have seen her. She was so brave."*

"She is very lucky that you had stayed with her," he moved toward the steep path that led to their quarters. *"I was very relieved to see that you were also unhurt."*

"As I with you," Drago followed his father up the path. *"Who were they?"*

"Changelings," he said.

"Changelings?" But Why? How?" Drago asked incredulously. *"How could they have gotten past the magic protecting us from changelings?"*

"Our Spell of Deception was broken by a powerful counter spell. But the Oracles and sorcerers have now put a spell to protect us from that ever happening again."

"Who could have placed such powerful magic against us?" Drago asked.

"Byla, the previous Oracle was called back to help penetrate their mental defenses. She found that a Master Demon now controls all the demons. They were sent to kill the new Oracle and all our dragonets. And, just as frightening is the fact that this Master Demon now controls the mindless dragons of the Blue Sea and has managed to turn the Spree dragons into our bitter enemies, again."

"If it can control the dragons of the sea and forest why aren't we controlled?" Drago approached the opening of their dwelling close behind his father.

"Because we have evolved mentally further than the other dragons. We and the silver dragons of the North have educated our young in all things." He stopped

Drago cocked his head waiting for his father to continue.

A deep sigh escaped from Zaatyr. *"There is much I have to tell you. So, I guess now is as good a time as any. Sit down, my son."* He turned and sat next to Drago, who peered up at his father.

Zaatyr looked down into the questioning face of his son. *"There was a time hundreds of years ago that we all, meaning all of us dragons, lived in a place called Earth.*

"Earth!" Drago said startled. *"But that is where Mac is from."*

"Yes," he continued. *"We were friends of man for many years, and then man turned on us and began pursuing and killing us."*

"But why?"

"Rumors. Stories of dragon treachery." Zaatyr looked away sadly. *"I suppose we did have a few dragons that may have been less than worthy. However, I believe that most of the dragons were honorable."*

"But we are very powerful, and man is so small," Drago shook his head.

"Man developed great weapons to destroy us. It was an evil time upon the land where everyone suspected everyone of something bad. Maybe it was because we were so powerful that we threatened man

without knowing it. Whatever the reason, we had to escape man and find a place where we would be safe."

"How did our ancestors find Mystovia?"

"I am coming to that," Zaatyr placed a claw gently on Drago's scaly knee. *"It was a time of war. It was a time of man against the beast, as they began to call us. All the dragons; the blue dragons of the sea and the green of the forest united to save our kind. We were losing, and all seemed lost until one fateful day a stranger came among us."*

Drago listened intently to every word his father was saying.

Zaatyr continued, *"He was a traveler. A traveler from another world. For days, he watched our war with the humans, and finally, he could take it no longer and tried to stop the destruction. It almost cost him his life."*

Drago sat quietly listening with fascination to his father's story.

"Instead of embracing his wisdom the humans feared him and imprisoned him. They sentenced him to be burned at the stake. The day before his execution a great storm raged through the village. It toppled their weapons and caused mudslides and water to slam into their village, toppling homes and buildings. The dragons seized that moment to rescue the strange little man who tried to save them."

Zaatyr moved toward the tunnel entrance to their dwellings. *"Someone is coming."*

Drago glanced at the opening and back at his father, *"I care not. Please, continue."*

"This little man had a strange glowing Orb in his hand and told all of those that were left to follow him to a safe place." Zaatyr shook his head and laughed softly. *"That they trusted him and did not question him was a great feat in itself. So, they followed him through a strange barren land to Mystovia, and this has been our home ever since that day."*

"So, all the dragons came to Mystovia?"

"I believe they did," he put his claw to his chin. *"Although, there were many smaller dragons with no intellect or thought process at all who were not brought over. After the dragon clans reached Mystovia*

each of the dragon groups chose their area to breed and live. Our clan chose the Arega Mountains and took that name as our own."

"You have not mentioned the Silver dragons of the north. Were they not with you?" He asked.

"No, they already lived in Mystovia. They were great friends of the little wizard, which proved to be a good thing for all of us." He nodded and smiled. "It was then that the Silver dragons of the North came to visit all of the new arrivals to Mystovia. They are dragons with great magical powers. After they tested all the new dragons that entered their world, they chose us to breed with and only us."

"Why is that?"

"Because the other dragon clans were not to be trusted," Xen's thoughts startled Drago.

He jumped up to see Xen standing in the entranceway of their dwelling. "*Xen,*" his heart soared at the sight of her.

"*Please enter our meager dwelling,*" King Zaatyr gestured for her to enter the room.

"*And I said 'I care not' who is coming up the passageway. I am so embarrassed. It is not true where you are concerned.*"

"*I know,*" her thoughts were like sweet music to him. "*You asked your father why our clan chose the red dragons of the mountains. If I have your permission, I would like to continue.*" She directed her request to Zaatyr.

"Yes," he nodded in acquiescence. "*It would be an honor.*"

"*I was told that the Haquada dragons of the sea were not of our liking, and they had no interest in mating with the silver dragons of the north. They thought us inept because we could not live underwater. We could have if we had so chosen, but they were dragons of a mean nature. As for the Spree dragons of the forest, they tried to control us and tried to find a way to take our powers from us and use it for them.*"

"*So, why did your clan choose the Aregas? Were we that different?*" Drago asked.

"*I was told that both the Haquada and Spree dragons were quick to wage wars; sometimes for no reason at all. My clan was impressed with the golden dragons of Arega, who embraced and craved knowledge. They did not try to take our powers or use them for their selfish reasons; instead, they chose to live beside us in peace and as equals."*

"We are thought of as 'golden' dragons," Drago looked puzzled. "We are mostly red."

"We have red markings, but if you look at the undercoat of a red dragon you will see we are really more golden," Zaatyr said lifting one of his scales to show the golden color beneath it.

"*But that is not the reason I have come here,*" Xen looked up into Zaatyr's face. "*Drago must leave immediately to help our friends. I am afraid they are in grave danger.*"

"*I will send my best warriors with him,*" Zaatyr began to call out to his warriors when Xen stopped him.

"*You will have much need of your warriors here,*" she looked downward for a moment and slowly lifted her head to stare into Drago's face. "*The enemy is massing for another attack. I see a vision. It is not as clear as I would like, but it will have to do. Drago will be needed to accompany his friends. I see him safe. But Mac is in danger as well. A betrayal of some kind.*"

Drago tried not to think of what Xen had told him about choices, and that they could affect the future of what she saw. "*I must go. Besides, Father, it will be easier for me to sneak out of here unnoticed than having the larger warriors flying with me. I will be careful. I promise. You must take care of yourself as well.*"

"*Why is it so important that Drago goes by himself? Surely, we could spare one other warrior?*" He asked skeptically.

"*Father, with their homes and families at stake, which warrior would you ask to go? What if something happened and his or her family was attacked? How would they feel being so far away and unable to protect them?*"

"*Drago is right,*" she said. "*Also, his future is not seen staying here. He will be needed more with his friends.*"

"*But I thought the humans were to come here?*" Zaatyr questioned.

"Yes, I know. They were coming here to help guard our Chan-Draa. But she is not here right now and does not need their help at this moment." Xen shook her head. *"My vision is clear on this. His friends are heading into grave danger. Drago's ability to read minds may save them."*

"Of course," Drago agreed. *"I will be of more use to them than I am right now. I am too small to fight, and if I did try to fight them; you would be more concerned about my safety and not thinking of your own."*

"You are right," Zaatyr finally said, hedging somewhat. *"We will prepare a diversion so that you may leave undetected."* He moved toward the entrance to the cavern and called out for his Royal Guard.

"Xen, have you seen where my friends are at this time?" Drago asked.

"Yes. Yes, I have," her voice faltered slightly.

"Right now, I see them inside a mountain." She said grimly, *"Many demons are looking for them. They are safe for now, but not for long. Once they leave the safety of the wizard's room they will be in deadly peril. And, Drago, they are preparing to leave that room."*

"What mountain are they on?" Drago asked.

"They are near the Rils forest in the southern Xelrils Mountains."

Drago thought for a moment and then declared in satisfaction. *"I know where that is."*

King Zaatyr walked over to Drago, the muscles in his jaw tightened slightly. *"I have made the arrangements. It is time for you to go. Be careful my son."*

"I will, Father, and you be careful as well."

Drago and Zaatyr moved to the lair opening. Drago stopped and looked back at Xen. Their eyes met briefly, and they knew something special had happened between them. Somewhat reluctantly, he turned back and followed his father.

$\mathcal{M}$ac and Sirel met the rest of the Ankhourian warriors at the stables in the castle. Freak winds overhead caused a change of plans from engaging the Gralcons.

"At least we're not going to run all the way," Mac mumbled. He turned to Sirel and asked, "Where are we going again?"

"We will be going through the tunnels of the Xelrils Mountain."

"How do you pronounce that again?" Mac queried.

"Zel-rils," Sirel explained and continued, "From the Xelrils Mountain we will make camp at a Tahotay village for the night. I believe Kess and the others are taking the tunnels to the south of the mountain; we are taking the ones north."

"Isn't there a Tahotay village somewhere on the banks of the Zanadur Lake?"

"There are many Tahotay villages along the eastern part of the lake," Sirel said. She placed her foot in the stirrup and swung up on her horse with ease. "We are going south to the mouth of Lake Zanadur from there we head northwest."

"Okay, you can stop now." Mac looked over at Sirel and threw up his hands. "I am so confused with who is heading east, west, north, or south. All I know for sure is that I'm in a stable and haven't a clue where that even is." He shook his head and gently nudged his horse toward Sirel. "I'll just follow your pretty face in whatever direction you want to go."

They moved through several large openings before they finally reached the grand tunnels beneath the Xelrils mountains where four sorcerers were waiting for them. They were to accompany Mac and the others through the maze of passages and create an opening to the outside for them to ride through when they reached the end of the tunnels.

"I have to ask," Mac looked over at Sirel. "Why are there no Men fighting? You know like me. I see Indian, Elven and Ankhourian warriors, but no Men."

"The Men join us from time to time. But mostly they partner with other villages that are nearby. They have a vast network of friends and family. And they occupy most of the top part of Lake Zanadur. If ever we needed help, which most of the time we do not, they would be there to help us," she looked at Mac and smiled.

"Thanks," he returned the smile. "Just curious."

They traveled side-by-side into the vast cavern under the castle.

"Look at the size of this place," Mac said in awe. "Does it stay this large to the end?"

"Only until we enter the passageways," Sirel said.

"Was this man-made or was it here?" Mac asked.

"It was here," she stated. "And magic protects it."

"Do the demons know about this specific place?"

"I think not," she gestured toward the sparkling, silvery walls lining the entire cavern. "The protective magic has been in place for hundreds of years. However, even if they did find this cavern it is a complex place with false passages that lead to nowhere."

"Who uses this?"

"We all do from time-to-time, and only with a guide," Sirel leaned back in the saddle. "There are many ways to get lost or worse down here."

"You mean they have booby-traps around here?" Mac questioned her softly.

"What is a 'booby-trap'?" Sirel cocked her head and looked in his direction.

"It means that there may be spells put on passages that lead demons or people astray, or they may explode or do something to stop someone from going any further." Mac shrugged. "That's the best I can do to explain it."

"Yes," she smiled. "That is exactly what will happen. This place is booby-trapped in many places."

"So, how do we avoid them?"

"That is why we have guides to lead us through," Sirel leaned forward and patted the neck of her horse. "I believe these horses know the way with no help."

They continued for miles deep in the mountain. Along the way, there were stops to water, feed, and rest their mounts, as well as the riders. They traveled until they finally reached the outer wall and the end of the passageway. A large rock creaked open, and instantly they were engulfed by the cold air outside.

They thanked the four sorcerers for their help and rode into the frigid weather. The sorcerers waited until the last rider was through and then sealed the opening with their magic. Mac turned to see where they had come through, but there were no signs of an opening ever being there.

"Wow," Mac shivered. "It sure got cold."

"As we travel north it will get a lot colder," Sirel said and motioned for her warriors to follow her down a narrow path, away from the mountain.

The Rils forest seemed barren of life and color, except for the occasional fir trees. Sirel called a stop about a mile from the Tahotay village and sent two scouts out ahead. A short time later the two scouts returned.

"The village is empty, Captain." The first scout's report was brief.

"Are there signs of a struggle or fighting?" Sirel's asked. Her eyes narrowed at the possibility of trouble.

"We saw no signs of either," the second scout reported stoically.

She turned to Mac. "There is a well-built fort in the middle of the town. We will camp there for the night."

"Do you think it will be safe enough for us?" Mac asked.

She paused in thought. "Camping out here in the open would be dangerous. We need the protection of the fort."

She motioned for her warriors to head in the direction of the empty village. The horses moved at a fast clip over the well-trodden path. Sirel stopped at the edge of the woods just outside the village and held up her hand for the warriors to stop. She climbed off her horse and crept through the trees to check out the village.

"It is too peaceful there," Sirel studied the village as her horse pawed at the ground behind her. "I don't like it."

"The scouts said nobody was in there," Mac shrugged. "Wouldn't that make sense that it's peaceful because nobody's in the town," he stated more than asked. "And the two scouts came back unharmed."

"The demons may know they were only scouts and let them go so that we all go into the village." She moved stealthily closer to the edge of the village. "There! Look!" She pointed to a pole with a flag hanging upside down. "They left us a warning."

"Warning us of what?" Mac asked.

"Not to enter the village," Sirel said.

Rustling sounds around them caused the warriors to bring out their swords and prepare for battle.

"Captain," an Indian warrior moved swiftly through the forest. "It is a trap. Don't go into the village."

Mac was startled to see several other Indian warriors joining them. Immediately, the Ankhourians went into a full-alert status.

"Walking Tall, what happened?" Sirel knew and trusted the Indian warrior well."

"We were out hunting and in the distance, we saw a huge contingent of demons moving toward our village. We raced back to the village and warned them. Everyone left quickly to join the main village further north. We knew you were coming and hid from the demons in our hiding places among the trees until they passed. We stayed so that we could warn you just in case you missed the upside-down flag."

"How many are there inside?" Sirel moved away from the edge of the village and signaled for everyone to follow.

"Too many for us to fight," he said.

"I wonder if they know we are here," Mac looked down at his amulet that lay dormant against his chest.

"I think they are waiting for us to come into the village, or they would have attacked already."

"They know we're coming because they spotted the scouts," Mac said.

"It just doesn't make any sense why they're playing this cat and mouse game," Sirel patted the side of her horse absent-mindedly.

"Unless, it's the Master Demon, you know, that Zetche thing that's doing all the manipulating." Mac touched the amulet against his chest. He sighed with relief that it was cool to the touch.

"I still have a couple of scouts who have not reported back. We will wait until they return, and then we must find shelter for us and the horses." Sirel looked at the Indian walking next to her. "Walking Tall, is there somewhere we can rest for the night safely?"

"We have several hiding places, but none big enough for a horse." He shrugged and shook his head.

"We need Maaleah," Mac said matter-of-factly.

"Captain Sirel," an Ankhourian warrior pointed in the direction of two riders on horseback. "Our scouts are returning."

"It appears they have a rider," Sirel squinted against the cold winds to make out the passenger on the back of the horse. Suddenly, her face lit up, "It's Maaleah."

The two scouts pulled their mounts to a halt in front of Sirel. The scout with Maaleah as a passenger waited until one of the warriors assisted Maaleah in getting off the horse and then dismounted. "Captain," she said. "We heard her calling out to us and found her running toward us in the Rils forest."

Maaleah appeared disheveled and tired as she held on to the warrior until she felt steady on her feet. "I was in a Dak tree and using my spells to see who was walking around up here. Luckily, I saw these scouts riding pretty close to my Dak tree."

"We heard her call out and found her racing toward us," the second scout said dismounting from her steed.

"I had some urgent matters to take care of before I could make this journey. Anyway, I found this Dak tree, and oh," she held up her finger as she thought of something else she wanted to tell them, "While I was in the Dak tree, I put a magical spell around the Groglemytes homes and nursery as I promised. The spell will turn people from its path, so nobody will accidentally stumble anywhere near the nursery."

Maaleah put her hands on her hips and arched her back. "Okay, I'm ready to ride again. The demons are everywhere. Come on, we don't have much time before they realize we are on to their scheme and come looking for us."

"Where can we hide from them?" Mac glanced around at the sparse trees.

Maaleah smiled weakly. "We're not far from the Rils River. I think we can make it there before they realize what's happened."

One of the scouts spoke up, "No. They have made encampments along the basin of Zanadur Lake. They will be waiting for us."

"Well, we can't just stay around here," Mac looked nervously around. "How is it they seemed to know where we are headed?"

"There is one other place we may be able to go until we figure out what to do," Maaleah pointed toward the Evoos swamps.

"Wait. Isn't that going near the Evoos swamp?" Mac asked incredulously. "I may not know my north, south, etc., but I do know that smell."

"No, but it is close to Evoos lands. We will have to hurry. There is a place in the middle of the Rils Forest that we can use for protection.

No one knows about it except the Sabbots, and maybe a handful of others." She gave a slight laugh, "Well, that's about to change with all these warriors. Alright. Let us ride."

A warrior helped Maaleah sit up behind Sirel. She was about to give the order for the Indian warriors to double up with her warriors but smiled when she saw all the warriors had already done so. "Tell me where I'm going, Maaleah," Sirel said.

"That way," Maaleah's pointed in the direction she wanted them to ride.

Sirel prompted her horse to race through the woods in the direction Maaleah had indicated. When they came to the end of the foothills of the Xelrils Mountains, Maaleah had them turn toward the Rils Forest.

Mac kept in pace with Sirel, only occasionally dropping back when the trees got too close to travel side-by-side. "We are in real trouble if we have to hide in between these sparse trees." Mac shook his head and hoped that wherever they were going had more cover.

The riders steered their horses clear of the hanging branches and jumped over small streams as they headed deeper into the woods. They rode for a while until Sirel held up her hand for everyone to stop at a small stream. "We need to rest here a moment for the horses," Sirel climbed down and helped Maaleah off.

Mac jumped off his horse and led it to the stream while he held its reins. He stood next to Sirel and Maaleah.

"I know I wasn't a great geography student, but aren't we headed in the wrong direction?" Mac looked around at the thinly treed area.

"Never underestimate a Sabbot, my friend," Maaleah turned and smiled at him.

"I wouldn't think of it," he nodded and returned the smile.

After the horses had eaten, rested, and been watered, they started their journey again. Suddenly, two scouts came riding hard toward the group. "Move out. The demons are behind us," they yelled.

"We don't have far to go," Maaleah said pointing to the direction they should be heading.

The group rode hard into the Rils forest following Sirel and Mac. When they came to a small clearing, Mac could see a large ravine straight ahead. Smoke billowed from a deep crevice, and as they approached the edge of it, Mac could see lava flowing at the bottom. The smoke blocked his view from what was on the other side of the ravine.

Demons were screaming behind them and closing in fast.

"This ravine is too wide for us to cross." Mac shook his head. "Our horses can't jump that."

Maaleah had Sirel stop just at the edge of the deep precipice. "Get me down, quickly," she yelled. Mac jumped from his horse and helped her down. She was holding a couple of stones in her hand. She closed her eyes and chanted quietly.

A whirling mist began to form, and soon it spread into a thick smoky haze that flowed across the ravine and disappeared into the misty smoke on the other side. When the smoke finally dissipated, a large wooden bridge appeared. Quickly, she was helped back onto Sirel's horse and led the riders two-by-two across the bridge into the dense smoke on the other side.

Once they were off the bridge and through a large metal gate, the smoke disappeared around them. The drawbridge was pulled back up, and the metal gates secured.

"Now this is really something," Mac's mouth was agape at the scene in front of him.

They were inside the huge courtyard of a castle. Maaleah directed them to the large stables where the warriors immediately took care of their horses before venturing back into the vast courtyard.

Maaleah pointed to the four, long barracks for the warriors to sleep in. "Come on. I'll show you where the warriors will bed down." Each of the four barracks was laid out the same. There were six-foot walls between each bed, and a curtain was used as a door for privacy. In each eight-by-ten-foot stall, there was a long bed with a small table on one side of it and a couple of hooks on the other side to hang their capes and shelves to place their weapons.

Down the wide center aisle were eight metal rods jutting from the floor. They were enclosed by several intricately woven metal strips. Heat rose through these pipes from the lava beds below making the long barracks warm and dry.

Maaleah led Sirel and Mac inside the main castle where they were met by a couple of Sabbot witches who showed them to their small private rooms.

Mac was pleased with the large bed and fireplace inside of his room. He placed his weapons and cape in the room and opened his door to find Sirel waiting there. She motioned for him to follow her up a flight of stone steps.

"From my room, I can see steps leading upward," she headed up the stone stairs. "Let's see what this place is all about."

They reached the top and were amazed by the terrain around them. A lava moat circled the castle, and the smoke from the lava hid the castle from view. The area the moat circled was vast. There were orchards bearing fruits, a stockade for farm animals, and various buildings occupying the area.

"We never heard of this place or knew of its existence." She placed her hands on the stone parapets and looked over the side of the castle. Mac did the same.

"I wonder whether the demons will be aware of this place. Although, I think it would be difficult to get across that ravine, even for a demon. Well, at least I hope it would be," Mac looked up in the sky. "The Drakluf dragons could still get in here very easily."

"There is a spell around this castle that makes it invisible to demons," Maaleah said joining them on the castle wall. "The demons cannot smell or see us. Even if the Drakluf dragons flew overhead they would only see smoke and rocks. There is a powerfully strong spell to keep demons out."

"I have been this way many times with my warriors. We have seen the circle of hot lava and gone around it."

"At first, we used magic to make it look like lava, but with the help of the Arega dragons, we turned it into a real lava moat." She smiled and gestured at the smoke rising from the ravine. "The smoke you see is half from the lava and half from our magic. This is where the most powerful witches of the Sabbots live. Come, you must meet them, and I am sure you are hungry."

They walked down the steps to the main hall where all the warriors were waiting for them.

The hall had a fireplace large enough for a man to stand in. Several metal rods lined the walls jutting up from the floor. They were exactly like those that heated the warriors' barracks.

The Sabbots welcomed Mac and the others and went about getting food prepared for the large contingent of warriors.

"This is quite an interesting place." He looked around the room at the poles sticking out from the floor. "What are they for?"

"Those are used for heating the castle. There is a metal plate covering the opening. You can pull it open, and the heat from the lava warms our rooms. When it is warm we slide the metal plate back over the opening, and it stays cool in here." Maaleah moved toward the fireplace. "We use them instead of a fireplace. However, this fireplace has its' uses."

"I hear the demons," Mac moved toward the large wooden door that led to the courtyard. He was quickly called back by Maaleah.

"Mac, you won't be able to see them through the smoke. But you will be able to see them this way." She pointed to a large round stone sitting on a high pedestal in front of the fireplace. The images of the demons approaching the ravine appeared. They divided into two groups and raced around the castle to join forces on the other side. They never stopped as they raced into the woods looking for Mac and the others.

Then everyone went silent as a lone, tall figure in a black cape stopped in front of the ravine. Its cape billowed and whipped around him as he stood on a chariot pulled by four snarling demon creatures. He was looking directly at the castle as if he sensed them.

He held something in his hand as his thin gray arms began to rise above his head. He stopped when several of the demons raced back to him. They seemed to be telling him something. Slowly, he dropped his arms. He grabbed the reins and pulled back away from the edge of the crevice. He rode around the deep moat and disappeared with his demon legions into the dark woods.

"You see," Maaleah smiled and heaved a sigh of relief. "We are quite safe here."

"Are you sure he didn't sense something? He sure looked like it," Mac said with a little worry in his voice.

"I do not think he knew what he was sensing," Maaleah shook her head. "Although, he may have sensed our Spell of Seeing. Let us hope he just thinks whatever he was feeling came from the ravine, not from our magic."

After their meals, the warriors left the hall and went into the courtyard. Sirel and Mac walked outside into the orchards. They hadn't gotten far when a young Sabbot Witch came running to get them.

"Maaleah said you must come quickly." Her voice was filled with urgency.

They ran to the castle hall where the Sabbots were congregated around the pedestal. The images were small, but they could make out the forms of several women and children racing toward the ravine and into the open. The witches expanded the spell to see they were being chased by Evoos. There was nowhere for them to run. The crevice with its lava was directly in front of them, and the Evoos' was closing in from behind them.

"Do you think this is a demon trick?" Mac asked. "I mean that big gray thing left only a few moments ago."

There was a brief silence as the witches quickly threw some stones on the table. Nothing happened.

"No," Maaleah shouted. "We don't see any demons around them. Quickly, clear the smoke and drop the drawbridge," Maaleah yelled to the other witches as she hurried behind Mac and Sirel out of the hall into the courtyard.

The warriors saw them racing out of the castle and came to full alert. They knew something was wrong.

"Warriors!" Sirel yelled. "We have women and children being chased by about fifty Evoos. Follow us. A couple of you get to the walkways above and stop as many as you can with arrows."

They raced to the large wooden draw bridge and watched as it was lowered down. The women and children were too far away from the bridge for them to reach it before the Evoos' would overtake them.

"What can we do? They'll never make it to the bridge in time?" Mac raced toward the bridge as it dropped slowly.

"We must help them," Maaleah said. "No matter what the cost to our sanctuary."

The warriors divided themselves into separate factions. Some ran up the stairs to the castle walkway; others followed Mac and Sirel to the bridge. The smoke had cleared, and the warriors on the walkway could get a clear view of the approaching women and children. Before the drawbridge was completely down, Mac, Sirel, and the warriors jumped off of it landing on the solid ground. Maaleah could not make the jump but stood on the edge of the drawbridge as it descended slowly with her stones readied.

Mac and the others raced toward the stumbling women and children. The warriors on the wall of the castle began shooting arrows over their heads hitting the Evoos' closing in behind them.

Mac and the warriors' war cries filled the air as they passed the women and children and charged straight for the Evoos'. The Evoos were startled to see the warriors. They stopped chasing the women and children and exchanged quizzical looks with each other. They would be evenly matched, but only in numbers. The fierce fighting power of the Ankhourian and Tahotay warriors was enough; the Evoos' turned and raced back into the forest.

Sirel halted the warriors. "Let them go. It could be a trap in the woods. Let us get the women and children into the castle."

Keeping a careful eye on their surroundings the warriors led the women and children safely into the castle compound.

Once inside the castle, the smoke billowed up from the ravine, and the spells were resumed to hide and protect it.

"What good are those spells going to be? The Evoos know the castle exists now," Mac quipped as he pulled out a chair for one of the women to sit. Her body was trembling so badly he had to help her sit in the chair.

"I think they were in such shock at the sight of the warriors coming from seemingly nowhere that they didn't notice anything else. I hope," Maaleah patted Mac's arm.

"If this Zetche is controlling them, they may say warriors came out of nowhere and this Zetche may investigate," Sirel said.

"If I know Evoos' they are still running and won't stop until they are home," Maaleah laughed. "Anyway, we have many defensive spells for this castle. We are safer here than anywhere else."

"What were you women doing in the Rils forest?" Sirel turned her attention back to the women and children.

All the women and children were seated around the table as the Sabbots brought them food and drink.

"We are from the Dahvat Village. Our homes were attacked by demons," a stocky, middle-aged woman said. She stopped and drank greedily from a cup placed before her. After she was done, she wiped her mouth with the cuff of her dirty sleeve and continued. "Our husbands have been missing for weeks, and we had no way to protect ourselves."

"How did you escape them?" Mac queried.

"We live on the border of the Dahvoos swamp, and the Evoos are a constant threat to us. But it had the best farming land in the country, so we stayed. Our husbands built a connecting tunnel to each of our homes as a safety measure. The passageways to the tunnels are very well hidden. We have a special spell we purchased from the

Sabbots. It gives a warning when any Evoos or demons approach. So, when the warning went off we took our children to the tunnels and hid until they were gone."

"The Dahvat Village is a long way off. How long have you been traveling?" Maaleah asked.

"We have been traveling for a couple of days," she grabbed a piece of bread and took a large bite from it. "I am sorry; we have not eaten for a while. We kept our food mainly for the children."

"Finish your meal," Mac said. "When you are done we will talk."

After the meals were done the women and children were taken to rooms in the castle for them to sleep. The woman who had been talking did not leave. Her long, brown hair, streaked with gray, was hanging in sloppy strands all over her head, and down into her eyes. She brushed the hair from her eyes and continued. "My name is Nayu. My husband and I have no children."

"Why didn't you stay hidden until your husbands returned?" Sirel pulled a chair out and sat next to the woman.

"As I said before, our husbands have been gone for several weeks. We waited as long as we could. But the children were getting anxious, as were we. Then the Evoos came. We fled to the tunnels. The Evoos stayed in our homes until they had eaten everything we had; livestock and all. We thought they would never leave. Finally, we saw a chance to get away and took it. We tried to make it to another village, but they too were under attack."

"What made you come this way?" Sirel asked.

"We thought it was a miracle: We saw you from a distance," Nayu wiped her mouth with the back of her hand. "We hid until the demons that were looking for you passed us. We thought it was safe to follow you. Then we were spotted by the Evoos. We ran as fast as we could."

"Where are your husbands now?" Mac sat down on the other side of her.

"Our crops were not doing well this year, so they went up into

Wolf Mountain to do some hunting. That was a couple of months ago. I have not seen or heard from Olo since then."

"Olo?" Mac's eyebrow lifted slightly. "Is Olo a common name in Mystovia?"

"I know not," Nayu replied. "Why do you ask?"

"We ran into a few hunters a while back, and I believe one of them said his name was Olo."

"Oh, that is good news for sure," Nayu smiled for the first time. "He is safe, then."

"Well, he was a couple of days ago, so I am not sure. I mean, I certainly hope he is safe." Mac looked over at Sirel.

"Your husband and his friends have been very clever in hiding from the Evoos and demons. I am sure they are alright." Sirel moved slightly to let a Sabbot Witch fill the woman's cup with water. "Tell me. What have you seen while you have been in the forest?"

"We have seen many strange things." Nayu drank from her cup as water ran down the sides of her mouth. Her dirty hand came up and wiped it away. "Many demons are roaming the woods, but they do not appear to be alone. One time I thought I saw a tall, gray creature glide . . . almost as if it were floating through the woods behind them. And, then it was gone."

"You were very lucky they did not spot you," Maaleah said.

"Oh, we had some close calls, especially when you travel with small children. But we managed to avoid them for a long time. That is until today. When we saw you, we almost cried out. But then we saw the demons coming after you. We hid and followed you from a distance. We were so busy watching you we did not see the Evoos coming up behind us. I shudder to think what would have happened."

"Well, you are safe for now. Why don't you go to your room with the others and get some rest?"

"Yes," she nodded weakly. "I could rest for a while."

Maaleah gently took her arm and eased her up from her chair and escorted her out of the room. She returned to a quiet dining hall.

"Well, Nayu and the others are resting. It must have been a very frightening ordeal."

"Yes," Mac nodded. "I can't imagine trying to hide the children from the Evoos and demons. I wonder how we can reach her husband. We can have them stay here with them. This would be a safe place for all of them."

"Yes," Maaleah smiled. "Our secret is no secret anymore. But we have all agreed it is for a good cause."

"I was thinking," Mac leaned forward on the table. "What if we went out looking for Olo? I mean, if those women could stay hidden with a bunch of little kids, we would fare even better. What do you think?"

"We have no idea where he or his men have gone," Sirel shrugged. "They could all be dead by now. But if you want to try to find them, I will go with you."

Mac looked at her beautiful face and realized he would be putting her and anyone else that went with them in grave danger. "Thanks, Sirel, but you're right they could all be dead by now. It would take warriors away from the castle and put their lives in grave danger. It was just a thought, and not a good one."

A Sabbot, who was monitoring the perimeter of the castle with their magic spells, called out to them. "You must see this."

A view of the forest edge showed movement. It was in the same direction where all the demons had disappeared. The figures of several men could be seen lurking between the trees.

"Call this a coincidence, or whatever," Mac got up from the table and walked closer to the images. "Isn't that Olo and his men? Someone get Nayu."

Nayu came down the steps, her eyes half-closed. "I was told you want me to look at something. What can I do to help?" She said rubbing her eyes.

"Is that Olo?" Maaleah asked.

"Yes, that is him." Nayu moved slowly to the vision on the table. "He is alive. I must go to him."

"We will send our warriors and bring them here," Sirel placed her hands on the table and stood up.

"No," Nayu spoke quickly. "He may think it is a demon trick. He knows me. I can take a horse and ride to them myself."

"We can't protect you at that distance," Sirel protested.

"She is right," Maaleah said. "Our magic can work wonders, but he is too far away."

"It is better for me to go," she smiled slightly. "There are things he can ask me, and I can ask him, to make sure that we are who we say we are. If all is well, I will signal you by raising my hand and waving my scarf. If not . . ."

"No," Mac spoke abruptly. "I am not sending a woman to find out what is going on."

"And, you think a 'woman' cannot do this," Sirel's brow rose sharply as did the edge in her voice.

Mac blinked a couple of times trying to regain his thoughts. "No, what I meant," he added quickly, "was an untrained, non-warrior woman should not go out there."

Sirel relaxed her stance, "Yes. I see what you mean."

"It has been so long. I am anxious to see my husband," she gestured toward the Sabbots. "Do you see anything else near them like demons or Evoos?"

"No," Maaleah shrugged. "I do not see any demons or Evoos. They're alone."

"There you see," Nayu pulled her cloak around her. "Let me ride quickly before the demons or Evoos come back."

"I will agree if we accompany you," Mac crossed his arms and stared down at the woman.

"Yes," Sirel agreed. "A couple of us will ride with you."

"Agreed," she nodded. "Thank you."

"When you ride out to meet him, we will put a protective spell against demons. However, do not travel outside of its protection. We will cast a slight mist in the spell, so you will know you are within the spell itself."

The drawbridge was located on the opposite side of where Olo and his men were standing. Five of the Ankhourian and Indian warriors accompanied Mac, Sirel, and Nayu around the castle toward the spot the men were last seen.

"Stay close everyone," Sirel shouted.

"Look, there they are," Mac was taken back a little. "There are more of them than before."

Nayu kicked her horse and charged toward the figures racing toward them. "Olo!" She shouted. "Olo! It is me Nayu. Your wife! Olo!"

Mac started to chase after her as she raced out of the protective spell when Sirel stopped him.

"Stay!" Sirel ordered everyone to halt. "Stay within the mist."

Nayu stopped in front of Olo, her horse reared, and neighed almost throwing her from its back. "NO!" Nayu screamed.

A Drakluf demon soared overhead, and its demon rider fired one of its poisoned arrows striking Nayu down. As quickly as it had appeared it disappeared into the gray skies above. Nayu grabbed at the arrow in her chest and fell from her horse in front of Olo. Her terrified horse ran back toward Sirel and the others without its rider.

It happened so quickly the warriors did not have time to draw their arrows and fire at it.

"Nayu!" Mac started to move toward her when Sirel grabbed his horse's reins.

"We stay here!" Her words were sharp.

"Quick," Mac yelled to Olo and his men. "Get into the mist. It is a magical spell against demons. Hurry!"

Olo bent down and picked up the lifeless body of Nayu. "We must get back into the woods. The Drakluf demon will have warned the others. I will take her with me."

"No," Mac protested. "We have other women and children in the castle. They are wives and children of your men. We have powerful magic protecting us from demons. Come with us."

"We will stay and fight them in the woods. Thank you for

offering us sanctuary. We had no idea this castle you spoke of existed. We will be near if you have need of us." Olo and his men turned and headed back toward the woods. He carried the lifeless body of his wife with him.

"We must get back to the castle," Sirel said softly. "I am sorry, Mac. I could not risk your life or that of the warriors."

"I understand," Mac said sadly. "It's such a shame. She was so excited to see him, and had waited so long, just to be killed like that."

"Come," Sirel motioned for the warriors to return to the castle. "We do not want to weaken the Sabbots by sustaining their magic out here too long."

They turned their horses toward the castle. Mac glanced behind him and was startled to see that Olo and his men were gone.

"Man," Mac smiled. "They're really good." He looked over at Sirel who had turned to look back at Olo and his men. A deep frown crossed her face, but she said nothing. "I know," he gave a half-smile to Sirel. "It is a very sad thing."

As they rounded the castle moat to cross over the bridge, they did not see the shadow moving in the trees. Two red eyes, filled with hatred, peered out from a dense copse, and watched.

CHAPTER NINE

*D*oc looked around nervously. "Okay, you sprinkled that magic stuff on us, and the demons are nearly here. Now what?"

"Quickly, everyone back against the stone wall," the wizard stopped and looked quizzically at the small party of warriors in front of him. "Who are you? And where did you come from?"

"It doesn't matter right now." Kess grabbed his arm and led him to the stone wall.

"It doesn't?" He said somewhat befuddled.

"No, we'll introduce ourselves later." Kess, with Kybil's help, pushed the tall, frail man against the wall.

A few small pebbles and dirt from the ledge above them fell over the side causing everyone to look up nervously.

"Oh, great," Doc said scrambling to find a place to stand with his back against the wall. "I'm going to be demon food. They must be on the ledge above us."

Rakmor yanked Doc next to him. He gave a quick check and a short sigh of relief to see that everyone was plastered up against the rock wall. "Here's hoping he didn't forget any ingredients."

"If he did we're all going to become human piñatas very soon," Kess held her breath as the demons poured into the opening.

The demons sniffed and scoured the entire area. One of them moved close to where Doc was standing. It sniffed the area and then moved away. Finally, they appeared to be convinced that no one was in or around the area, the demons raced down the mountain to search elsewhere.

"I almost wet myself," Doc said slumping to the ground.

"Wow," Kess exclaimed. "We were invisible. I mean really invisible."

"Well," Rakmor remarked. "We were invisible only to the demons."

"And your point?" Kess said, still reeling from the experience.

"I guess I don't have one," he shrugged and laughed.

"We must get off the mountain," the wizard exclaimed. He pointed to another group of demons searching the mountain and heading toward them.

"We can't go down that way," Kybil said as he peered at the demons that had just passed left them.

"Nor, that way," Rakmor said at the collapsed part of the mountain they had just come from.

"Say," Doc looked at the wizard. "Can this stuff make us fly?"

"No," the wizard snapped. "But I am working on that. Come, I know another way down."

"Well, which way?" Kess shrugged.

"Let's get going." Doc's eyes widened with terror. "The next wave of demons is almost here."

More pebbles fell and a scuffling sound could be heard coming from the ledge above them.

"What was that?" Doc looked above him.

"The demons may be above us," Kybil said. "We have to get moving now."

"Where are we going?" The wizard asked.

"Away from here. I hope," Kess said.

"Oh, yes," the wizard scratched his head and then nodded as if he remembered something. "Follow me." He hurried along a path and after a while, he stopped in front of a wall of stone. He studied the wall for a moment and then his face broke into a big smile as he pushed on a large stone embedded in the mountain. It was a small, wide stone door that groaned as it swung open. "There, this is the way," Baalizar said more to himself than the others.

"Say," Doc looked at the steps. "We just escaped from a cave-in inside this mountain. What are you thinking?" He exclaimed.

"It is only for a short way," the wizard ducked down as he briskly walked through the small opening. "We must hurry. Last one through push it closed."

Kybil stood by the opening hurrying everyone through. Once inside they found themselves in a large open area. He was the last to enter, and quickly pushed the stone door closed.

Baalizar tapped the bottom of his staff on the stone floor, and the whole shaft of his staff lit up. He put a finger to his lips for everyone to be silent.

Kess opened her mouth to say something and then closed it. Scurrying sounds could be heard from the other side of the stone wall.

A shrill scream caused the warriors to draw their swords and take a fighting stance. Then, there was silence.

"Hmmm! Very interesting. Very interesting," Baalizar said. He turned and began walking down the steps. "Follow me."

"What was very interesting?" Kess asked following Doc down the steps.

"He must be talking about this infernal steep staircase we get to go down. If this mountain shakes while we are on it, you can kiss your ascot good-bye," Doc said looking over the side of the steps.

On one side of the stone steps was a stone wall, the other a precipice so deep they could not see the bottom. Single file, the warriors walked carefully down the steps.

The warriors continued down until they came to a plateau deep

"Okay," Kess whispered. "Do you think they're gone?"

"I'll bet there are no more steps beyond that door," Kybil said. "Nordaal. Yaneth," Kybil spoke softly. "Let's see if we can open it from this side."

They found the edge of the door and carefully pulled on it. It moved toward them, and Kybil glanced out. "Let it go."

"Let it go?" Doc said. "And why are we letting it go?"

"Just like I figured there are no steps outside for us to use," Kybil leaned against the door and sighed.

"That was just enough light for me to see what may help us," Rakmor said. "Everyone stay where you are."

"I don't think any of us is going anywhere," Doc said in the darkness. "Why aren't you using your magic wand thingy to light up this room?"

"I dropped it during the last powerful shake," he said. "It went over the side. But hold on. I saw a symbol of light on one of the stones in the ground."

All they could hear was the rustling sound of Rakmor's cape and a couple of thudding taps of something against the stone floor. Soon, a faint light began to glow in the darkness, until it was bright enough for everyone to see their surroundings. They were in a small, square room about ten feet wide.

"Wow," Kess's eyes blinked at the brightness and glistening room. "Look at this place."

Embedded in two walls of the room were diamonds and quartz of every size. The third wall was in the form of a triangle made up of gold. The fourth wall was made of rocks and stones.

"Look," Rakmor said excitedly as he worked at releasing the glowing stone from the ground. "I can pull this stone out. It will be able to light our way."

"Well, that is all well and good, but how do we get out of here," Kess turned looking at the four walls surrounding them.

"He said to push on the wall of rocks," Kybil moved toward the only wall with rocks on it.

"I did," Doc said. "And it brought us in here. I mean, how could he have known that I would rest against that particular wall, at that particular place and time?"

"How indeed?" Kybil ran his hands over the rocks. "Nordaal. Yaneth."

He did not have to ask them what to do. The three of them began pushing on the rock wall, and it started to move. "One more time," Kybil grunted, as he pushed.

Kess, Rakmor, and Doc rushed to help. The wall moved a little more and then stopped.

"Okay," Kybil turned and put his back to the wall. "Let's try this again." The wall moved a little further.

"Alright everyone, one more big push should do it," Kybil grimaced as he pushed harder.

Suddenly, the door swung open so fast everyone was thrown beyond the door. But the other side of the door was not a flat surface. Instead, a short, steep embankment awaited them as they fell and slid down. They came to a stop just before they dropped off into a precipice. Everyone scrambled back away from the edge. They were on a stone shelf about twelve feet long and six feet wide.

"Oh, my gosh. Is everyone okay?" Kess gasped.

"Were all fine," Kybil said as he walked around the small rock platform. "Rakmor, bring that light to the edge over there. I think I see something."

They moved toward the edge of the stone shelf. "There's just enough light to see some more steps."

Rakmor peered over the side. "I wonder how far down these steps go. It looks pretty dangerous."

"Having a mountain come down on our heads is far more danger-ous," Kybil stated and returned to the anxious group. "Here's the plan. I think it'll work."

"I can hardly wait," Doc said. "It's the 'I think' that gets my heart palpitating."

"There are few options here," Kybil knelt on one knee in front of the group. "There is no easy way out of this. There is no platform or shelf above us. The only way out seems to be over the side. There are steps cut into the side of the ledge which takes us down to a larger ledge."

"Where does that ledge take us?" Kess asked.

"I don't know," Kybil shook his head. "But we can't stay here."

Doc got up and inched his way to the edge where the steps were honed into the side of the mountain wall. "Are you kidding me?" He gulped. "There's nothing to hold onto. What if the mountain starts doing its rumba in here? Anyone going down those skinny steps will certainly fall."

"We can try to find some way to tie our capes together like a rope and use our quivers to connect them just in case the mountain starts to move again. At least, there would be something to grab," Rakmor suggested as he began taking off his cape.

"It's a good idea Rakky, but I think the capes are too thick for us to tie them together. We have to think of something else." Kybil sat down rubbing his chin.

"Is there any way to time the mountain shakes or whatever they're called?" Kess asked.

"They seem to come in spurts," Doc thought for a moment. "But if we go fast we could probably make it before the next quakes start."

"But what if the ledge below isn't as wide as this one, and where will it take us?" Kess asked.

"I don't see any way to go up," Kybil spoke to the group. "I'll leave this up to all of you. What do you want to do?"

"I think we should wait for the next quake to pass and then go for it," Kess said. "You know we could use our belts. Slip them through the cape openings. Just in case someone starts to fall they will have something to grab onto."

"That's a good idea." Rakmor smiled. "It's worth a try."

They quickly looped their belts through the cape slits and dropped them over the side.

"Nordaal and me stay here ta ya be safe," Yaneth grabbed the edge of the capes and handed part of it to Nordaal. "Den we come down."

The mountain shook again as everyone braced themselves. When it stopped Yaneth spoke to Kybil. "Kybil be first, and he sees if der be room fer us down der."

Kybil patted Yaneth's arm and quickly climbed down the steps and onto the ledge below. "There's plenty of room. Hurry."

The next was Rakmor, followed by Kess. Now, it was Doc's turn. He looked down and started to back away from the edge. "I can't do it." His eyes were wide with terror. "I can't do it. I'm sorry."

Without hesitation, Nordaal picked up Doc, slung him over his shoulder, and started down the rough-cut steps on the side of the ledge. Kybil and Rakmor grabbed Doc from Nordaal and hauled him on the ledge. Nordaal looked up and yelled to Yaneth. "I be here. Now you be here."

"Wait!" Kybil screamed. "A quake should be coming soon." No sooner had he said it when the mountain shook.

"I trow down da capes," Yaneth yelled from above. "Ya better catch dem."

Nordaal reached out and grabbed the capes and pulled them safely onto the ledge.

Yaneth started his climb down and was just getting ready to step onto the ledge when another shake hit the mountain. Kybil and Nordaal were quick to grab his jacket. With all their strength, they yanked Yaneth toward them, and he fell like a stone on top of the two men. Kybil and Nordaal finally succeeded in getting Yaneth off them without accidentally throwing him over the edge.

"This ledge looks just like the other one, only bigger. Maybe there's another rock wall we can push on somewhere." Kess said feeling the sides of the stone wall.

Doc put his hands on his hips and walked to the edge. "I can't be doing this; my ole heart can't take much more here."

Kess wandered to the back of the ledge pushing on the wall as she went. She was startled when she felt a part of the wall give way.

"Hey, I was just kidding, kinda, about another moving rock wall, but this one did."

Everyone raced to the wall and began pushing on it. It opened to reveal a tunnel about six feet in diameter.

"We could crawl through this. It's going down, which is in the right direction." Kybil sighed deeply. "Again, we have no idea where it'll take us."

"As you said," Kess gave a half-smile. "It's going in the right direction."

"Let's get our belts back on and capes," Kybil said. He helped Kess with her cape and then secured the clasp on his.

"Look," Rakmor pointed down the tunnel. "There appears to be light coming from somewhere. Alright, I'll lead the way on this one." He put the glowing stone in his cape pocket and got down on his hands and knees. With one last look at everyone, he began to crawl through the tunnel.

The wide tunnel twisted and turned a couple of times but was on a steady decline. They were making good progress when the mountain began to shake again. They all froze in place. When the shaking stopped Rakmor began to crawl faster. But he was not prepared for the steep incline and the more he tried to stop sliding the faster he slid.

"Don't come any further. I can't stop sliding," Rakmor yelled as he watched the black hole getting closer. He let out a short scream, as he burst through the tunnel and was suspended in the air for a moment, and then, fell into the blackness.

"Rakmor!" Kybil yelled after hearing his friend scream. But now he found himself and Kess being pulled down the shaft with no way to stop. He tried bracing his legs and arms against the sides of the tunnel, but it only seemed to make them go faster. He grabbed Kess's arm as they broke through the tunnel opening. They hung in the air for a moment and started to fall.

It was a shortfall. Kybil grabbed Kess as they scrambled out of the way. Doc broke through sailing into the air and landing inches away from Kess. Kybil and Rakmor grabbed Doc just as Nordaal hit the floor. Yaneth slid down just missing Nordaal.

"What the heck was that all about?" Kess said trying to catch her breath.

"Dat be some ride." Nordaal beamed a huge smile at everyone.

"Where we be?" Yaneth asked.

"You're guess is as good as ours," Kybil walked over to the edge and peered upward and then down. "It looks like we covered a lot of territory during that slide." He stopped abruptly. "Hey, wait a minute. It looks like a path winding its way down through the mountain over there."

Everyone moved to the side of the rock platform and looked down. A wide path meandered through the large stalagmites jutting up from the bottom of the mountain floor.

"Are those steps?" Doc asked in surprise. "They look like their cut into the side of this ledge."

"It appears to be going downward," Kess sighed with relief. "Now, maybe we can get out of here."

"Okay," Kybil touched Yaneth's arm. "You and Nordaal go down first and help Kess and Doc."

Yaneth and Nordaal hurried down the steps and waited at the bottom for Kess and Doc to climb down. Soon, everyone was on the path and heading downward.

"This is much better," Doc said. "At least we won't fall off this darn path. If we're lucky nothing is going to fall on our heads."

They traveled past odd formations and strange alcoves cutting deep within the mountain. A dim, eerie, green glow came from the rocks outlining their pathway.

"We need more light. Rakmor. The stone might help here," Kess said.

"Stay on the path," Kybil ordered, as he led them through the stony maze.

"Hope this stone is still working." Rakmor reached in his cape for the stone.

"Kybil," Kess whispered. "I don't think we're alone."

"I've had the same feeling for quite a while," he whispered back.

"There! It still works." Rakmor shouted pleased with himself. A bright light burst from the stone in his hand. He almost dropped it in shock at the sight in front of them.

Screams came from hairless creatures as they quickly disappeared into the blackness around them.

"Let's get out of here," Doc pushed on Kybil to get him to start running. "I'm hungry and maybe they are, too."

"Okay," Kybil said, as they raced down the wide path toward a huge cavern ahead.

"What are they?" Kess yelled as she ran keeping up pace with Kybil.

"I've never seen anything like them before," Kybil said.

"Dey be da Arachmires," Yaneth said running behind everyone.

"Yeh," Nordaal kept up a steady pace with everyone else. "Dey lives in da mountains."

"What kind of creatures are they?" Kess looked back at the dwargers. "I mean they had no hair, that I could see, and it looked like they had a bunch of arms or legs or something."

"Yep," Yaneth quipped. "Dey has a lotta arms and legs. Sticky feet, too. Gotta stay away from dem. Specially when dey be hungry."

"Keep running," Doc yelled back. "I don't like being on the bottom of the food chain here."

"Dey won't bodder ya," Nordaal trotted up near Doc. "Da light hurts der eyes. Dey won't eat us unless da light goes out again."

"Rakmor?" Doc's voice was an octave higher.

"This light should hold out for a while, Doc. I hope."

"A while? I hope? Oh, boy. I don't like the sound of that. And look at the huge cavern coming up. We'll be out in the open, just ripe for the plucking," Doc's voice was coming in gasps. Nordaal reached over and quickly grabbed his arm to help him run.

"Wait," Kybil put up his hand for everyone to stop.

"Wait?" Doc stopped and bent over trying to catch his breath. "What? Are we going too fast for those things?"

"Douse that light Rakmor. Quickly!" Kybil ordered.

"Douse the light?" Kess chimed in. "Are you crazy? Those hungry things are right behind us."

"And, maybe right in front of us, too." Kybil pulled out his sword.

"I hear someting," Yaneth said.

"Me, too," Nordaal agreed.

"Everyone get behind that boulder and be quiet." Kybil reached Kess's side and noticed she had already drawn her sword as well.

Suddenly, a thunderous clapping sound echoed throughout the cavern and followed by a brilliant light that encompassed the entire space. Shrill screams filled the air and the sound of scurrying feet disappeared into the black recess of the cave.

Lone footsteps headed toward the hiding group. They stopped just short of the rock they were all hiding behind.

"Come. Come!" The wizard Baalizar spoke briskly. "What took you so long?"

"What took us so long?" Doc asked incredulously.

Everyone came from around the rock and stared in disbelief at the wizard. He continued to chastise them for not being punctual. "We have been waiting for quite a while. I had your warriors wait by the cave entrance. I heard you in the chambers here. What were you doing?"

"We had to climb and slide down several hundred feet to get here," Kess said agitatedly.

"Why you silly fools," he shook his head in disbelief. "Why didn't you ride down the mining shaft car? I told you to push on the golden triangle in the room."

"What?" Doc's eyes widened. "What shaft car?"

"We must go," Baalizar headed back toward the entrance to the cave. "The shaft car would have taken you down to the level where we were waiting."

"You told us to push on the rock wall," Kybil said firmly.

Everyone agreed.

"I did?" Baalizar shrugged. "Well, it was wrong."

"Yeah," Kess said. "We found out the hard way."

"Well, it was a small mistake, and everyone is just fine. Come, your warriors are waiting for you."

"How did you find us?" Kess asked.

"I began searching when you did not come down the riding shaft car. When I got to this cavern, I heard you. It echoes quite nicely and makes sounds much louder than they really are. Luckily, you were only a couple of levels up. Come. Come. We must make haste." The wizard moved swiftly through the cavern opening, down a few tunnels, and to the nervously waiting warriors.

Kybil and the others were relieved to see the warriors who appeared to be just as relieved to see them.

"Follow me," Baalizar said. "We have to get to the witches' castle in the Rils forest before nightfall. I have very important information for them, and it is a long journey."

"Got any 'shaft cars' we can ride?" Doc said sarcastically.

"Not necessary right now," Baalizar said matter of fact as he walked them out of the cave into the bright sunlight. "Now, you can explain to me who you people are and where did you come from."

"Fine," Kess scanned the area. "But where did all those demons go?"

"Not to worry," Baalizar smiled. "I sent them on a false trail. It will be a long while before they figure it out. But still, we must hurry. When we were at the top of the mountain, I happened to read the mind of a master demon. Awful creature. Not a nice creature at all. I remember it from long ago."

"We got the point," Kess said even more annoyed than before. "What did this awful creature say?"

"It didn't 'say' anything, my dear. I read its mind, and I must warn the witches. Someone called Mac, I think that was the name, is in grave peril."

"Mac?" Kess gasped and grabbed at her throat.

"I take by your response you know this, Mac, person." He adjusted his cape and walked away. "Well, let us go and warn this fellow, creature, or being while we can."

"What did you hear about Mac?" Kess quickly moved in front of him blocking his way.

"Hmmm," He stopped and looked down at her with disdain. "Do not be annoying."

"Annoying?" Kess's voice raised an octave. Angrily she said, "You have no idea how annoying I can become if you don't tell me what you heard."

Baalizar crossed his arms and tapped his foot as he studied Kess.

"Come on, tell her what you heard," Kybil said, his voice was anything but friendly.

"You have to know right this very minute?" Baalizar unfolded his arms and put his hands on his hips as he looked down at Kess.

"Yes," Kess, Kybil, Doc, and Rakmor said at the same time.

"Well, if it's that important to you," Baalizar stepped back and looked at the warriors. "Wait a minute! Why am I helping you? I don't even know who you are."

"Who cares?" Kess said crossly. "I want to know what kind of trouble Mac is in."

Kybil quickly told him who they were, and why they needed to know why Mac was in danger.

"Why didn't you say so before?" Baalizar huffed. "Well, it appears that there is a Master Demon loose on Mystovia."

"Yes, yes," Kybil said. "We are aware of that."

"What you are not aware of is that it now possesses the body of a human."

"That is impossible," Rakmor said. "They can only possess lesser beings and demons."

"This Master Demon has an object that enables him to do so, but not for long. I read its mind, a very nasty demon. It can only possess a human body that is not alive."

"You mean this thing is a zombie," Kess shivered involuntarily.

"I have no idea what a 'zombie' is," Baalizar stared at Kess. "What is a zombie?"

"It's a walking dead thingy. But I don't care if this thing can possess a dead body or shoot carrots out its butt." Kess snapped.

"Now, that's quite a visual image," Doc said with a tone of amazement.

"One I wouldn't particularly like to see," Kybil said.

"All I want to know is what danger Mac is in," Kess said defiantly.

"It appears this 'zombie' is preparing a great force to attack the witches' castle in the Rils Forest. It has an object that has great powers and can penetrate the strong powers of the witches. And somehow it knows that this Mac, and a little dragon, is responsible for killing its mate."

"Kybil! Rakmor!" Kess looked into their faces. "Is there any fast way to get to the witches' castle?"

"No,' Kybil said. "The air is full of the Drakluf dragons, and between the Evoos' and demons, we are greatly outnumbered by land."

"By sea. That is how we go," Baalizar turned and began walking back toward the cave opening.

"What we see?" Nordaal asked.

Yaneth shook his head. "I dun't see nuttin."

"I dun't see nuttin' eider," Nordaal concurred.

Baalizar did not look back at the stunned group behind him as he turned and re-entered the cave.

"Go by sea?" Kybil shook his head in disbelief. "First time for everything! Okay," he yelled to his warriors, "let's follow this wizard and see what he's up to."

"Back into the mountain with those spider thingies," Kess followed Kybil into the cave. "Great! Simply great. I hope this wizard knows what he's doing."

"I just hope he can remember it," Doc said nervously as he entered back into the cave.

CHAPTER TEN

Olo stood at the edge of the woods and watched Mac, and the others ride out of sight. Safely hidden among the trees, and out of view from anyone, Olo looked down at the woman he carried in his arms, and with no effort, he slung her lifeless body into the bushes.

A black mist rose up and around the woodsman and when it cleared the Zetche stood above the lifeless body of Olo. He reached into his cape and pulled the Skull of Semetter out. His hand gently caressed it.

"It is good to see you again, my friend." He held the skull out in front of him, turning his head from side-to-side as he gazed into its empty sockets.

His black lips smiled slowly. "I am sure you have powers that even I am not aware of yet. We did not have much time to talk while we lived in the cave. I was too weak. I could hardly kill my prey. But I believe if it had not been for you, I would not have gathered the strength I have now. And now, I am the power to be reckoned with."

The Zetche stopped and continued sadly. "I was lonesome until I felt your company. You have all the power I shared with my mate and more."

He squatted on his haunches, still stroking the skull's face. "When I got back to Mystovia and found that my mate was not with me, I had to gain my strength so I could look for my mate." His eyes turned from orange into a bright red as hatred spewed from his black lips. "Then, this Mac told me that he and that vile, little dragon are the ones responsible for the death of my mate."

He pulled the skull close to him and stroked it. "They thought I was this Olo person and that my demon changelings were human, and they had saved us from the demon attack," he snarled. "My payment for their 'rescue' will be their destruction." His face registered a smile, but his eyes were filled with loathing. "I shall repay them by killing them."

"Excuse me, Master," a demon spoke softly to the squatting figure. "We have lost them, Master," the demon's face was contorted and mangled. When the demon spoke, spittle erupted from his mouth that held long sharp fangs. Its arms fell well beneath his knees, and his eyes were a steady yellow.

"You have lost them? Where?" Instead of anger, there was a ring of curiosity in his voice.

"We chased them through the mountain and over the mountain, but they were gone." The grotesque demon paid no attention to the skull in his master's hand.

The Zetche stood up towering over the demon as he carefully cradled the skull. When he spoke, it was to the skull, not the demon standing in front of him. "I encountered two powerful beings. I was almost destroyed by their magic. But they do not know the power I have acquired. They are no match for me now."

"Yes, master," the demon replied with no emotion.

"But I have to understand this myself if I am to destroy all of them," he pointed a long gray finger toward the demon and motioned for him to sit

The demon moved further away than his master had ordered and sat down among some bushes.

The Zetche kicked the lifeless, decaying body of Olo out of his way as he moved toward the demon and sank to the ground next to him. "I am the last of the great master demon Zetches. How sad is that?" he said looking down at the skull. "With you, and my mate, we would have been the most powerful ever to reign in Mystovia." His head slumped against his chest.

"Master," a demon called hurrying toward him. "The demons are amassing in the forest, along with the Evoos."

"Yes. Yes," he waved the demon away. He was too deep in thought to destroy the annoying demon who had interrupted him. His hands came together, as he clicked his long black nails against the skull.

The Zetche began to pace. Absorbed in his reminiscences, he did not care about anything or anyone around him.

———

Quietly, in a small, dense copse of trees, a couple of small figures huddled together. Their bodies were completely hidden by the thick branches and bushes. They listened intently to the loud ravings of the Zetche. Ensconced in a magical barrier, that not even the Zetche and all his power could detect; they listened, watched, and waited.

———

"Where was I, oh, yes, I have been very clever in setting traps for the unwary. I sensed many warriors riding on horseback through the woods. I had no idea where they were going, and I was anxious to try out one of my new magical powers." He laughed and continued, "They were going to be such fun to destroy." He pulled on his cape, throwing it over one shoulder.

"I wanted to toy with them. So, I assumed the body of a woodsman I had killed. The skull gives me that power. I had my minions pretend to be chasing humans," he chuckled. "What a surprise that would have been. I was longing to see the horror on the rescuers' faces when they realized they had ridden to the rescue of changeling demons and into my trap."

He paused and rubbed his gray chin. "I had forgotten the ferocity of these fighting warriors," he thundered and stomped his foot. "I was about to have my demons surround and destroy them when this Mac and Kess came out of nowhere with their friends. I remembered the strong power of those two sorcerers, and I knew I had to withdraw. I was not prepared for them. Not then. I would have to fight them with far more powerful forces to win against them."

He breathed in deeply. "But I cannot figure out where they came from. They came out of nowhere. Where did they come from?"

The Zetche began to pace again. "This time I will destroy them both. And," he whirled around so fast he startled the bored demon sitting on the ground, "I am not forgetting that nasty, little red dragon. I will destroy him for taking my mate from me."

He motioned for the seated demon to get up. "We must go now. I have settled my thoughts by bringing them out in the open. Now, we must attack the invisible castle. I will lure this Mac and his pitiful warriors out and away from the castle. There my hundreds and hundreds of legions, hidden from view, shall strike them down. Except for this human called Mac, he will not die that quickly. And, before he dies, I will absorb his powers."

The Zetche laughed, looked down at the demon, and a bolt of red light shot out from his eyes killing the demon. "I can't have anyone knowing all of my weaknesses and strengths now, can I?"

He headed back to the waiting mass of his legions. The two hidden figures, cloaked by magic, lay still in the dense bushes.

As the Zetche passed the area where the two figures were, he stopped. He did not turn his head. His eyes narrowed, and a small smile crept over his face. He called for his chariot and his demon warriors. When he stepped onto the chariot, he immediately ordered his demons to surround the dense copse. He raised his hand and pointed for his forces to charge. Hundreds of demons hacked and screamed as they entered the small space.

"Bring them to me before you kill them," he yelled.

It was not long before one of the demons approached the Zetche. "Master, we found nothing, but this." He held up a small blue-gray amulet on a silver chain they found lying on the ground.

"Give it to me," he ordered. The Zetche grabbed the amulet from the demon. "A Sabbot witch's amulet. That must have been what I sensed when I passed by the bushes. Or it could be just a trick to make me think that is all that was in there. Check out the area. Check it out thoroughly."

He rode in his chariot through the trees as he scanned the area for any more signs of magic. After several minutes, finding no other signs of magic, he waved his legions on toward the witches' castle.

The Zetche reached the edge of the forest and called forth the demon changelings. He had demons bring the lifeless body of Olo to him. "It is time for you to fulfill your destiny." His black lips smiled as took out the Skull of Semetter and placed it on top of the still form.

Black smoke began to rise from the skull. It swirled and undulated, encompassing both the Zetche and the dead body on the ground until only a thick cloud of black smoke was visible. When the smoke cleared, the form of the Zetche was gone and the lifeless body of Olo stood erect. The rotting flesh and stench of the corpse were gone. The body of Olo looked alive and healthy. Except, if you looked closely you could see the dark, depth of blackness in his eyes.

The demon changelings were now in a human form and followed him out of the woods. They ran around the edge of the castle to the drawbridge that would lead them across the lava-filled moat.

The Zetche had not seen the drawbridge or the castle when he rode past it before. It was not until one of his demons encountered an Evoos and was told of a drawbridge that came from out of a mist that he realized a castle must be hidden by magic. He called upon the Skull of Semetter to alert him to the magic. It told him it sensed magic coming from beyond the ring of lava. The Zetche ordered it to reveal the hidden magic, and the castle appeared.

"Mac," Olo yelled. "Mac come quickly." His voice filled with urgency.

Mac ran to the parapet and looked out to see Olo standing in front of the drawbridge. "Olo, what is it?" He yelled down.

"We need help from you and your warriors." Olo's voice rang with urgency. "A village is being attacked by Evoos, and we can't fight them alone."

"Quickly, you and your men come inside, and we will equip you and get you horses to ride," Mac hollered.

"We will wait here," Olo said. "We will keep watch for any demons or Evoos headed this way."

"We'll get our horses ready and be with you in a moment," Mac raced down from the parapet and had the witches drop the drawbridge.

The warriors inside the castle ran to get their weapons and hurried to saddle their horses. In a short time, they were all ready to leave the protection of the castle.

"Mac," Maaleah ran to him, just as he was getting ready to mount his horse. Her hands rested on his chest. "You cannot go."

"Maaleah," Mac patted the top of her hands. "We'll be okay. It's just Evoos."

"No," She grabbed his hand. "It is more than that. It is far more than that."

"All the more reason we should ride to the village and help them," he looked down into her worried face.

"We have thrown the stones, and they have the signs of demons written all over them," her fingers gripped his tunic. "Please, they are trying to warn us of something."

"Maybe the stones are telling us to hurry before the demons attack, Maaleah." He spoke quickly, but softly.

"Mac?" Olo's voice called out. "What is keeping you so long?"

"No!" Maaleah shook her head. "It is you, and the warriors,

riding out there that are in danger. I do not need the stones to tell me this. I can smell it."

"Maaleah," Mac gently pulled her fingers away that tightly gripped his tunic. "We must go. Sirel has excellent scouts; they will keep us warned of any dangers." He went to mount his horse when another witch came running out of the castle.

"Wait!" She screamed. She ran as fast as she could to reach Mac. Her long, gray braid that hung over her shoulder flew back to flop against her back. "You must wait! There are deception and danger outside the castle walls. It is in the stones." She reached Mac out of breath.

"Look," Mac put his foot in the stirrup and swung onto the horse. "I am sure the stones are warning us of danger, in fact, when hasn't there been danger in Mystovia. We will be extra careful, that's all. Now, thank you ladies for your warnings, but if we are to help that village then we must go now."

"Mac! Don't go!" Maaleah pleaded.

"Sirel," Mac turned to her as she listened and waited. "What do you think?"

"We always listen to the stones," she said. "Although, we do not always understand what they mean."

"You see," he carefully maneuvered his horse around Maaleah and the other witch. "The reading from the stones could mean anything."

Olo and his changeling demons had moved back closer to where his legions lay hidden. He needed Mac and his warriors away from the drawbridge and the safety of the castle. Once they reached him, his demons would cut off any retreat to the castle. The Zetche smiled, he knew there would be no way for any of them to escape.

Mac started over the drawbridge, and Sirel gave the signal for the warriors to follow. He waved at Olo who had moved a good distance from the castle and was standing at the edge of the forest.

CHAPTER ELEVEN

*E*arlier that Same Day

King Zaatyr moved to the edge of the cave and saw the Spree and Haquada dragons attacking from all sides. *"Drago,"* Zaatyr said. *"You must move quickly and stay in the shadows as much as you can."*

"I will be back as quickly as I can to help you, Father," Drago said sadly. He did not want to leave his father and the other warriors, and yet he had to warn Mac.

The King and his dragons flew into the midst of the battle and began to fight fiercely. They began to pull the enemies away from being too close to the cave entrance.

Drago did not fly, as the air was filled with the enemy. Instead, he crept down the side of the mountain hugging the dark crevices.

King Zaatyr watched his son moving in the shadows and shot high into the air. His warriors followed him. Higher and higher they went in the opposite direction from Drago. And, just as Zaatyr had planned, the enemy dragons followed them thinking they were running away.

"*I am clear, Father,*" Drago's voice drifted into his mind. "*I am safe.*"

"*Now!*" Zaatyr yelled to his warriors. They turned and attacked the dragons that had been chasing them. The enemy was caught off guard. King Zaatyr's group attacked ferociously from the front while other Aregas attacked from behind.

The Haquada dragons were now battling against great numbers. Those that could retreat quickly did so.

Drago carefully studied the sky trying to find any enemy in it. He felt and saw nothing. At first, he kept low to the ground and then he began to fly upward until he cleared the clouds. His father suggested instead of flying south, where he was supposed to go, that he should fly north for a while and then turn east, where he could fly over safer territory as he headed back south.

Drago flew close to the top of the clouds, making it easier for him to see any Drakluf dragons and their demon riders. He traveled north for a while, turned sharply to the east, and began his journey south.

He kept a watchful eye on the clouds below him and the sky around him. Then he saw something moving toward him. It was not one dark figure it was many. He quickly dipped down into the thick clouds for cover. The figures were getting closer to him. Drago used his telepathy to see if it was an enemy or friends. To his chagrin, it was the enemy. Several Drakluf dragons were flying directly toward him. Even with all his cleverness, he knew he was no match for that many Draklufs.

Drago sighed. He would fight them and do the best he could against them. The Draklufs closed in on him and he turned to fight when the Draklufs and their demon riders passed directly overhead. He could almost reach out and touch them. He was puzzled. Why didn't they see him? He stayed in the clouds and watched the Draklufs fly frantically in and out of the clouds, and all around him. Not one of them even looked his way. He held his breath, afraid to

the mountain first. He looked down and saw the mountainside covered with demons. They were scouring every facet of the mountain and heading directly toward the top.

"*Here,*" Xen said. "*They will not see us from here.*"

"*You don't want Kess and the others to see us? Why?*"

"*Because there will be no time for us to explain. Look.*" Her head gestured toward the demons almost on top of Kess and the others. "*No matter what happens do not make a sound. Do not let them know we are here. It could mean their lives and ours.*"

Drago and Xen landed on top of an overhang causing a few stones to fall over the side. He noticed that the top of the mountain had a flat spot on it. It was large enough for many people to stand. Two sides of the flat space had large stone overhangs like the one they were standing on.

Suddenly, a door formed in the rock wall, and when it opened Kess and many warriors raced through it. There was a little confusion and then everyone ran under the ledge and stood with their backs to the wall.

Drago moved closer to the edge causing more stones to filter down. He turned and looked at Xen. Her eyes were closed, and her head titled slightly back. She did not move.

The sound of hundreds of demons racing below them got his heart racing. He watched in horror as they ran straight for Kess and the others. Then, miraculously, they just looked and sniffed around. He caught his breath as one demon seemed to have sensed Doc, but after a brief, scary moment the demon scurried over the mountainside with the rest of the demons.

He was about to say something to Zen when he noticed another wave of demons heading their way. He quickly looked down and saw the wizard had opened a doorway into the mountain and everyone disappeared.

Drago turned to Xen. She was unconscious. Panic gripped him. The other demons were almost on top of the mountain and heading right for them. He was even more terrified at the close sound of the screeching Drakluf dragons. Drago opened his large wings and covered her with them, tucking his head inside. He closed his eyes and thought of rocks. Nothing but rocks. The sounds of the demons and the Drakluf dragons were deafening to his ears. But he continued to think of nothing but rocks and boulders. He did not move. Then, there was quiet. He waited a few more seconds and slowly peeked above his wing. There were no signs of demons or Draklufs to be seen anywhere.

He kept his wing covering Xen until she opened her eyes. She looked into his face and smiled. *"You are very brave, little Drago."*

"I would never have left you," Drago said.

"Thank you. We must go now," Xen began to move.

Drago pulled his wings back. *"I am confused. I am not sure what happened. I kept thinking if we could just blend into rocks, you know, look like nothing more than a pile of rocks. I just knew I had to think of rocks. Just rocks."*

"You have great powers, Drago. Powers you are not aware of." She smiled and pulled herself to a sitting position on her haunches. *"Now that I know you have the power within you, I shall trust in you to help me when you can. It will take less out of me."*

"All you need to do is ask," Drago said moving to the edge of the ledge. He looked down the mountainsides and up into the sky. *"I think they are all gone."*

"Yes," Xen stretched her wings and pulled them back in toward her. *"Drago,"* she looked into his face. *"While I was unconscious, I had a very strange vision. There is a deceiver, a dangerous deceiver in Mac's company. But I could not make out exactly who it was. The image of this deceiver was blocked from me."*

"How can we find out?" Drago asked.

"We must seek out the Zetche. It has the key."

"Zetche!" Drago was startled. *"What does the Zetche have to do with this?"*

"I don't know, but we have to find out," she thought for a moment.

"There is another who can warn Mac. He knows. But can he get to him in time."

"I may be a young dragon, but I don't think the Zetche is going to volunteer to tell us anything," Drago said.

Xen gave a small laugh, *"Drago we are not going to go up to it and ask. We must seek it out and find out what it is up to."*

"Xen, this Zetche demon is dangerous and powerful. One that is too powerful even for us."

"Are you getting hungry?" She said teasing him about the Zetche he had consumed in Mac's world.

"That was different," Drago said. *"It was in a mundane world, and its powers were greatly diminished. I was told that the Zetches feed off each other for their magic, otherwise, whenever they use it, it makes them weaker. And, that was how I destroyed that Zetche. Not because I am stronger or wiser."*

"You are much stronger and wiser than you know, my dear, Drago."

"Besides, Xen, how will we ever find this Zetche demon? I don't know where he is, do you?"

"As a matter of fact, I do," Xen pushed off the ledge and flew into the sky. *"Are you coming?"*

"Like I have a choice," Drago flew next to her.

They flew carefully through the sky, always watchful for any Draklufs flying near them. As they neared the Xelrils Mountains they could see thousands of demons on the ground.

The screech of the Draklufs broke through the cold, blue sky. Drago knew they had to find a place to hide . . . and quickly. After a brief search, they spotted a thick group of trees and bushes on the ground.

"Between the two of us, we have enough strength to keep us unnoticed," Xen said, as they dove into the trees knocking down some branches and limbs.

"Unnoticed from what? Wait, I hear something," Drago moved

closer to Xen as they crawled to the edge of the trees and bushes to peer out.

"Drago," Xen sent him a message. "*When it gets too hard for you to listen and concentrate on hiding us, don't worry. I will have enough strength. This is all new to you.*"

"Look," Drago said incredulously. "*It's the Zetche. How can that be?*"

"*I told you I knew where he was,*" Xen said.

That sat for a long while and listened to the Zetche rant and rave about his past, present, and future. The present and future were the most important and upsetting things to hear.

"*I feel he has sensed us. I am not sure.*" Drago looked worriedly at Xen.

She reached behind one of her scales and dropped a necklace with a small, softly glowing stone set in the middle of it to the ground. "*This may help give us more time.*"

"*I have heard enough,*" Drago motioned for Xen to move out of their cover and away from the large demon. "*We must hurry and warn Mac.*"

"Yes," Xen reached over and grabbed Drago's wing. "*Think with me. Think with me. They cannot see us. They cannot smell us. They cannot hear us. They cannot sense our magic. Keep thinking with me, Drago.*"

Their thoughts worked as they moved through the throng of demons. Once they were clear of them they flew into the sky unnoticed. A blaring sound erupted from below and the legions of demons began to move out.

"*How can we possibly get to Mac and warn him?*" Drago was beside himself with worry for Mac.

"*Drago, I had a vision that he was at the witches' castle in the Rils forest. If we can get close enough to the castle we can send Mac our warning.*" Xen flew down and landed near a small tree. A gurgling brook flowed nearby and she began to drink from the cool water.

Drago landed next to her and after he had his fill of water he sat down under the tree.

"We are too far away to reach Mac and I sense thousands of demons surrounding him," Xen said as she sat next to Drago.

Immediately he stood up and began to pace back and forth. *"We need what Mac calls a miracle."*

"Drago?" Xen's eyes were wide with surprise at something behind Drago. *"What's happening there?"*

Drago turned and saw an undulating wall forming in front of them. Suddenly, a doorway appeared and at least a hundred people came through. They all had their weapons drawn, as they cautiously entered Mystovia. The last to come through were the four youths from Earth. Danny, Brody, Marcus, and Naomi stood eyeing their surroundings when they spotted Drago.

"Hey," Danny pointed excitedly as his red hair whipped about from the cold winds. "Is that you, Drago?"

"Wha . . .?" Drago was speechless.

"Hey," Naomi said pulling her cape around her heavy-set body. Strands of her curly, black hair worked their way from under the hood of her cape. "It is you, isn't it? Who's your beautiful friend?"

"Yes, yes," Drago said excitedly jumping up and down. After he regained his composure he spoke quickly to the group. *"It's me, and my friend Xen."* He looked at Xen. *"These are my young friends from Earth and the others are friends from the Land Between."*

"Yes, I see. Welcome," her thoughts were soft and sincere.

"Dude, this place is cold," Marcus's dark hair and eyes were hidden by the hood of his cape as he shivered against the freezing temperatures.

"I think it feels invigorating," Brody said rubbing his hands together and blowing on them trying to keep them warm.

"You're either one hot blooded Asian or crazy," Marcus groaned.

"It is good to see you, Drago," Jhondar stepped forward. The silver coating was gone and a tall, lean man with blue-grey eyes stood before him.

"Oh, it really is wonderful to see you again, Drago," Jainy's face broke into a big grin.

"*It is good to see you, too. All of you.*" Drago sent his thoughts to all the people who had come through.

"Drago," Etheria stood before him, her blonde hair streaked with silver, and her vivid blue eyes deep with worry. "The Zetche has stolen a very powerful object, and he is going to use it against Mystovia."

"Yes," Drago nodded in agreement. "*We have seen the skull he carries in his cape. He is planning on killing, Mac, Kess, and me for killing his mate.*"

"He is a very powerful demon," Xen explained. "*Even without this skull he carries.*"

"Yes, my dear," Etheria said softly. "We have had quite a few years of fighting both of the Zetches. We have come to help."

"*It is wonderful that you came to help,*" Drago just shook his head. "*But we have seen his demon legions. He has gathered thousands of demons to fight against us. And, now with this new powerful skull, I don't know how we can stop him.*"

"Let us worry about that," Jhondar said and motioned for the others to come closer. "We must get to a safe place so that we can plan our attack."

Drago thought for a moment and then smiled. "*I know of just the place. Follow me. But we must hurry because they are going to attack Mac.*"

"You have many brave and loyal friends, Drago." Xen hurried next to Drago as they came to an extremely wide tree trunk.

"*Oh, oh,*" Drago's smile faded. "*I don't know how to open it.*"

"A Dak tree," Etheria said, with awe. "It has been many, many years." She sighed and pulled a pouch from her cape and opened it. A stone fell from the pouch and rested on the palm of her hand. "This is a very old stone. I hope there is still magic it in and that I still know the right incantation." She spoke the words to create a door in the Dak tree, but nothing happened. Etheria took a deep breath and began another incantation. She sighed with relief as a door formed in the tree. "But Drago, I'm afraid there is not room enough for all of us in there."

"Drago will show you plenty of room. Just keep your magical stone ready." Drago and Xen walked down the wooden steps. Etheria and Jhondar followed. *"Now, you say the words you said up there down here."*

"But" Etheria's hand went to her throat. "There are creatures in there that will kill us."

"No, they are friends of Drago's."

"Alright," Etheria shrugged uneasily and spoke the incantation to open another doorway. It appeared and opened into a vast cavern. Jhondar called for those waiting above that it was safe to come down. Everyone filed down the steps and into the warmer shelter.

"Say," Marcus said, nervously. "It's really dark down here. Anybody got a flashlight on them?"

"One moment, please." Drago sent a message to everyone. *"I must warn the Groglemytes that we will be down here and that we are going to light our way."*

"Did he say we're going to have a warm groggy night?" Marcus moved closer to Naomi.

Naomi snapped as Marcus brushed up against her. "That's close enough, dude!"

Scurrying sounds could be heard all over the cavern. *"They say it is okay now to use the hurtful light. They are far enough away so that it will not hurt them."*

"So, what are these groggy things again," Brody asked.

"They live down here and feed only from the Dak tree roots. Light hurts their eyes. Anyway, they are our friends and we do not want to hurt them." Drago said as he waddled next to Xen.

"Gotcha little buddy," Brody said. "So, does anybody have a flashlight, candle, or matchsticks . . . anything that lights up so we can see?"

"Please wait. There is a little light from the inside of the Dak tree.

I have to close and seal the doors. We don't want demons or anyone coming down here." Etheria said a few words and the grinding sound of the first door they came through closed, and then the second door that led them into the cavern slowly shut.

"Oh, man, this is so totally dark," Marcus moaned.

"I took out a potion and put it in my hand before the door shut enclosing us in darkness," Jhondar replied.

His words were barely audible as Jhondar started the incantation. At first, there was just a faint flickering from the stones. Soon small embers began to travel upward from his hand. The embers twirled and twisted over their heads. Soon the embers meshed together giving off just enough light for everyone to see where they were.

Etheria laughed, along with Jhondar, "It is good to be home," she said.

"This light will stay with us until we can find some torches or other things to use." Jhondar looked at the deep, twisting roots all around him. "Now, which way, my little friend?"

"*Follow me!*" Drago led the group down a path deeper into the cavern.

"*The Zetche, as you call it, is preparing to attack Mac at the witches' castle in the Rils Forest. We must get there to warn him. There are thousands of demons laying a trap for him and the others.*" Xen sent her message to everyone.

"Where is this Witches castle?" Brody asked.

"*It is where Mac is at,*" Drago exclaimed.

"Of course, it is," Danny shrugged and looked over at his friends. "I've got nothing," he whispered.

"That makes two of us," Brody whispered back.

"*We must hurry,*" Xen quipped excitedly.

"Does mother, I mean the Imperial Sorceress know of the problem?" Etheria queried.

"*I don't know,*" Drago said. "*We are too far to get a message to her, and we don't know if Mac sent one or not.*"

"How long will it take us to get to the witches castle from here?" Jhondar asked.

"If we don't have any problems it will take us a short while," Xen said.

"Well, that helped narrow it down," Naomi said sarcastically.

"Okay, anybody else wondering why we're walking underground with a bunch of earth overhead that could collapse on us at any time?" Marcus eyed the dirt-packed ceiling with its twisting roots.

"We are perfectly safe," Etheria said. "We are down far enough that there is no fear of the earth caving in on us."

"Do you have earthquakes in Mystovia?" Marcus tripped over a root and was grabbed by Brody before he fell.

"We have quakes, but mostly they are in the mountain area," Jhondar half-smiled. "Unfortunately, that's the way we should be headed."

"Huh?" Marcus stopped abruptly.

"Get going, dufus," Danny did not see him stop and collided with him. "Did it ever occur to you that the sooner we get outta here the better?"

"Yeah, goober," Marcus snapped. "That's exactly what I'm thinking."

"Where's Jainy?" Danny looked around until he spotted her. "Hey, Jainy! You get to see Mystovia from the bottom up. Cool, huh?"

"Yeah, dude," Jainy laughed. "Cool!"

"Oh, my," Etheria said softly to Jhondar. "She picks things up quickly, doesn't she?"

He chuckled, "She sure does, dudess."

"This is where we must turn to get to the witches' castle," Drago moved toward a massive tree trunk. *"We will have to leave this area pretty soon as the Dak trees only go so far. So, if you want to talk about what we are going to do, we had better do it now. The area up ahead is not very wide, and it will take us pretty close to the castle. At least that is what they told me."*

"Who told you? Those groggy creatures?" Marcus asked.

"Yes," Drago nodded. *"They say after the great water, there is a great fire."*

"Fire?" Marcus' eyes widened. "Did you say 'fire'?"

"Yes," Drago said. *"The fire is far off, and they do not go near it. The water is where the Dak trees end and that is coming up pretty soon."*

"Here we go with a definitely-maybe time frame again," Naomi sighed.

"Are there any other beings down here besides the Groggy people?" Marcus asked.

"We have no idea," Jhondar said. "We have never traveled down here before. We always stayed in the base of the Dak tree, never beyond it."

"Alright," Etheria put up her hand for everyone to stop. "Gather around. Let us join our minds and thoughts and come up with ideas to help Mac and the others."

Everyone sat, knelt, or squatted around in a large half-circle, except Marcus.

"We are outnumbered, but I don't think that will be a problem," Jhondar said.

"You don't?" Marcus raised an eyebrow. "Am I the only one who thinks that maybe a problem? A very big problem."

"You're our problem," Danny grabbed Marcus's cape and pulled on it for him to sit down. Reluctantly, Marcus knelt on one knee.

"First of all, let us see where and what we are up against. I am pretty sure I can remember the layout of the witches' castle and where it's located. Etheria and I were privy to its location, and it came in handy quite a few times. But, . . ."

"Oh, boy! I hate it when someone says 'but,'" Marcus shook his head.

"As I was saying," Jhondar looked over at Marcus, smiled, and then continued. "But I have no idea how to get there from beneath it."

"Oh, boy!" Naomi moaned.

Jhondar picked up a small stick lying by his side and began to draw a crude layout of the castle, the moat, and the surrounding terrain. He asked Drago to show him where they were now. Drago studied the drawing for a few moments and with one of his claws, put an X to show where they were.

"*We may be more over here,*" Xen said drawing another X further away from Drago's.

"Either X looks like we are not too far away," Etheria said. "I should probably say - at least they do not look that far away."

"*I hear something,*" Drago said.

"*I feel danger,*" Xen sent out her thoughts to everyone.

"That's good enough for me." Marcus stood up. "Let's go."

"Silence," Jhondar whispered. "Listen. I do not hear anything, yet. We can hide until we see what is coming this way. There are plenty of places to hide for all of us. Quickly, find a spot and once everyone is hidden I'll douse the light."

They scrambled to seek hiding places away from the path. Jhondar waited until everyone had found a place to hide and waved his hand making the light disappear. Darkness quickly enveloped them all.

Soon, they could hear the pounding sounds of footsteps and something dragging. Long shadows flowed ahead of the torches they carried. The footsteps and dragging sounds got louder until they reached the cavern where everyone was hiding.

There was a sniffing sound that got closer to the hidden group.

Marcus could not stand it any longer. He had to see what was coming closer to him. The dragging sound stopped. He peered around the large root of a Dak tree and came face-to-face with one of the biggest and ugliest things he had ever seen. He let out a scream. It startled the troll who let out a scream as well.

The other trolls moved toward Marcus, who promptly fainted.

CHAPTER TWELVE

*K*ess shuddered slightly as the door behind them disappeared. "Are we going to have to meet up with those spider thingies again?"

"No," the wizard moved down a long tunnel.

"Hey," Doc said. "Before we start going downward, do you know of any more of those mine carts nearby, you know those things that take you down to the bottom fast and safe. I don't think I could climb down another ledge."

"No," Baalizar said briskly. He hurried down the dark hallway, his hand would move over darkened torches on the walls that quickly burst into flames.

"Great," Doc sighed and hurried behind the fast-moving wizard. "At least with all this light we can see ourselves falling off a ledge.

The tunnel emptied into a vast room. The wizard had everyone stop. He raised his hands and torches in the room burst into flames.

"Wow," Kess exclaimed. "What is this place?"

"The Temple of Iszel." Baalizar gestured toward the grandeur of the temple. "Is it not beautiful?"

Statues of Sorcerers, Sorceresses, and other inhabitants of

Mystovia were set back in niches lining three sides of the room. They must have stood over twenty feet high, and were covered in shimmering gold, Kess thought.

A large marble fountain dominated the room with the image of a dragon embedded in it. It almost reached the top of the ceiling, and it ended on the bottom of the floor. Water flowed out of the mouth of the dragon and down into a narrow river that disappeared beneath the rocks.

Their padded footsteps echoed softly as they walked down the steps of the temple. They reached the bottom and walked across to the dragon fountain.

"This dragon is fantastic," Kess managed to say.

"That dragon has to be over 30 feet high," Doc scratched his head. "Wonder how they did it? I mean it looks like it was cut into the stone."

"Yes, yes," Baalizar muttered. "But we must go."

"Who uses this place?" Kess looked at the water running from the dragon down into a basin and disappearing under some rocks.

"It was used by the worshippers of Iszel," Baalizar said. "That was centuries ago, and they are no more."

"What happened to them?" Doc asked.

"Wars and hatred of them," Baalizar shrugged. "I am not quite sure which, but probably both."

"Does anyone use it today?" Kess said quietly, almost if in reverence to where she stood.

"No one knows of this place," Baalizar said.

"Umm," Doc bent down and looked at the water racing under the rocks. "We're not going to have to swim under that, are we?" He turned to the wizard just in time to see him heading for the steps next to the dragon fountain. "Now, where's he going?"

Everyone stood and watched as Baalizar walked up the steps, around the pillar, and out of their sight. They waited a moment and when the wizard did not reappear, they hastily followed him around the marble pillar.

They stopped abruptly. The water dripped on their heads as they moved along the narrow path behind the fountain. The path ended with two ways to go; one led to a path on the right and one on the left.

"Anybody have a clue where 'Mr. Now-You-See-Me-Now-You-Don't' went?" Kess asked trying to figure out which way to go.

"Which way he went?" Doc said exasperatedly. "I'm hoping he just remembers we're with him."

At that moment, one of the wizard's hands came from around a large flat rock at the end of one of the hallways. The hand flapped back and forth gesturing for everyone to follow him.

"I hope the wizard is attached to that hand," Kess mumbled as they turned down the hall toward the waving hand.

"Wait here. We'll find out," Kybil moved ahead of Kess along with a couple of his warriors.

They ran down the hallway and around the corner where they had last seen the wizard's waving hand. Within seconds, they returned around the corner signaling everyone to follow them.

Steps carved out of stone led down to a small, underground sea. Stalactites hung from the roof of the cave almost touching the water. The current was fast as it poured around the boulders and stalagmites that stuck up periodically through the dark water. Little eddies formed, and in some cases, they would break into larger whirlpools.

"Well, unless we have some boats or scuba gear, we're not going anywhere." Kess looked down into the muddy water at the edge of the river. "Can we wade in this? I mean, how deep is it? This is a spooky grotto. How are we going to get downriver?"

"Patience," Baalizar snapped. "Patience."

"I'm gonna make you a patient if you don't get us out of here. We have to get to Mac. Remember." Doc snapped back.

"Of course, I remember," Baalizar said. "I am forgetful at times, but only with unimportant matters. Now, follow me and be quiet."

They walked cautiously along a narrow ledge on the edge of the underground sea. The slippery rocks beneath their feet made walking difficult.

If someone made a noise, Baalizar would quickly shush them, so everyone tried to be as quiet as possible as they slipped and slid.

They traveled quite a while when the ledge opened up to a large cave. The startled and relieved group moved away from the ledge and stood in front of several enormous boulders. Before anyone could say anything, Baalizar put his finger to his lips to signify silence. He took out a pouch and whispered a few incantations. Sparkling dust flew out and above the boulders and into the cave. Several loud thuds were heard beyond the large rocks.

"Quickly," Baalizar whispered loudly. "Quickly!" He raced around the boulders as everyone followed him.

"Oh, my gosh!" Kess stopped in her tracks. Several trolls were lying on the ground unconscious. A fire had been built and something foul-smelling was cooking on a spit.

"Did you kill them?" Kess whispered.

"No, no, just made them sleep. Quick," Baalizar jumped into one of their large canoes tied in a slip. "Everybody. Get in. Start moving."

"Everyone into the boats," Kybil ordered.

They grabbed four of the six troll canoes. They were large enough so that there was room for everyone. They untied the canoes and pushed off into the churning water. It took three warriors to work one oar on each side of the canoe, as they dropped them into the water.

"How long will that spell last?" Rakmor asked.

"I have no idea," Baalizar said. "But it should be enough for us to get away from them."

"Should be?" Doc's voice raised an octave.

"Yes," Baalizar said nonchalantly. "Yes, I think it should be."

It took the warriors a while to figure out how to maneuver the giant oars through the rocks and racing water. And a couple of times the oars struck something in the water that almost threw everyone out of the canoe.

All around them dim lights emanated from some of the stalagmites casting eerie shadows in the water and rock formations.

"Something is moving over there," Kybil pointed to his warriors. Pull back."

The giant oars disappeared deep into the cold, dark waters, as the Warriors struggled to control them. But the current was too strong for them to pull the heavy oars back.

Kess stood up next to Kybil and spotted the moving object. It was an enormous whirlpool. The canoe that Kess, Rakmor, and Kybil were in was being sucked into it. No matter how hard the warriors tried to paddle back the force of the whirlpool was too strong.

The first three canoes had managed to escape the deadly, spiraling water, and looked helplessly at the canoe behind them being pulled deeper into the powerful force of the swirling water.

The centrifugal force of the whirlpool sent their boat spinning around and around as it sucked them down into its deadly core. Suddenly, the canoe shot upward and out of the middle of the whirlpool. The waters around them became smooth.

"Hurry," Kybil yelled as he helped the warriors struggling with an oar. "Let's get out of here while we can."

They paddled with all their strength. Everyone, including Kess, grabbed part of a mammoth oar to paddle away from an almost certain watery death. They reached the other three canoes safely when the whirlpool began to form again.

"Come on," Kybil said. "Let's get away from here."

The water current was so strong that the warriors no longer needed to row with the oars. Instead, they began to use them to navigate around the boulders and objects sticking out of the water and avoid hitting the things hanging down from the ceiling.

"Listen," Doc said.

The cave began to resonate with deep guttural sounds.

"Where's it coming from?" Kess asked.

"It may be that the trolls just woke up," Kybil said, alerting his warriors.

The warriors knew just what to do. They pulled out arrows from their quivers and watched for any signs of danger.

"Hey," Kess grabbed Kybil's arm. "This canoe is going too fast. I mean really fast."

"I noticed," he shook his head. "I don't like this."

"Oh, oh!" Kess stood up and looked ahead. "I've heard that sound before."

It was the roar of a waterfall, and it was directly in front of them.

Behind them, the roar of guttural screams was getting closer. The trolls were now awake and in pursuit of their four missing canoes.

Kess and the others were trapped in the dark grotto with forward as their only option.

"They're gaining on us," Rakmor looked behind and saw a couple of canoes closing in on them.

"There's no place to hide in here," Kybil yelled to the wizard. "Is there?"

"No," Baalizar said. "No place. Pull the oars in. We are going over a waterfall."

"Of course, we are," Kess sighed.

"Great," Kybil sighed. "Okay, do as he says. Pull in the oars and everybody grab onto something and hold on."

The roar of the waterfall drowned out the roar of the trolls behind them. The strong current thrust the first canoe over the falls. It hung in midair for a second and then began its fall down the steep waterfall. It hit the water at the bottom of the falls amid the frothing, roiling water, but did not break apart. The canoe was grabbed instantly by a swirling mass of rapids and pulled uncontrollably down the river. Each canoe landed safely only to be pulled into the powerful force of the rapids. Slowly, the rapids began to diminish in force enough that they could manage to navigate the underground river.

"The trolls are going to be on us anytime now," Kess moved the wet hair from her eyes. "What are we going to do?"

"Over there," Baalizar pointed to a small cove. "Pull in and get out of the canoes, and as soon as everyone is out push the canoes back into the river."

Kybil gave the order. "Let's do it."

The canoes were quickly emptied and pushed back into the racing water by the warriors. Instead of moving away from their landing point the canoes bumped and jostled into one another.

"Oh, my," Baalizar looked at the canoes, gave one long sigh, and pointed his finger. A white light shot out pushing the canoes into the rapids and down the river out of sight.

"Come on," Kybil yelled. "Let's get out of here."

Everyone scurried to hide from the approaching trolls. The guttural sounds were now deafening and echoed loudly as they got nearer. Kess carefully peered through a couple of boulders and watched as the two canoes, with three trolls in each one, passed by. They had no trouble manning the heavy oars as they pushed toward the three empty canoes racing ahead of them.

"You could have warned us about the falls," Doc said wiping his wet face with an even wetter shirt.

"It was unimportant. I do not stuff my brain with insignificant things. Well, we're almost there," Baalizar crept along the boulders until he came to a very narrow path far away from the river. He straightened up and began walking briskly along the path. "Come. Come." He said with annoyance. "We have to get moving. We have to warn this Mac person."

"Doesn't anybody use transportation around here?" Doc said out of breath.

"We just took a boat ride," Kess said.

"Oh, yes, fun wasn't it." Doc chided. "Now if we could just find a limo."

The narrow path meandered downward ending onto a wide plateau in a cave, with several tunnel openings. The wizard stood for a while looking around. "Hmm," he said. "I am afraid I do not remember which one we should take. Hmm."

"I know da way," Nordaal moved past him and headed toward one of the tunnels.

No one questioned him as they followed him into the tunnel and down to an intersection where Nordaal turned with confidence. As they approached the next intersection, they could hear the noise of people shouting, and a male's voice yelling for help, and what sound like smashing noises. Everyone began to run toward the sounds and came to an alcove where it had become pitch black.

Baalizar's cape rustled as he pulled one of his pouches out and said a short spell. Suddenly, light exploded in the cave. Everyone was aghast at what they saw when the flames from overhead lit up the cavern.

Two trolls were swinging their clubs madly around in the air, sometimes hitting each other.

The two trolls were beating their clubs at the large roots of the Dak trees and trying to rip the roots from the ground to get at their quarry.

The sight of Drago and a silver dragon flying over their heads breathing flames on the trolls stunned everyone.

It only took a moment for the startled warriors to regain their thoughts and jump into the fracas. They pulled out their arrows and swords to fight the trolls who had now turned their attention toward them.

The two trolls realized there were too many for them to fight and charged toward the advancing warriors with their clubs swinging. The warriors jumped out of reach as the trolls fled past them.

Slowly, people began to come from around the Dak roots. Kess spotted Danny and Naomi.

"Oh, my stars!" She exclaimed. "How did you get here? Drago? When did you all get here? Why?"

A woman with shoulder-length, graying blonde hair walked toward Kess. "They came with us, Kess." Her face broke into a huge smile.

"Mother?" Kess stared in disbelief. "Is it, you?"

"Yes," she reached Kess and embraced her. "Yes."

"Thank goodness you came along," Jhondar said to Kybil. "We placed a spell to douse their torches. We did not dare to give those trolls any light. It was so dark in here we could only poke at them when Drago and Xen flew overhead and lit up the area with his fire breathing."

"Mac?" Jainy looked from face-to-face for Mac.

"We're going to find him now," Kess said gently.

"Is everyone okay," Kybil asked.

"Yes," Naomi saw the handsome elf, and her mouth fell open. She turned her attention to the other elven warriors. "Like, wow! I think I'm going to like Mystovia."

"I'm thinking jail sounds much better every day," Marcus stumbled from around a large tree root. "That big, ugly thing nearly killed me."

"Aw, quit complaining," Danny said. "This is wild. Man, did you see the size of those things?"

"How could you not?" Marcus quipped.

A couple of the older elves from the Land Between began to walk toward the younger elven warriors. The older warriors studied them carefully, while the younger warriors looked at each other wondering what was going on. Then the older warriors began talking to them, suddenly the room became filled with shouts of excitement as some of the warriors found part of their lost family.

"You know," Kybil broke the revelry, "I hate to break up this reunion, but those trolls are going to be back and bring some friends with them. They looked mighty hungry to me."

"Hungry?" Marcus's voice jumped several octaves.

"You'll get used to it, son." Doc patted his shoulder.

"We had better get out of here as fast as we can," Kybil looked at Baalizar. "Do you still know the way out of here?"

"I remember, now," Baalizar said. He pulled a pouch from inside his cape pocket and threw silvery sand against a large boulder next to him.

"Wait," Kess exclaimed. "Will the Groglemytes be in danger from the trolls?"

"I do not know. The trolls do not know of the Groglemytes existence, because they have stayed hidden from them for centuries. And the trolls usually do not come this far into the caves. I think they must have smelled your presence and came in here to have a meal." Baalizar said shaking his head. "Unfortunately, for the Groglemytes the trolls will be back and venture further into these caves now that they have smelled food in them."

"Well, can you zap a little protection for the Groglemytes right now?" Kess asked.

"Of course," he said. "I already did." He put the pouch of silvery sand back into his cape pocket. "We must go past the Dak trees, back to the river, and across the bridge of doom." Without waiting for anyone, Baalizar headed away from the Dak trees and toward the river.

"The Bridge of Doom?" Marcus looked around at everyone. "Does anyone else think that sounds pretty dangerous? You know the word 'doom' kinda just, you know, jumps out at you."

No one was paying any attention to him as they followed the wizard. It wasn't long before they were away from the Dak trees and heading toward the river. The excitement was in the air as Kess, and the others were caught in deep conversation with their newly found family members.

"Listen," Kybil said loud enough for all to hear, but not loud enough he hoped, for the trolls to hear. "I think our 'friends' are back, and it sounds like they bought some more friends, a lot more friends."

"The path to the Bridge of Doom is just ahead," Baalizar whispered. He walked a few feet and pointed down a path leading to a tunnel.

"I think I can help with this one," Rakmor smiled and patted Kybil's shoulder. "Get everyone started down the path to the bridge. I'll give them something to concentrate on for a while."

"I'll stay with you," Kybil said and motioned for everyone to hurry after the wizard.

"I'm staying, too." Kess moved to stand next to Kybil and Rakmor.

"No, you're not staying this time," Kybil turned her around and gently pushed her toward Etheria, who stood waiting for her. "We'll be with you in a moment."

"But" Kess started to protest.

"No, buts," he looked at Etheria and motioned for her to come and get Kess. She acknowledged the look.

"Come dear," she said loudly and then whispered in Kess's ear. "We will stay by the entrance to the tunnel. If they get into any trouble, we will be there to help them."

A broad smile crossed Kess's face. "Thank you," she whispered back.

Just as she had promised, they waited by the tunnel entrance, along with Jhondar, Drago, Xen, and the teens. The darkness and silence were interrupted by a burst of light and the sounds of yelling and screaming. Kybil and Rakmor came running down the path toward the tunnel.

"Nice work," Kybil laughed. "I never would have thought of giving them a hot foot." Kybil looked up and saw everyone standing there. "Get moving."

Rakmor was the last one to enter the tunnel. He stopped and turned. He said a few more words, and the rocks began to spin and roll toward the tunnel opening. Soon, the entire entrance was covered by rocks and stones.

"Don't know how long Baalizar's spell will last. Can't have them going back in there to snack on the Groglemytes," Rakmor stood there smiling to himself.

Kybil tapped Rakmor's shoulder and motioned for him to get moving. "You can admire your handiwork later."

It did not take long for Kess and the others to catch up to the rest of the group.

"Say," Marcus said. "Is it getting warmer in here?"

"Of course," Baalizar nodded. "It is going to get a lot warmer, young man."

"Great," Marcus plodded after him. "By the time those big, ugly, hungry giants get to us, we'll be cooked to perfection."

Baalizar stopped everyone at the edge of a cliff. About a hundred feet below them was a moving river of lava that spewed and spit its hot contents upward.

Marcus walked to the edge and looked down. "You got to be kidding me! We're not going to have to jump this are we?"

"This way," Baalizar walked them down to a spot where a stone bridge crossed over the lava bed below. "We cross here."

"Looks like we're gonna join the trolls with a hot foot," Doc said looking at the steaming bridge.

"No, no," Baalizar said a few words and the bridge began to sizzle and spit. Clouds of dense steam billowed up almost blocking out the view of the bridge.

"Oh," Doc said sarcastically. "That's so much better. We don't have to worry about getting a hot foot because we're going to fall into the lava."

"That isn't a very wide bridge," Kess said looking at the now steaming bridge. "It doesn't look like more than two people at a time can cross."

"Double up. Be quick about it," Kybil sized up the situation. "Grab onto the person in front of you and follow them. But you must move quickly."

"Oh, that makes me feel so much better," Marcus snapped. "If one falls, we all fall."

"You should be able to see the bridge once you're on it," Danny said, smacking Marcus in the back. "If no one slips, or makes a wrong step, we'll all be fine." He chuckled as he grabbed a hold of the belt on the warrior in front of him and the person next to him.

"You're a dufus," Marcus snapped. Reluctantly, he grabbed the belt of the next warrior to cross the bridge. He closed his eyes and followed him across.

Drago sent a message telling everyone, that he and Xen would fly on both sides and catch anyone who would happen to slip and fall.

Danny turned and looked at Marcus as he stepped off the bridge onto land. "Are you nuts?" Danny yelled, perspiration dripping down his face. "You had your eyes closed? You could have gotten killed, and everyone around you."

"I figured there was a warrior ahead of me, one behind me, and one next to me. I figured they weren't about to drop into a river of lava." Marcus sighed with relief, "it worked. I got here okay."

"Yeah, but" Naomi walked up to Marcus. "The wizard just said he made a mistake. We have to go back across it again."

Eyes wide with terror Marcus whirled around to look at the steaming bridge. "You're kidding!"

"Yeah," she laughed. "I am."

"That wasn't funny," he glowered at her.

"Come on, guys," Brody yelled. "They're moving out of here. Man, it couldn't be fast enough for me. Now I know what a grilled hamburger feels like."

Baalizar pulled on a large stone latch. It creaked and groaned as the door opened to a wide set of steps. Just as the door opened a small rumble shook the ground. The bridge they had just crossed over broke in the middle and crumbled into the lava below.

"Did you see that?" Marcus said in a high-pitched voice. "We could have all been toasted by now."

"*Yep,*" Drago said landing next to him. "*But you made it.*"

"*I did not think the bridge was strong enough for everyone to cross,*" Xen flew down beside Drago.

"Now she tells us," Doc said widening his eyes.

"Come, come," Baalizar said. "Up the steps with you now."

The further up the stairs they went, the intensity of the heat decreased until a draft of cool air wafted down to them.

The group entered the large stone hallway of a castle startling a group of witches.

"Sorry," Kess said. "We didn't mean to scare you. We're looking for Mac and the others."

"You are too late," a witch of light blue coloring and white hair said.

"Yes," said another witch standing next to her. "We tried to warn him, but he wouldn't listen."

"No!" Kess screamed and grabbed one of the witches' arms. "Which way did he go?"

She pointed toward a huge room with two large wooden doors that were wide open. Kess and the others raced through the room screaming Mac's name.

"We can't be too late!" Kess cried. "We can't be!"

CHAPTER THIRTEEN

$\mathcal{K}$ess and the others tore out the castle door screaming his name. "Mac!"

Drago and Xen were already in the air.

"*Stop! It's a trap!*" Drago's voice came loud and clear to Mac as his horse trotted to the end of the wooden drawbridge. Mac pulled back on his horse's reins.

Drago flew in front of Mac blocking him and the other riders. Mac's horse reared up nearly knocking Mac off. Xen flew to the battlements to keep a watchful eye on Olo.

"Drago?" Mac steadied his horse. "Drago?" He repeated. He looked back and saw Kess and others racing toward him. "Kess?"

The horses became skittish, and the riders had to dismount and steady them.

Kybil was already giving loud chirping signals that Sirel heard.

"Retreat," Sirel ordered. "Get back in the castle. It's a trap." The warriors turned their horses and headed back into the castle.

Mac was still so stunned he couldn't speak as he dismounted. He looked at Olo standing by the edge of the forest and down at Kess and back at Drago.

"Mac?" Olo yelled with frustration. "What are you doing?"

"I'll get back to you on that," Mac yelled, and turned his horse toward the castle.

"Close the drawbridge!" Maaleah ordered the witches who were working the drawbridge.

"What's going on, Drago?" Mac asked.

Maaleah put her hands on her hips and nodded, "You see, there was something wrong."

"Mac?" Olo's voice rang with anger. "The women and children are going to die."

"Drago? Kess? What's this about a trap?" He stared in wonder. "How did you get in here without anyone seeing you?"

"That's a long story," Kess sighed. "Right now, Drago and this wizard person have something to tell you."

Baalizar moved out from the group and approached Mac. "What I have to say is redundant. Ask your little dragon friend here."

"Baalizar?" Maaleah's mouth dropped open. "I thought you were dead."

"I only feel like I am," he looked down at his wet and dirty robe. "I probably look like it, too."

Mac turned to Drago, "Well, little buddy, what is this about a trap?"

"*The man you see outside is not a man,*" Drago saw the confused look on Mac's face. "*He is one of the not so good-tasting Zetches. Xen and I were hiding when we heard the Zetche talking about how he was going to trick you into coming out of the castle. He stole some kind of object, a skull of some kind that gives him great magical powers. He killed this woodsman named Olo and gets into his body and wears it. That's the best way I can explain it.*"

"Mac," Sirel touched his shoulder. "That would explain a lot of things. When we first met this man called Olo, he was being chased by demons. Yet, when we fought the demons, I do not remember seeing him or any of his men fighting with us against the demons, nor do any of the other warriors."

"I don't remember any of them fighting either, but I attributed that to my being too busy trying to fight for my life. Although, there is one thing, okay a couple of things I kinda noticed." Mac raised his hand and tapped his chin. He wanted to say that if he had not been so interested in Sirel, he would have caught all these incidents and put it together himself.

"Mac!" Olo called. "Why have you pulled up the drawbridge?"

"Are you going to share the 'couple of things' or not?" Kess asked.

"Olo's wife said she hadn't seen him in months, and Olo said it was just a couple of days. Then, there was them not coming into the castle. I mean he was going to come in and balked when we said it had a protective shield against demons entering."

"Yes," Sirel said. "He seemed shocked that there was a castle behind us. Remember the look on his face."

"Right." Mac shook his head. "I thought it was because he wanted to come in, but felt he had to stay outside with his men to keep checking the perimeter."

"He showed no reaction when his wife was killed," Sirel said.

"And another thing, now that we are remembering things, it looked like his men bowed to him. Is that normal around here.?" Mac asked.

"It is not a usual practice among the common folk," Sirel said.

Kess looked at Mac. "Remember when we fought the demons at the Dak tree. When it was over Olo, and his men took off running into the forest. I mean, like in a blink of an eye they were gone."

"Mac!" Olo's voice rang with impatience. "What are you doing?"

"Hello, Mac," Jhondar stepped forward.

"What the . . .?" Mac's voice faltered. "How the. . . where the. . .?

"It's good to see you, too." He laughed and walked over to Mac. He gave a quick hug and stepped back to talk to him and the others. "Drago mentioned a skull. The Zetches stole one of the three Skulls of Semetter. He would have stolen all three if he had known there were three. But we had it arranged through technology and magic that it would appear there was only one Semetter Skull."

"But the silver coating stuff." Mac could not help but stare at his father. "You said it would take a couple of weeks. Trust me I am very glad it didn't."

"The Plexias knew of the problem and released the ecoplasm coating faster than normal. It would endanger us if we did it all the time, but they said it would not harm us if we used their release formula once in a while."

"Do you think the Zetche can see the castle now? I mean he has the Skull of Cemeteries with him." Kess asked.

Etheria gave a small laugh, "Semetter, my dear, the Skulls of Semetter."

"What is our 'woodsman' doing out there now?" Mac shouted snidely to one of his warriors stationed outside on the battlement.

One of the warriors called out, "They are just standing there, at the edge of the woods."

"Unfortunately, he is going to catch on very quickly that you have discovered who he is and what he is up to." Etheria moved up the stairs to the castle walkway.

"I am still trying to remember just exactly how things work here in Mystovia," Jhondar laughed. "It's going to take me a while getting used to this world again. However, it is a wonderful 'getting used to'."

———

Olo stood looking at the castle. He turned his back and took the skull out to look at it. He spoke softly to it, stroking it gently. "I have no idea if you are powerful enough to overcome all the witches' spells. You have enabled me to see the castle, but my minions cannot see it. I am not even sure if I can go inside of the castle, but I know my thousands of demons cannot."

His mind raced to try to figure out what to do. "What were little dragons doing in the castle? I do not have to worry about the dragons, because I know they cannot speak. No. No one knows of my plan. The only witness to my thoughts is dead," he mumbled. "I will call for my Draklufs. They will not be able to see the castle or its occu-pants, but they will attack any area I instruct them to. I will wear their magic down." His black lips curled up into a smile.

———

Maaleah studied Olo and his men on the other side of the moat. She looked around sadly at everyone standing on the parapet. It was then that she spotted Xen.

"Is that you?" Maaleah called out.

"Yes," Xen said. "*We can talk of this later. Right now, we must worry about the treacherous master demon.*"

"Do you think he is aware that we know about him now?" Kess asked.

Just then the witches gave the alarm that Draklufs were headed straight for the castle.

"I'm not taking any chances," Mac shouted. "Everyone get into the castle, now!"

The parapet wall-walk was cleared as they raced into the castle. They slammed the castle door shut just as the Draklufs, and their demon riders flew overhead. The dragons spewed fire, and their riders shot poisonous arrows. But because they had no idea what they were shooting at, or what they were supposed to burn they were inef-fectual.

Maaleah and the other witches immediately released a poisonous spell to eliminate the deadly riders. A couple of the Draklufs fell from the sky into the burning moat of lava; the others turned and flew away.

When it appeared safe to come out of the castle, Mac and the others raced to the parapet. They were not surprised to see that Olo and his men were gone, and in their place stood the Zetche and thou-sands of demons surrounding the castle. There was a glowing red light around the Zetche as he stood with the skull pointing directly at the castle.

"It is time for all of you to die," the Zetche smiled. "You cannot win against me and my minions. Not even your greatest and most powerful witches can stop my power." He held up the Skull of Semetter.

Danny, Marcus, Naomi, and Brody joined the others on the castle walkway and looked out at the demons waiting across the river of lava.

"What are those things over there?" Marcus asked.

"Those are the demons waiting to attack us," Maaleah said.

"They don't look human," Marcus exclaimed.

"They're not, dufus," Danny looked at Marcus and shook his head. "That's why they call them demons."

"There sure are a lot of them," Naomi said looking nervously over the wall.

"Yes. But we have brought help," Etheria felt the skull in her cape pocket. "We can only hope there are not too many for us."

"I've never seen so many ugly things in my life," Marcus' eyes widened with amazement. "We're not going to have to touch those things, are we?"

"No, only when we have to fight them," Brody and shrugged.

"Fight them?" Marcus looked at all the faces around him. "Oh, boy, this isn't going to be fun is it?"

"No," Mac patted his shoulder. "It's not going to be fun. Let's get back inside."

"Oh, boy," Kess came back from walking around the castle. "There are thousands of those nasty creatures all around the castle. Even you and I will have a hard time fighting them with our amulets."

"Look what he has in his hand. Is that what I think it is?" Mac asked.

"Yes," Jhondar said. "I think our Zetche is over-confident. He only has one. We left the most powerful of the three in the Land Between. It has been moved to a safer place and is heavily guarded."

"With our amulets and your skull we should be a pretty fair match against this Yahoo," Kess said moving toward the teens. "I would appreciate your help here."

"Sure, what?" Brody asked enthusiastically.

"Remember that door we came through in the castle, well, the trolls we were fighting down there have surely alerted their friends. They are probably down there looking for us now. If the trolls aren't down there, then I have to worry that the demons may find it and may try to sneak up behind us. There is protection around the castle, but it is losing its power."

"Yes, I'm afraid it is," Maaleah said.

"Are you trying to put us out of harm's way again?" Brody put his hands on his hips. "And besides, the bridge we crossed fell into the lava, remember?"

"The Trolls can pick up boulders and use them to put across the lava, so that will be no problem for them." Maaleah moved toward Brody and the other teens. "Your positions by the door may be very dangerous."

"She is right. If they know of that entrance, we wouldn't stand a chance if they infiltrate the castle from below. If nothing happens for a while, and we need help, trust me, I will be the first to come and get you. On the other hand, if you sense danger from either the trolls or the demons come and get us immediately." Kybil crossed his arms and looked at the young teens in front of him. "Will you help us with this?"

"Yeah, fair enough," Brody motioned for the others to follow him. "We've got your backs."

The teens headed down the winding castle steps while Kess and the others went back outside to the battlement.

Suddenly, a loud piercing scream erupted from the Zetche. They watched as his staff began to emit billow clouds of smoke, and within seconds, the entire castle was surrounded by a thick, swirling black smoke.

"What is he doing?" Kess asked. "I can't see a thing beyond the moat."

"Hmm," Baalizar rubbed his chin. "Very interesting diversion. Let me see if I can remember how to break that spell."

"Well, I hope you can remember one of your spells correctly," Maaleah sighed.

"Whatever do you mean, witch?" the wizard stopped rubbing his chin and looked down at her.

"Hey," Doc said indignantly. "Don't call her a witch?"

Baalizar and Maaleah looked at Doc and spoke at the same time. "Why?"

"Because, well. . . er," Doc fumbled for words.

Mac and Kess laughed at Doc's attempt to protect Maaleah from being called a witch.

"Maaleah, in our dimension calling someone a witch can be considered a derogatory word," Kess said.

"Who be da 'rotten Ory'? What be an Ory?" Nordaal asked.

"If I knew I'd be telling ya," Yaneth shrugged.

"Why, Doc," Maaleah smiled broadly. "That is very sweet of you to try to protect me from this old reprobate." She patted Doc's arm. "Thank you, but we have known each other for a long time."

"I thought he was a hermit and never left the mountain," Mac said, somewhat confused.

"Oh, that," Maaleah said. Now it was her turn to laugh. "He visits us quite often really. Well, at least eight or nine times a year. Where do you think he gets his food and supplies from?"

"You mean he goes through that tunnel with the trolls and the lava bridge all the time?" Kess asked incredulously.

"Heavens, no," Maaleah patted Kess's arm. "He usually comes by Pegasus or Gralcon. I think he came through the tunnels three or four times since he has lived on the mountain."

"It is very dangerous to come that way," Baalizar snapped. He moved to the parapet, while he fumbled with trying to open one of his pouches. "Three times it was. Humph! Well, four times now."

"So, what's with this black smoke surrounding the castle?" Mac gestured wildly at the dense, dark mass with his hands.

"I am not sure what he is planning. Anyone have any ideas?" Kybil asked.

Xen hopped up on the battlement wall. She stared into the black smoke that circled the castle. After a while, she pulled away and lowered her head. "*I know what he is planning on doing.*" She shook her head slowly, "*It is not black smoke; it is the Hvarth Wraiths. They will wear down the protective spell, and the Zetche will attack with his demons.*"

"Where does he get all those demons from? I mean if they keep replenishing themselves all the time we can never defeat him." Mac stared into the swirling mass of Wraiths.

"He does not have unlimited demons. As we destroy them, he calls forth more, but they are not limitless. And, the Dark Lords of Hvarth will not take kindly to having all of their minions destroyed." Maaleah began pacing on the wall-walk.

"That is true," Baalizar said walking next to her. "I believe he has made a pact with the Dark Lords. They are probably helping this Zetche because they believe he can defeat us humans, and then they would split this world into two sections. Each one would take half and rule it. Nasty buggers." He stopped Maaleah from pacing. "Why am I walking with you?"

"Why don't these 'nasty buggers' just take Mystovia for themselves?" Brody queried.

"Yeah, why should these Dark Lords split up the world when they can have it all?" Naomi asked nobody in particular.

"Because the Dark Lords of Hvarth cannot set foot on Mystovia soil. They once roamed the lands and almost destroyed Mystovia. They were defeated by the power of Mystovia's two moons and the two Crystal Orbs. They were forced to dwell in the deepest, darkest region under Mystovia; the realm of dark shadows called Hvarth. If the Zetche wins against us, he will break the spell that surrounds the Lords of Hvarth setting them free."

"Why can't these Dark Lords of wherever disguise themselves like that Zetche thingy out there?" Kess asked.

"If the Lords of Hvarth set foot on Mystovia's soil, they would be destroyed instantly. Mystovia's powers are great and would recognize their magical signature immediately no matter how they were disguised." Etheria said.

"But even though they reside in the dark, shadowy world of Hvarth, they continue to try to find a way back to Mystovia. That is why they will help this Zetche, in hopes he will defeat us, and destroy their spell so they can return to the lands of Mystovia." Jhondar shook his head. "They are a very powerful and dangerous force we do not wish to fight again."

"Why don't their demon armies just take over Mystovia? I mean there are enough of them," Naomi said.

"Hmm," Jhondar pondered for a moment. "Let me see, oh yes. The demons you see surrounding us have no thought processes and would never know how to design a strategy to win a battle, and even if they did they have no power to release their masters."

"As far as having their minions conquering Mystovia it would be useless as they have no magical powers. Our magical powers would destroy them and the Lords of Hvarth know this." Rakmor placed his hand gently on Naomi's shoulder. "That is why they use demons that have strong magical capabilities as well as a brain. Very good question." He smiled and patted Naomi's shoulder.

"Okay, so let's do something," Kess's hand began to tap the hilt of her sword. "Maybe we should give them a taste of our magical powers and show them we're not to be messed with."

"I wonder if that is what he is expecting us to do," Rakmor said. "If we use your powers it might open a pathway into the castle. He would seize on that in a moment."

"Rakmor may be right," Etheria nodded as she lowered the skull and carefully replaced it into its pouch. She quickly descended the stairs following Maaleah and the others into the courtyard.

"So," Mac was behind Sirel as she walked down the stone steps. "Now, what?"

"This is not of my liking." Sirel moved her lithe, muscular body down the steps. "I do not trust this foul master demon."

"Let's get into the castle and see what we can do," Maaleah moved quickly through the doorway. "I have a feeling we don't have much time. And, I am afraid they will find out about the tunnels below. Our magic has hidden it for many, many years, but it can only do so much, and our magic is being drained. And, we have trolls down below who are looking for their next meal. I'm sure they have alerted the others, and the tunnels will be crawling with trolls."

"We have enough magical power between us to come up with a plan that would fool even that foul creature." Rakmor walked to the fireplace and pulled down a map of Mystovia. He placed it carefully on the large table in the center of the room. Everyone converged around him. "Let's see." He pointed to the spot where the castle was located. "We're here and are surrounded by Wraiths circling the castle, and there are hundreds of demons waiting to attack us."

"Umm," Mac said correcting him. "Make that thousands."

"We could escape down through the tunnel." Kess looked over at Danny standing at the top of the stairs. "But there would be no way for us to get the horses down that winding staircase."

A murmur rippled through the warriors at the thought of leaving their horses behind.

"*We cannot go back that way anyway.*" Xen sent a message to all.

"*That's right!*" Drago sat back on his haunches. "*Remember the bridge across the lava is now gone.*"

"We could use one of our spells to create another one," Maaleah said, tapping the table anxiously.

"Yes, but that would alert the Zetche immediately. He carries the skull. It may alert him of our whereabouts the minute you use your magic." Etheria pulled away from the table and began to pace the floor.

"We have enough magical power between us to confuse our whereabouts. Even with his magical skull, he would not be able to trace all the spells we could create to confuse our trail."

"It's a good thought," Mac said. "Going back down the tunnel and confusing our steps might work."

"Even if we could use the tunnels, there are bunches of trolls down there waiting for a meal. And, we don't want to leave the horses and other animals here for them to destroy." Kess shook her head. "It appears we are trapped."

"I don't think so. I have an idea," Danny was at the top of the stairs listening to them discussing their plight. "I wasn't eavesdropping. You were all speaking very loudly.

"Hey, we have no secrets from you anyway," Mac motioned for him to join them. "We're up to listening to any ideas."

CHAPTER FOURTEEN

"We're all ears, Danny," Mac said.

Danny called down for the other teens to hurry up the steps. When they reached the top, they stood for a moment conversing with each other.

The warriors looked at one another in confusion and back at the teens.

"It would help if we all knew what your idea was," Mac folded his arms and leaned back against the table. "We're running out of time pretty fast here."

"Oh, yeah," Danny smiled sheepishly. "I was just checking with them to see if it would work. They think it will, too."

"Come on over and share it with us," Mac gestured for the teens to join them.

Danny hurried over and grabbed the map on the table. "Okay," he turned the map around a couple of times. "Umm, show me where this castle is on the map."

Maaleah pointed to the area the castle was situated on.

"Okay, now show me where the enemy isn't," he stood back so that Maaleah could reach the map.

"Say what?" Maaleah asked confused.

"I know where the enemy is but are the demons everywhere on this map. Is there one place they're not? I mean a place pretty close to us." Danny pursed his lips and waited for a reply.

"Young man," Maaleah sighed. "They have us surrounded by the thousands."

"Well, it's just this. I heard Kess tell of the Unicorn in the briar patch or some such place, and I heard the old wizard say you had a lot of powerful magic between all of you." He flipped the map around and then pounded his fist on the table. "I've got it."

"Let's have it, Danny," Mac said raising his eyebrow.

"Can you teleport us, and the animals, so we are all under the castle? You know near the groggy thingies." Danny started to laugh. "And maybe at the same time teleport the trolls up here."

"What does teleport mean?" Maaleah asked.

"What I mean is," Danny said gesturing frantically. "Move everybody down below and the trolls up here by magic."

"I understand," Maaleah smiled and nodded.

"Yes, yes, it just may work," Kess said. "Rakmor you transported at least thirty of us at one time, and a horse by yourself. Do you think all of you could work together to do this?"

"Hmm," Maaleah brought her finger up and began tapping her chin.

"Hmm? What do you mean by that?" Baalizar questioned irritably. "Of course, we can. There is a lot of powerful magic between all of us."

"Yes," Maaleah said. "That is true, but by doing that we have to pull the magical spells protecting the castle away. And, won't the Zetche see that the castle is empty."

"Please," Naomi spoke up. "Haven't you guys ever seen a movie or television show? Oops, guess not. But there is something we could do that won't cost you any magic. We have some dummies to make and quick." She grabbed a startled witch's arm. "Get us some clothing and a few hats, bonnets, helmets, head covering, or whatever you call it. Oh, and something to stuff in them."

"Okay," Danny smacked the table with his hand. "That's settled. You magic people or whatever you're called get your potions or spells together because we are going to have to synchronize everything."

"Sink our eyes? Why we sink our eyes?" Nordaal began blinking rapidly.

Mac looked down at Nordaal. "Nor, I haven't a clue what the heck you're talking about. Nobody is going to do anything with your eyes. Okay, buddy?"

"Yeh," Nordaal looked up and smiled. "Dat's good. So, when dey tries ta take yours, I protect ya."

"Okay, then," Kess patted Nordaal on the arm. "I think I have an idea of what you kids are thinking. We gotta move fast. Everyone who doesn't have something to do come with us."

"Xen," Maaleah turned to her. "We will need your help as well. We'll do the stuffing, and you do the placing of the stuffed figures."

"*Of course, I have read your thoughts. How very clever of you. He will think we are still here.*" She nudged Drago to go toward the door leading to the courtyard. "*We will put the stuffed figures on the parapet for the Zetche to see.*"

"*Yes. We can do it faster than having them run up and down the steps.*" Drago agreed.

"Get your horses and all the other animals and meet in the court-yard as fast as you can. Make sure everyone is accounted for before we leave. We don't want to leave anyone behind. Get the women and children up. We have to be ready in a couple of minutes." Kybil grabbed the map and lit it on fire.

"Maaleah," Rakmor yelled. "Be sure you and the other witches get as much of your magical potions as you can carry. We are going to have to work fast."

The warriors ran to the stable to get their horses, and witches grabbed their livestock and brought them into the large courtyard. The women and children, still groggy from little sleep, moved slowly into the center of the group. The teens and several others helped finish placing dummies along the wall-walk. They raced down the steps of the battlement to join the strange ensemble gathered there.

Anyone possessing magical abilities joined the Sabbot witches. They stood in front of the gathered group of people and animals.

"Listen up," Mac yelled to the group. "What they have to do is going to be difficult at best. Do not speak or make a sound until you are told it is okay to speak. Mothers, the witches have cast a small spell that will not hurt your children in any way. It is a spell of feeling safe and unafraid. They have placed it on the animals as well. Just in case."

One woman spoke out from the crowd, "thank you, but these children know when to be quiet. Unfortunately, they have had a lot of practice."

"Alright. Are we ready?" Rakmor asked his colleagues. They all gave him an affirmative reply. "We must do this quicker than ever before. Understood? If we fail to do so, it will mean our deaths."

Several witches surrounded the entire group and began the transporting spell. The ground underneath their feet began to shake, and instantly a misty, magical shield was sent over and around the group. Encased in a cloudy mist the ground seemed to give way. No one spoke or moved except the spell makers. Their soft chants grew louder as a white vortex began to form.

The wind from the vortex began to whine and as the vortex grew and moved away from them; it began to shriek. Guttural sounds of the trolls could be heard and grew in intensity as did the vortex. After a few moments, there was a popping sound, and the sounds of the vortex and the trolls ceased.

———

The Zetche stood with his arms spread wide as the Wraiths continued their circling of the castle. "Yes! He screamed. "Your powers are almost gone. I can see you now," a hideous laugh escaped from his black lips. "I see you on the castle wall. You cannot fight my armies. You are doomed. I shall make a bridge to span the entire width of your moat, and my demons will be able to attack from all sides."

He held the Skull of Semetter high in the air. "The minute you sense their power has been completely removed, form a bridge for my demons to cross. I have sent a message to kill all that they find in the castle. Spare no one or nothing. I cannot bother with you anymore Mac. It is a shame, I will not be able to pull your powers from you, but I realized with this skull, I don't need your puny powers." His black lips cracked into a smile. "They will not escape me this time."

At that instant bridges appeared over the moat, and the demons converged on the castle. The air filled with their war cries as they filed across the bridges and began crawling over the walls. The sound of fierce fighting could be heard as the Zetche threw back his head and laughed.

"Wow, that was great," Danny said as he jumped up and down on the solid earth. "Hey, this is where we first met those trolls. We're not far from the...Groggy...whatevers."

A light grew around them as the witches cast a bright light in the dark caves below. They walked for a while until they came to the opening that would lead them through the Dak tree roots. The tired children and women were put on the backs of the horses, and the other animals were tied with ropes and led through the spacious caverns. The soft sounds of something scurrying off to the side of them caused anxious moments for those that had heard the terrible tales of the Guardians of the Dak trees.

Xen and Drago left the group to find the leader of the Groglemytes. In a short time, they returned to the group.

"They say the Dak tree we seek is far away, but there is another

place that would enable us to take the four-legged beasts through," Drago spoke to everyone.

"It is not far from here," Xen stopped and turned toward the opening to the Dak tree caverns. *"Drago and I must go and close the entrance forever. The Groglemytes said that the trolls had ventured into their territory and left signs along the way leading to it."* Xen stood next to Drago. *"We must destroy all the signs they have left. If just one of the Groglemytes is detected it would cause a feeding frenzy among the trolls."*

"You and Drago cannot go alone," Mac said. "I will go with you."

"And I as well," Sirel quickly added.

"Hey, der." Nordaal grabbed the cap from his head and smacked it against his hand. "I be der wid ya, too."

"Yep," Yaneth said loudly.

"Hey, this sounds like another adventure. I'm in!" Danny said.

"Yeah," Brody moved toward the two dragons. "I'm in."

"Trolls?" Marcus walked slowly toward his friends. "Do you think there are other trolls down here? I mean," he stammered. "I'll go, too, just asking." There was less enthusiasm in his voice than his friends.

"Didn't you close the entrance to the Groglemytes?" Kess asked, "And Maaleah didn't you put a protective spell around them?"

"Yes, but that was on the other side, which is far from here," Maaleah shrugged.

"There is only one other entrance that the trolls use that will lead them to the Groglemytes," Baalizar said.

Maaleah nodded. "If the trolls are venturing further into the Groglemytes domain, they may discover them. And, Miri and Drago are right they need to be protected."

"We all can't go," Mac looked around at the others. "We need to have protection for this group because we don't know what lives down here other than the Grogles. So, we have to make some choices here." Mac stopped abruptly and looked at Maaleah. "You just said 'Miri and Drago'. Did Miri join us? I didn't see her."

"Come forward, Miri." Maaleah's voice was soft with love.

Xen moved away from Drago and stood next to Maaleah.

Mac tried looking past them for Miri.

"Miri," Doc called out. "Where are you, child? Oh, no, we didn't leave her up there, did we?"

A soft laugh came from Xen, *"No. I am here."*

"Who said that?" Doc looked around. "Where are you?"

"I am right here, Doc," Xen said. *"I am here standing next to Maaleah."*

"Huh?" Doc was startled.

"Miri, it is time to tell them," Maaleah said nodding toward the startled group.

"Yes, mother."

"Miri?" Kess and Mac gasped along with everyone else as they stared at the beautiful silver-blue dragon.

"Did we hear you right?" Mac asked. "Did you call her Miri? Our little Miri?"

"Yes," Maaleah reached up and stroked Miri's face gently.

"How can that be?" Kess smiled at the little dragoness that was a head taller than her.

"Her father was a Dragling. And, her mother was a young, beautiful, and powerful Sabbot. She was killed shortly after Miri's birth by a Spree dragon. I chose to accept the egg and raise the child/dragon within it as my own. After a year and a half, she emerged from the egg as one of the most beautiful of dragonets I have ever seen. Miri grew incredibly fast, as do all young dragonets, and she is extremely smart." She turned to Drago and smiled.

"But she was in a human form? Why is she in dragon form now?" Doc questioned.

"It was my doing," Maaleah said. "She emerged in a human form, and I used magic to keep her in a human form. Her father felt great powers coming from his off-spring and worried that if her powers were detected by the demons, they would destroy her. He knew the demons would be looking for a dragon, not a human child. And, it was easier for me to take care of her."

"Where is her father?" Mac asked.

"*I have met him,*" Xen replied. "*He is a silver dragon. A silver Dragling.*"

"The silver Draglings are the most powerful of all Draglings," Maaleah shrugged. "Even I do not know all the powers they hold."

"Can she turn back into her human form?" Doc said staring into the blue eyes of Xen.

"Yes, of course," Maaleah reached up and gently stroked Xen's face. "I am very proud of her. She is only three years old and has learned very quickly."

"Three years old?" Kess, Mac, and Doc said together.

"Oh, brother," Doc shook his head. "Now I'm doing it." He looked at the confused faces around him. "You know, talking at the same time as Mac and Kess. Anyway, back to Miri."

"You see it takes a very long time for a dragon to emerge from their egg. . ." Maaleah was interrupted by Doc.

"I don't mean to ask this, but her human mother laid an egg?" Doc's eyebrows rose slightly.

"Laid an egg?" Maaleah threw her head back and laughed. "No, she was not a chicken. It is hard for those from another world to understand some of our ways."

"Boy, I'll say," Marcus said and was elbowed by Naomi to be quiet.

"You see Miri was born small, like any other normal human child, but almost immediately she began to change into a dragon. Her father and the other Silver Dragons quickly placed her, by magic of course, into an eggshell large enough for a dragonet to grow." Maaleah spoke as if it was the most normal thing in the world, and it was in Mystovia. "After her mother was killed, they brought the egg to me, and I kept her safe and warm until she emerged a year and a half later."

"But why did Miri have to change now?" Doc asked staring at the dragoness as if trying to find a sign of Miri in there.

"Xen," Maaleah gently corrected him. "She became of age and has become the Oracle for the Arega dragons and her name as an Oracle is Xen."

"Will we be able to see her often? Is she leaving us for good?" Doc's voice filled with concern at not seeing little Miri again. "I don't care what form she has taken." He turned to Xen. "I would miss you terribly if you were not around."

Xen moved past her mother and stopped in front of Doc. "*I will always keep you in my life, for as long as you will have me. You have become very special to me in this short time.*"

A huge grin spread across Doc's face. "Well, good. That is settled. Miri, I mean Xen, you have made this old man incredibly happy."

"Right now, we must deal with the problem at hand. We still may have trolls lurking about down here, and for sure we have demons running around above. We must consider the safety of the women and children. My warriors will stay with the main party. It would be better to have them with you to help fight, just in case." Sirel moved to stand next to Mac.

Kybil smiled at Xen and looked back at the group. "My warriors and I will also stay and help protect the women and children."

"I will stay with Kybil," Kess said. "Mac and I have our talisman to use in case it is needed."

"Our warriors will stay with the women and children as well," Walking Tall nodded toward the group.

Naomi was still ogling some of the tall, handsome elven and Indian warriors, and opted to go with them.

Drago and Xen both agreed to travel with Mac.

"I agree that Drago and Xen should accompany us," Mac nodded in agreement. "It's done. Sirel, Yaneth, Nordaal, Brody, Danny, and Marcus will come with us as well. The rest will travel down here."

"Wait a minute young man," Baalizar shouted. "I am the only one that can lead you through this maze and get you out of there safely."

"We are going to block the entrance to the cavern permanently. We cannot use magic because the Zetche or demons would sense it and know that there is something to hide behind the barrier. We must try to find all the markers to the entrance, then and only then will the Groglemytes be safe." Xen nudged Maaleah gently good-bye and headed back toward the cavern opening.

"Be safe," Maaleah called out.

"I will protect her," Drago said as he followed Xen.

"I know you will," Maaleah smiled warmly at him. "Protect each other."

"Yes, mother, I shall be there for him," Xen said only for her mother to hear.

"Oh," Drago stopped and turned. *"The Groglemytes said to be very careful when you go through the large, open place. They hear strange sounds coming from deep within."*

"Don't they know what is in there?" Kybil asked.

"No, the entrance to their domain is hidden out of sight, and they stay away from the opening because of the light. Their ancestors long ago had special protection placed on the opening. Something can go into the cavern, but nothing from the cavern can come into the Groglemytes domain. Once you are in the cavern you cannot return." Drago turned and followed the others. *"Be careful."*

"You as well," Kess said.

"Well, let's get moving and everyone stay close together." Kybil made a chirping sound, and quickly the women, children, farm animals, and horses were gathered into the center as the warriors walked on the outside of the group. They walked for quite a while before the light from the cavern started to filter toward them.

"Okay! We are entering the cavern now," Kess remarked. "Wow, is it huge."

It was tall and wide enough for the horses to walk three abreast. Now and then, they had to be careful of the stalactites that hung low from the cavern ceiling.

The cavern floor began to slope downward making it difficult at times to maneuver around the large stalagmites jutting up from the floor. Shadows appeared and disappeared above the weary group as they trudged on toward the end of the mammoth cave. Faint scuffling sounds began to filter down to the nervous, tired group of travelers. The horses started to act skittish and a couple of the dogs led on leashes, began emitting low throaty growls.

Kybil made a low whistling sound that meant for the warriors to draw their weapons.

Quickly, and silently, the warriors withdrew the swords from their scabbards. Others pulled arrows from the quivers on their backs and held them next to their bows. The horses were made to walk two abreast instead of three.

Kess nudged Kybil and pointed to something wrapped around one of the stalactites. It looked like a tail.

Kybil gave a low chirping signal, which meant high alert, as the warriors began visually to scan the area above and below. The passageway through the cavern was getting narrower the deeper they went.

A bright green, fluorescent light began to emanate from the fossils embedded in the stone giving them plenty of light to travel through the rocky terrain.

Soon, warriors began spotting shadows moving among the stalactites on the ceiling. They were prepared and ready for an attack. The women and children were lifted off the horses and placed in the middle. Each warrior instructed their charges on being quiet and to stay by the horses.

The passageway through the open cavern turned into a maze of high walls. There were weird carvings on the stone walls of strange-looking creatures.

"Kybil," Kess traced an etching with her finger. "It looks like a cross between a very mad monkey and a lizard. Have you ever seen any creatures like this before?"

"No," he shook his head.

"I have heard tell of a race that dwells within one of the mountains that . . ." Rakmor was interrupted by the shouts of warriors being attacked.

One of the warriors called out, "They're after the children."

The lizard-monkeys were as tall as the warriors, and their grey and brown mottled bodies blended in perfectly with the rocks in the cavern. At the end of their arms, which hung to the ground, were sharp claws. Their tails were long and whipped out at the warriors.

The seasoned warriors could not maneuver well between the high rock wall and the horses. Some of their swords were ripped out of their hands by the long tails of the monkeys. The screeching of the monkeys was almost deafening as it reverberated throughout the cavern.

The best defenses the warriors had were their bow and arrows. Kess spotted several monkeys above getting ready to drop down near the children. She let out a blood-curdling scream and charged straight for them.

Rakmor had a potion in his hand and threw it up toward the advancing monkeys. Fire exploded all around them. Most of them escaped and fled to the protection of the rocks. Those that caught fire could be heard jumping into a pool of water somewhere in the cave. The flames of his potion circled over the heads of the women and children.

"They won't be coming at them from above anymore," Rakmor said confidently, but as he was taking out another potion, a rock glazed his head. Startled he looked up to see that a couple of the monkeys were trying to stop him by throwing rocks. If he had not moved to take out the potion, it would have hit him square in the head.

"Got 'em," Kybil yelled and took out the monkey-lizard with his bow and arrows. "Hope you got something else to get us out of here."

"Working on it," Rakmor yelled. "Just keep those things from cracking my head open."

Kybil took out another monkey holding a large rock in his hands. "We've got to get out of here. We can't keep fighting them like this."

"There is an amply number of us witches to rid us of these nasty things, at least long enough for us to get out of this cavern." Maaleah and the other witches hurried to Rakmor's side. "How's about an old and hardly ever used spell? The Dragon's Breath."

"I think that is an excellent suggestion," Rakmor concurred.

Without saying another word, the witches pulled out a bright-red stone. "Now," Maaleah yelled and they all began to chant.

Suddenly, the once brightly lit room became pitch black. The monkeys stopped their screeching. A small red light began to appear overhead, and then it grew into hundreds of tiny, twinkling red lights. The little lights grew until they took the form of two red dragons. The dragons roared and spewed fire from their mouths and began chasing the monkeys around the stalactites.

The light from the dragons gave Kess and the others enough illumination to hurry through the maze of rocks to a large opening with huge columns of rocks on either side. Warriors grabbed the younger children, and everyone raced toward the exit.

After the last person passed the column, Kess turned to see some of the monkeys coming toward them. At that instant, a large explosion shook the ground. Stalactites shook and began to fall from the ceiling. The monkeys were not only being chased by fire breathing dragons but were dodging the deadly falling stalactites.

"Kess," Rakmor shouted. "Get away from the entrance. We're trying to close it."

Kess raced to the group and watched as Rakmor and the witches held the gleaming brown stones in their hands. They chanted quietly as the dirt and stone at the entrance began to fall. The advancing monkeys stopped in their tracks as the entranceway collapsed and was now closed under mounds of debris of rocks and dirt.

"I am sure they have other ways out," Rakmor shrugged. "If not, it will take them a while to dig through this stuff."

"How long will those dragons last in there?" Doc asked.

"Oh," Rakmor said nonchalantly. "We probably have about an hour before the spell wears off. It may give us time to get out of here."

"What do you mean 'may'?" Doc looked back at the pile of rocks. "It looks pretty solid to me."

"True," Kybil interjected. "But there may be more of those lizard-monkey beings on this side of the entrance."

"Yikes," Doc exclaimed. "I never thought about that."

"And I thought it would be safer going with all the warriors," Naomi sighed.

"I sense that we should go down this path," Maaleah said. "I think it will open out near Fort Ankhouri."

CHAPTER FIFTEEN

A horrific scream ripped through the cavern.

"What was that?" Marcus grabbed at his heart.

Mac started to laugh, "I believe it is our 'friend Olo' finding out his demons are fighting the trolls and not us."

"He's going to be using his magic to try to find out where we went. So, I suggest we keep on moving." Sirel said walking at a fast pace.

Xen and Drago flew back to Mac. *"The opening of the cavern is just ahead, but unfortunately, we saw other trolls on the river headed this way. If they pull into the bay, they will see the markers pointing in this direction."* Drago nodded toward the entrance.

"What kind of markers?" Danny asked.

"There are some rocks with lines on them, pointing in the direction of the cavern," Drago said.

"How close are they to us?" Mac picked up his pace.

"Doesn't matter how close." Baalizar's head shook. "We have to get rid of those markers."

They reached the cavern entrance and found several large boulders lining the pathway.

"Rocks?" Marcus gulped. "Those are fricken boulders. We can't move them."

"Move aside young man," Baalizar pushed past Marcus. In his hand were glowing stones. He said a few words, and the stones began to swirl around in mid-air. "Oh," he said as an afterthought, "I think we had better seek some protection."

"Move it!" Mac yelled.

Everyone scurried behind the sides of the cave entrance and waited. They heard several explosions and watched as rocks and dirt flew past them slamming into the cave. When the noise died down, and there were no more flying rocks, they came from around the cave entrance to see that all the boulders were gone. Rocks were strewn about in all shapes and sizes, but nothing on the ground was larger than a basketball.

"We need to close this entrance permanently and without magic." Mac stood with his hands on his hips and stared at the huge cave opening.

"There are trolls headed this way, and you are going to cut off our only way out?" Marcus gasped.

"Yeah. It kind of looks that way," Mac said. "But I am not sure how we can do that without magic."

"Maybe we can help," Yaneth eyed the cavern opening and smiled. "Yep, we can."

"I dink you better stand back . . . way back," Nordaal said.

Mac and the others hurried down the path until they came to the river's edge.

The pathway was filled with small rocks, but off to the side of the path were hundreds of different-sized boulders. Yaneth picked up a small boulder and threw it at the side of the cavern opening. Yaneth did the same. They continued to slam the large rocks at the opening until a rumbling sound began, and the sides of the cavern began to crumble.

Yaneth and Nordaal hurried back to the others as earth and rocks fell. Dust billowed out and enveloped the group, but when the dust dissipated the entrance to the cavern no longer existed.

"Wow," Danny exclaimed. "That was awesome."

"The entrance is gone, and the markers are gone." Baalizar thought for a moment. "I think those are the only markers in here because they didn't have much time to put others around before they were whisked up to the castle."

"You don't think other markers are leading to this spot?" Mac asked.

"I don't think so. They're not as stupid as Evoos', but they're not that intelligent either. But we should check the bay area and see if there is a bay where they land their canoes." He shrugged and moved down the path toward the river.

"What's this?" Mac pointed to a strange shape etched in the stone along the edge of the small inlet.

"This may be an old marking, but it is better not to take any chances." Baalizar reached down and picked up a rock. Thought for a moment and handed the large rock to Nordaal. "Smash this at the markings there on the edge." He shook his finger in the direction he wanted Nordaal to heave the stone.

Nordaal walked over to the edge and pointed down at the symbols," Dis where ya want me ta smash it?"

"Yes," Baalizar rolled his eyes in expiration. "Of course, that's where I want you to smash it."

"Easy there Baalizar," Mac crossed his arms. "He just wants to make sure. That's all."

"Dat's right," Yaneth growled toward the wizard.

"Now he knows," Baalizar snapped. "And I would prefer it if you quit growling at me. You sound like I am your next meal. Hurry up; we have to get across the river to the other side."

"Here it goes." Nordaal raised the rock above his head and brought it down with all his might. The stone edge with the markings shattered into what appeared to be nothing more than fragmented rocks.

"I don't mean to sound crazy or anything," Marcus said looking at the river. "But are we planning on swimming? I don't see any boats or bridges anywhere."

"We can fly each of you across with no problem," Drago said.

"It would take too long," Mac pointed up the river. "I can hear them. They're almost on us."

"I believe there is another path we can take," Baalizar moved toward a large boulder and motioned for everyone to follow him. Behind the boulder were steps worn into the stone that led to a bridge high over the river.

"Somebody sure was busy making all these steps," Danny said looking up at the steep stairway.

"I think we have to hurry. If I remember correctly, these steps will take us up, and once we cross the bridge we will be able to get out of here." Baalizar said rubbing his chin in deep thought. "I think."

Mac did not have to tell anyone to climb the steps as fast as they could. The steps that led up to the top of the cavern were not very wide, but wide enough to make it to the bridge spanning the river.

They had to duck when they reached the top step because the ceiling clearance was only about five feet high. Bent over they rushed to the other side of the river where Drago and Xen were waiting for them on a flat rock platform high above the river.

Everyone stopped and held their breath as a canoe of trolls passed under the bridge. The trolls did not look up, or they would have seen the small group hunched over and pressed against the stone wall. Then a second canoe of trolls followed close behind. Mac peered around the wall and saw that two canoes had pulled up to the inlet that he and the others had just left. The Trolls stopped for a moment, seemed to be saying something to each other, and then continued down the river.

"We had better get moving before they see or smell us," Drago said to everyone.

"How are we supposed to get down?" Mac whispered. "There are no steps on this side."

"*I flew around,*" Xen said. "*There is a ledge you can follow that will take you away from the trolls until we can figure out what to do.*"

The ledge was slippery and covered with moss as they maneuvered along it. They stepped through an opening onto a ledge on the other side of the bridge. It led away from the river and eventually, the ceiling of the cave became high enough for everyone to stand. But it left them completely exposed to any trolls that would happen to come down the river through the grotto.

Baalizar pointed to an opening at the end of the ledge that would take them into a tunnel leading away from the river.

Everyone hurried along the high ledge and into the cave, except for Mac, who was last in line. He spotted one of Baalizar's magical pouches lying on the ledge and stopped to pick it up when two canoes with three trolls in each pulled into the clearing below him. The trolls got out of their canoes and pulled them into the small inlet.

Mac froze; afraid if he moved they would spot him.

Six trolls began making grunting noises to each other, and after a short while they sat down making themselves comfortable.

Mac was high above them on the ledge. If one of them looked up, they would spot him easily. He did not want to move, but he knew it was only a matter of time before one of them spotted him.

Anxiously, the others in the group watched as Mac tried to edge little-by-little toward them and cave opening.

Brody peeked around the edge of the cave and froze. One of the trolls was stretching his arms and yawning; his head was tilting upward. He would spot Mac for sure. He reached down and found a large stone and threw it past the trolls. When the rock hit behind them, all the trolls stood up and turned around, giving Mac the time needed to get inside the cave.

After they checked the area and finding nothing, the trolls went back to prepare their food.

"Follow me," Baalizar said and mumbled quietly to himself. "This has to go somewhere."

"I think one of those trolls smelled us. I felt one of them thinking about human food." Drago said following Baalizar.

"Okay, let's get outta here," Mac whispered motioning for everyone to get moving.

Suddenly, a large troll hand reached inside of the cave. Mac jumped back, hitting his head against the stone wall.

Everyone turned around at the sound of the troll's loud growling at the small cave opening.

Immediately, everyone took off running. Soon, the hallway was raining down with earth and stone as more trolls began beating on the cave wall. But instead of knocking the stone from around the cave, it caused the roof of the cavern to shower down stone and dirt all over the trolls who finally gave up and ran for cover.

Mac and the others wandered through a labyrinth of tunnels, all ending nowhere. "Baalizar do you know where we are going?" Mac asked with annoyance as he turned down another tunnel.

"Down this tunnel," Baalizar snapped.

"Stop!" Danny said loudly. "Look at that scratch right there." He pointed to a long scrape in the wall of the tunnel. "I made that about an hour ago. We're going in circles."

Mac looked at the scrapings on the wall and shook his head. "I take it we're lost."

"Lost? You mean we're lost?" Marcus said looking down the tunnel in front of him and behind him. "We've been going through these tunnels and going nowhere?"

"That's about the size of it," Mac said crossing his arms and leaning up against the wall.

Baalizar threw up his hands, "Well, don't blame me. I have never been through these tunnels before."

"Then why were we following you?" Brody asked.

Baalizar just shrugged.

"So, we're going to be in here for eternity walking around?" Marcus' eyes widened in terror.

"Eternity? Don't be silly." Danny said.

"We won't?" Marcus asked hopefully.

"Heck, no. We'll die of thirst and hunger before we get to eternity."

Mac looked at Sirel hoping she had a solution, "Any suggestions on how to get out of here?"

"I've never been in here, Mac. I have no idea where we are. Anyone have any ideas on how we can get out of here?" Sirel asked the group.

Yaneth placed his hands on his hips. "Why didn't ya say someding sooner? Of course, we get us outta here."

"What?" Mac said startled.

"Sure," Yaneth pulled Nordaal over to him. "He can talk ta rocks. Dey tells us where ta go."

"Yep," Nordaal smiled his big toothy grin. "I get us outta here."

"Why didn't you do that sooner?" Marcus's voice was filled with relief and annoyance at the same time.

"Nobody asked me," Nordaal said.

"Besides, we tink dat Baalizar knowed da way. We not tink we be lost." Yaneth said and motioned for everyone to give Nordaal room.

Nordaal put his hand on the tunnel wall and stood there for quite a while before he finally took his hand away. "We gotta go back dat way," he pointed to where they had just come. "We be outta here in no time."

They headed back to another split in the tunnel where Nordaal placed his hand on the stone wall. Every time they came to a split in the path Nordaal would rest his hand on the wall, smile, and take them down another path until they came to a set of winding steps leading upward.

"Dat's the way out," Nordaal smiled broadly and then placed his hand on the rock wall.

"What's he doing now?" Brody asked.

"He be tanking dem walls fer helping us,"

Xen and Drago flew up the stairs. "We'll check everything out first."

Drago returned a short time later and motioned for everyone to continue. They climbed the winding steps for a short while until they felt a cool breeze drifting down.

"I smell fresh air. Is that fresh air?" Marcus said excitedly.

"It sure is," Mac smiled. "Good work Nordaal. We owe you one."

"What one ya owe me?" Nordaal asked confused.

"I'll tell you later," Mac quickly changed the subject. "I hope this leads us out of this mountain, and not down another tunnel."

It was getting late, and the sky was darkening as they reached the top and stepped out into the cold, fresh air.

Marcus fell to the ground kissing it. "I wouldn't do that," Danny said. "You don't know if there's something on the ground that'll run up your nose or grab your face."

Marcus jumped up and began brushing himself off. "I was just being thankful; that's all." He snapped.

"And I was just kidding," Danny laughed.

"What I'd like to know is what happened to Drago and Xen?" Brody asked looking around the area.

Everyone moved far away from the steps, not wanting anything to sneak up behind them. They sat down on a couple of small boulders to rest for a moment.

The sound of wings beating overhead caused them all to look up. Much to their horror two Drakluf Dragons were flying overhead surveying the area.

Everyone was out in the open, and to get to the stairs, they would have to cross the wide-open space in front of them. The demon riders spotted them sitting there and gave a blood-curdling scream to alert the Drakluf Dragons of their presence.

Sirel drew her arrow and aimed at the advancing Drakluf dragons and their riders. Her arrow bounced off the hard shell of the dragons. The demon riders were close enough for everyone to see their smiles spread across their ugly faces. Sirel kept shooting, striking her target every time, but to no avail.

Suddenly, the Drakluf dragons and their riders burst into flames.

The startled group watched as they sank like glowing splotches and fell down the side of the mountain out of sight.

Drago and Xen appeared from above, surrounded by several Pegasus. *"We bring friends to help,"* Drago said as he and Xen landed next to Mac.

"Are those for real?" Danny asked in astonishment. His mouth agape as he stared at the Pegasus.

"Of course, we are real." One of the Pegasus said while the others laughed.

"I meant no disrespect, honestly," Danny apologized profusely. "It's just where we come from you are . . . well you aren't . . . what I mean is you guys are fantastic looking."

"Some of us 'guys'," came a very soft and feminine voice, *"are not 'guys'."*

"Wow," Danny shook his head. "I think you all are fantastic looking. To me, it's just a small detail whether you are male or female."

"Lucky for us, we care about that 'small' detail," said one of the male Pegasus.

"Your friends here said you might require a ride." One of the Pegasus landed near Sirel and Mac, and the others followed.

"No way," Brody was almost jumping up and down with excitement. "You mean we are actually going to get a ride with you guy...oops, with you."

"I don't see any saddles," Marcus stared intently at the beautiful horses in front of him. "How are we supposed to stay on?"

"Don't worry, I won't let you fall," the same female voice said. She walked toward Marcus and nudged him gently with her nose. "I will take care of this one."

"We are supposed to meet up at Fort Ankhouri. Is there any way you can get us there, or close to there?" Sirel asked.

"We have seen a lot of demon activity going on at a new castle," a male Pegasus said. *"We have been that way many times and never knew it was there."* He gave a short laugh and shook his head. *"Anyway, we will fly you as close as we can to Fort Ankhouri. We*

have to be very careful because this new powerful demon has called many of the Drakluf demons into his service."

"Yes, we must travel in great numbers now for our protection and that of our colts." The female said.

"We don't want to put you in any danger or your families," Mac said. "If you could just show us the way to get down off this mountain and the way to Fort Ankhouri that will do us nicely."

The female Pegasus spoke quickly. *"He just meant we will take you as far as we can. We cannot leave our colts for any great length of time. They are heavily guarded now, and it is our turn to keep watch over our area for signs of an attack."*

"Oh, boy," Danny clapped his hands with the excitement of riding a Pegasus. "Let's get going before they change their minds."

Everyone climbed onto a Pegasus, and the Pegasus' that had no rider kept on the outside guarding them while they scanned the area for any signs of the Drakluf dragons.

"Stop pulling my mane," the female Pegasus said to Marcus. *"My magic will keep you from falling. Relax."*

"Sorry, sorry," he said letting go of his tight grip on her mane. "I am sorry. I didn't mean to hurt you."

"Enjoy the ride," she laughed and proceeded to dip and loop through the sky.

Once Marcus realized that he was not going to fall from the horse, he started to enjoy the trip.

Drago and Xen appeared ahead of the Pegasus and advised them that they could safely land a couple of miles from Fort Ankhouri. There were no signs of demons anywhere, but the Drakluf Dragons seemed to be heading back toward the Pegasus' home base.

The Pegasus' thanked Drago and Xen for their information and quickly landed in an open field close to the forest.

"We must get back and keep watch over our clans," the female Pegasus said lowering her body slightly for Marcus to climb off.

"Thank you for getting us this far," Sirel said. "This has been most helpful."

Everyone disembarked from their mount and watched the graceful horses take off and disappear into the darkening skies above.

"I hope they will be alright," Marcus said sadly. "I really liked the Pegasus I was riding on. She was great."

"They are not only brave but very intelligent," Sirel patted Marcus's arm. "They were anxious to get back and protect their families. Trust me when I say, they will be fine. They are a very clever lot and extremely fierce fighters. Now, we must get to the fort as fast as we can." She turned and ran into the forest, with everyone following behind her.

They reached Fort Ankhouri with only a few stops in between. A brick wall over forty feet high ran along the entire fort. Sirel walked to the main entrance to the fort. It was closed. Heavy steel and iron gates barred their way. She called out to the guards on the wall-walk.

"I am Sirel, Captain of the 1st Regiment, answering only to Commander Fraanel."

"Step into the light," a guard called out.

Sirel did not hesitate as she stepped into a niche in the rounded corners of the gate as light poured over her. An iron gate opened first, and another one after that. Sirel motioned for everyone to follow her.

"What was that light thing all about?" Mac asked.

"It is a magical light that can tell if someone is a changeling or a demon." Sirel smiled. "I am neither."

"Welcome back, Captain Sirel," an officer greeted her with a salute.

Sirel returned her salute. "Good to be back. Thank you."

Once everyone was inside, the gates were closed. "There is a strong contingent of demons heading this way," Sirel spoke to the officer. She looked around at the almost empty fortress. "Where are the rest of the warriors?"

"They are in the city fighting against a surge of demons near the port."

"So, we don't have a full-blown contingent of warriors in here?"

"No, captain, but we have a regiment that has been left behind to protect the fort."

Sirel nodded toward the warrior. "Also, there will be a party of Elven and Ankhouri warriors with others headed this way. They may be chased or in trouble so have the sentries stay alert. Have a potion of detection brought to the gate immediately."

"Yes, captain," she saluted and went to inform the warriors guarding the walls.

"What's a potion of detection?" Danny asked.

"It is a potion that they will shoot over the heads of the approaching party. It will burst into dust that will drift down and touch all that is coming this way. If they are demons or changelings they will begin to burn right away." Sirel answered.

"It will not harm any animals or humans," Baalizar said out of breath and doubled over from running too much. "Did anyone ever stop to think I am an old man?"

Marcus, Danny, and Brody were busy ogling the women warriors hurrying about in the compound. "Wow," Brody almost gave a wolf-whistle, but smartly decided against it. "Look at all those women. I sure would hate to have to fight them."

"Me, too," Marcus watched as some of the women were practicing their sword fighting in the middle of the compound.

"Captain!" A warrior on the wall by the gate called out to Sirel. "Captain, come quick. I think we have many riders coming at us pretty fast."

Sirel, Mac, and the others raced up the steps to the wall-walk and saw dust being kicked up. Something was coming out of the forest at a fast clip and heading straight for the gate.

The alarm was sounded, and warriors hurried to the battlements. Some ran out of a building, still dressing for battle as they took up their positions. Arrows loaded with the potion of detection were aimed high over the approaching horses.

Sirel waited until she knew the arrows would reach and gave the order. Arrows shot out and passed over the heads of the riders. The glowing dust could be seen drifting down over the riders; nothing happened. But shrill screams from something chasing behind them could be heard.

"Open the gates," Sirel ordered. "Be prepared to shut the gates fast when I give the order."

CHAPTER SIXTEEN

The further Kess and the others walked inside of the mountain cavern the larger it got.

"This is the largest cavern I have ever seen," Kess said. Her voice echoed eerily around them. The sound of the horses' hooves striking the hard ground made it sound as if hundreds of horses were walking with them.

"That is quite unusual," Kybil said looking up at the ceiling of the cavern. "I don't see any stalactites. I would think there would be plenty in here."

"You're right. There were so many in the last part we were in, it was hard to get through them. There are neither stalactites nor stalagmites anywhere."

"Yeah but look at how beautiful these rocks are. They sparkle like they are made of gold or diamonds." Naomi said walking next to Kess and Kybil.

"Yes, it is quite beautiful to look at." Maaleah spoke up from behind her, "I am hoping once we are through this particular cavern we will be out of here."

"Those kids are incredible," Kess said looking back at the children and women traveling with them. "They haven't fussed one bit, even when those monkey-lizard things tried to grab for them."

Kybil made another chirping sound, and the warriors began to spread out searching the surrounding area.

"What did you just tell them to do?" Kess asked.

"To check the area," Kybil said. "And, Jhondar went with them."

"He chirps and the warriors know it's some kind of signal?" Naomi asked, watching a tall, young, handsome elf disappear with several other warriors behind a large boulder.

"Oh, yes," Kess laughed. "They certainly have a way with words in Mystovia."

It was a long time before the warriors returned. "All is clear," Jhondar reported. "And we have found an opening that leads to the outside."

"Good work," Kybil said. "Lead the way."

It was only a short while later and everyone was standing outside of the mountain cave.

"You guys sure have a lot of underground passageways, and stuff going on," Naomi shook her head.

"That was my first impression, too, Naomi," Kess nodded. "But think about it this way, we have a lot of subways that take us from point A to point B, and a lot of tunnels – like through the mountains. Plus, in some States, they have shelters dugout to hide from a tornado, just as they have dugouts here to hide from Evoos or demons. And, we have many creatures that burrow underground for their place of dwelling."

"Yep! Okay, I can see that point of view. You're right. But we don't have any ugly monkey-lizard things trying to eat us," Naomi said scrunching up her face in disgust.

"I can agree with that," she smiled at Naomi. Kess quickly turned her attention to Kybil and Maaleah. "All righty then. So, where are we?"

"We are near a village where we can rest and eat," Maaleah said pointing down a trail leading through the woods.

"Yes," Kybil nodded. "I know this village. It is too far for the children to walk, get them on the horses. Move out." He waved his arm as they moved onto a path leading through the forest.

They traveled for a couple of hours stopping occasionally to rest the children and horses. Finally, they spotted a large village. But when they got there they found the townspeople hurrying around loading up wagons.

"What's going on?" Kybil queried a man running with his belongings to put in a wagon.

"We have word that the demons are headed this way. It sounds like way too many for us to fight, so we're headed to Fort Ankhouri for protection." He pushed the items in his wagon aside to make room for his family.

"We're headed that way," Kybil motioned to the warriors. "Let the women and children ride in the wagons. We'll help you where we can."

"We can use all the help we can get," Chief Wolfclaw yelled from one of the buildings.

Kybil laughed and greeted the chief warmly. "What are you doing here?"

"We are moving our families to the fort as well. I thought the people in this village could use some protection on the way. So, we joined up with them." He stopped and yelled at one of the men carrying a chair to his wagon. "You there. You won't be needing that right now. Leave it. It'll make more room for the children and women to ride."

"Wolfclaw?" Jhondar walked toward the Indian chief.

"Yes?" Wolfclaw's voice filled with curiosity as he stared at the man approaching him.

"It is I, Jhondar."

It took a moment for the stunned chief to respond. "What?" Wolfclaw exclaimed. "I cannot believe this. Is it true?"

"Yes," Jhondar motioned for Etheria to come forward. "And Etheria is with me, too."

It took the chief another moment for him to recognize his old friend. "Jhondar, it is you." He paused and looked at Etheria. "And Etheria as well. By the stars, it is you two. I do not understand. My friends, you are truly here." Wolfclaw quickly hugged Etheria and Jhondar. "This is indeed a happy day. We must talk later."

Jhondar motioned for some of the Indian warriors who had crossed over into Mystovia to come forward. "You might recognize a couple of others as well."

"No!" He yelled in excitement at the sight of the Indian warriors walking toward him. He rushed toward an older Indian warrior. "Bear Stalker? Is this truly you?" Tears began to form in his eyes. He embraced him and a couple of others he recognized. "I know the older ones," he said fighting back the tears forming in his eyes. "But the younger ones I do not."

"I am sorry to break up this happy reunion," Kybil winced as he spoke. "Really, I am. But we have to get moving. You can catch up with what has happened in the last twenty-five years as we travel."

"Yes, yes, of course," Wolfclaw said jubilantly slapping the back of Bear Stalker. "Jhondar, you and Bear Stalker must fill me in on what has happened. Where were you all this time? How did you get here?" Questions tumbled out of him as he mounted his horse. He placed his horse between Jhondar and Bear Stalker horses as they began to answer his myriad questions.

The large caravan moved out of the village toward the fort some miles away. All the warriors managed to get a horse to ride for themselves, but Kess and Naomi decide to ride in a wagon, driven by Rakmor.

Kybil rode his horse next to Kess's wagon. "This is the bad part coming up."

"Thanks for cheering me up," she looked over at his worried face and smiled. "Why is this the bad part?"

"Yeah, why is this the bad part coming up?" Naomi was sitting between Rakmor and Kess and had to lean around Rakmor to look at Kybil.

"I'm throwing in my request for an explanation, also," Doc said peering out from the covered wagon behind Kess and Naomi.

"We have to travel through the borders of the Rils and Myam forests where the Spree dragons live, and it's close to the Dahvoos swamp."

"Oh, no," Kess gulped. "The Evoos territory."

"What evil territory?" Naomi asked nervously.

"Not evil, Evoos," Kess corrected her gently.

"Okay, whatever you say," Naomi raised her eyebrow slightly. "What's with the evils anyway?"

Kess laughed, "I did the same thing before with the Dak trees. Anyway, it's E-V-O-O-S, Evoos. They're nasty little cannibals."

"Oh, great," Naomi looked down at her pudgy body. "They're gonna love me."

"These wagons make a lot of noise, so I don't know how far we're going to get without being detected. And, we do not want to have everyone go on foot, because that would be even more dangerous for them." Rakmor shook his head.

Maaleah, who was also riding in the back of the wagon, stood up and lost her balance. She quickly grabbed a hold of Kess's shoulders. Kess reached up and grabbed her hand to help steady her. Maaleah gestured toward the other witches riding with her in the back of the wagon. "We have a few potions that can help out."

"I may be able to help as well," Etheria chimed in. "Although I am not quite sure how."

"Just knowing you're there is enough for me," Kess peered back into the wagon at her mother.

The woods became darker the farther they traveled. A fetid, moldy smell began to permeate the air, and the horses were becoming more skittish.

"Maaleah," Kybil looked over his shoulder at Maaleah still standing behind Kess. "Can you put a spell on these horses to keep them from being so restless?"

"If she does that, it may slow them down when we have to make a run for it," Rakmor just shook his head. "Do we want to take that chance?"

"No," Kybil said. "We're going to need them to move like the wind."

He had no sooner spoken when one of his scouts rode up to him. "There are a couple of Spree dragons coming this way. They are flying overhead checking out the area.

"Rakmor. Maaleah," Kybil looked at them. "Any help would be appreciated at this point."

"We'll take care of the dragons; you just get us out of here. Signal your warriors to stay as close to the wagons as possible." Rakmor said. He handed Kess the reins and climbed into the back of the wagon with Maaleah and the other witches.

As directed, Kybil gave the signal, and all the warriors moved in closer to the wagons.

It was a few moments later when a bright light shot out from their wagon. It moved in both directions, covering all the wagons, from the first in line to the last. The light turned into a thick, hazy mist over their heads, and the sounds of the horses' hooves and the wagon wheels became silent.

Two dark figures loomed in the mist overhead as the wagons raced down the narrow path. Their blurry shapes passed over the wagons without hesitation and flew away.

"Kybil," Rakmor moved swiftly to the front of the wagon. "We have to get more potions. Or, we're not going to make it to the fort."

Maaleah stood up next to Rakmor. "We have been using heavy-duty potions, doubling, and tripling some of them. We are almost out."

"Is there any place nearby we can get more potions?" Kybil asked.

Maaleah thought for a moment. "Yes. There is a place I know. It is a Sabbot Village about a mile from here."

"And you're sure we don't have enough to get us to the fort," Kybil sighed deeply.

"I am positive," Rakmor shook his head. "Without more potions we will be at the mercy of . . . well just about everything."

"Then, we will head for the Sabbot village," Kybil signaled his warriors who rode back to him. "Listen up. We are going to head for the Sabbot village near the Dahvoos swamp. I want a couple of scouts in each direction to keep watch for any movements. Not only do we have to worry about the Evoos and demons, but we are deep in the Spree dragon country."

He sent eight warriors out: two in each direction. They rode through the trees and out of sight. Kybil gave the orders for the wagons to move out. "At the pace we are going, we won't be that far by the time the scouts return.

"We've come through this area before, and I don't remember having any trouble with any dragons," Kess said looking quizzically at Kybil riding on his horse next to her.

"We haven't had any problems with them until lately. We think it has something to do with the Zetche that is controlling the Evoos and demons." Kybil reached down and patted his horse's neck. "The dragons occasionally steal a horse or cow, although, it is rare. But they never bothered any of the people that live in this area or any other area for that matter. Except for now."

They rode for a while when the sounds of the scout's horses could be heard coming toward them. The first two scouts reported nothing unusual from the east. A few minutes later the scouts from the south appeared advising there was activity behind them, but it was not headed their way - so far.

The scouts from the west arrived and informed them that a few Spree dragons were flying around checking out the area. Much later, the last two warriors who had scouted north, the direction the wagons were headed, rode up to report.

An Elven scout stopped alongside Kybil. "We found the Sabbot village and went as we could. The village is overrun with Evoos."

The scouts dismounted as a couple of warriors appeared with buckets of water for their steeds. The warriors continued talking while they held the buckets up for their horses to drink. The Elven warrior continued, "There might be a possibility of getting into the village unnoticed."

"Yes," said the other warrior as she patted her horse's nose. "The Evoos are drinking the witches' wines and any other liquids they can find. Some are already passed out on the ground."

"How far from here?" Kybil asked.

"A half-hour by horse," the Ankhourian warrior said. "If you stay off the road you will not be seen. They have a couple of lookouts posted on the road, but we saw no sign of any in the forest."

"I'll take a couple of warriors into the village and retrieve the potions," Kybil started to select the warriors and was stopped by Maaleah.

"You do not know where we have hidden them."

"She's right," Rakmor said. "But I do."

"It would be easy enough for us to sneak in and grab the potions," Kess said climbing down from the wagon.

"Ah, Kess," Kybil looked down from his horse. "You're not going on this mission."

"Ah, Kybil," she smiled up sweetly at him. "Yes, I am. Besides, you may need the power of my ring, just in case we meet up with a few dragons."

"She's right," Rakmor said, climbing down from the wagon and standing next to Kess. "We will need a couple of warriors to go along as well."

Jainy jumped down from the first wagon. "I will go. I am a good fighter."

"Thank you for the offer, Jainy," Kybil said gently. "But if these wagons are attacked, they are going to need all the good fighters they can find." He looked over at Chief Wolfclaw and gave him a sign to help keep Jainy at the wagons.

Chief Wolfclaw understood Kybil's signal and spoke out loudly. "We will need all the warriors and witches we have to hold off any attacks until you get back."

Jainy looked down at the ground and said solemnly. "But I want to help."

"Wait," Naomi called out. "I will need someone to help me drive these horses. I am scared to death of these things. Can you ride upfront with me, Jainy?"

Jainy's head jerked up, and a giant grin crossed her face. "I would be more than happy to help. I have never seen such beautiful beasts before, but I am not afraid of them at all."

"Geesh thanks. I appreciate that." Naomi looked over at Kybil and gave a quick wink.

"If we get off the road and hide in that thicket of trees we can use what is left of our potions to protect us," Maaleah said. She looked up at Kybil, "Go, now. And, return as quickly as you can."

Kybil motioned for the two scouts who discovered the village to come with them. "We don't have a lot of time."

Etheria moved to the front of the wagon. "I hear wings beating. It sounds like the wings of a dragon."

Maaleah and the other witches quickly cast another spell clouding their view and scent from the dragon. Soon, the large form of the green dragon hovered overhead. It looked down at the road below and slowly flew away.

"He must have sensed us here," Etheria said. "The first two dragons were too far above us, but this one was flying very low."

"Yes," Jhondar joined them. "He will be back to investigate further."

"And, now we have even less magic to protect us." Maaleah shrugged.

"Get these wagons off the road," Chief Wolfclaw ordered. "Head for those trees." He pointed to the clump of trees deep in the woods. "Put the wagons facing the road, in case we need to move out quickly."

Kess and the others rode off toward the Sabbot village. Moments later, two figures, hugging the shadows of the forest, silently followed them to the village.

CHAPTER SEVENTEEN

ess rode beside Kybil as the small group headed toward the Sabbot village. The only sounds in the woods were those of the leaves and twigs being crunched beneath the horses' hooves.

Soon, the two scouts put up their hands and slid off their mounts.

"We have to go by foot from here," the Elven warrior spoke softly and motioned for everyone to follow him.

"Don't tie the reins around anything," Kybil told Kess. "If they sense danger while we are gone, they will be able to run. Plus, when we get back we might need to ride fast."

"Won't they wander away?" She asked anxiously.

"No," Kybil dropped the reins to his horse on the ground. "These are very well-trained horses. Come on, let's get moving. From here on out no one speaks unless necessary," he ordered. Everyone nodded and moved quietly toward the village.

Soon, the guttural sounds of the Evoos and the beating of their drums began to filter through the trees.

Kybil held up his hand for everyone to stop behind a large boulder and a tall clump of bushes. "I see some Evoos lookouts," he whispered and pointed to a group of bushes with the Evoos hiding in them.

"No," the Ankhourian scout said softly. "That is what we thought, too. But as we crept up closer it is just a decoy."

"They put up decoys?" Kess queried keeping her voice barely above a whisper.

"I thought they were kind of stupid."

"They that are. They are also very lazy and cowardly. My guess would be they probably were afraid to stay out here on duty." Kybil motioned for everyone to follow him. "Let's move a little closer."

Kybil stopped everyone as they reached a large boulder just outside the village. "Which building are the potions kept in?" He asked Rakmor.

Rakmor crept forward and peered around the boulder. He pulled back and looked at Kybil with concern. "The building we need to go into looks like there is a bunch of Evoos walking in and around it. But worse than that, there is a giant Spree dragon in front of it."

"Let me see," Kybil said. He moved past Rakmor and took a quick peek around the boulder. He shook his head. "This doesn't look too good."

Everyone took a turn looking around the boulder at the building with the giant dragon in front of it.

"There are so many of them, and what about that dragon, can't it smell us?" Kess asked softly.

"I don't think so; we're upwind from it." Kybil looked over at Rakmor. "But one of your spells to keep it from smelling us would help, and we need a distraction of some kind."

"Is there a back way into this place?" Kess asked. "Or, a tunnel of some sort? You guys have tunnels everywhere."

"This village is honeycombed with tunnels," Rakmor shook his head. "But unfortunately, we are nowhere near an entrance."

The sound of breaking twigs caused them all to stop and listen. Footsteps were coming their way. Everyone moved deeper into the bushes until their backs hit the boulder behind them.

Two Evoos' were patrolling the area. They seemed to be conversing in a strange guttural sound to each other as they passed the group hidden in the bushes.

The long hair that had been placed on the shrub to mimic an Evoos began to tickle Kess's nose. She brought her hand up to stop a sneeze and broke one of the branches off the bush in front of her.

The two Evoos stopped and peered into the bushes. Before they could let out a warning, the two scouts silenced them by throwing their knives and killing the Evoos' instantly. They fell silently to the ground.

The scouts pulled their knives out of the dead Evoos' and wiped them off on the Evoos' hairy body. They re-sheathed their knives and looked around for any other Evoos' that might be around. Reassured there were no more Evoos on patrol, they dragged the bodies into the bushes and left them.

"I have a crazy idea," Kess said.

"I will listen to anything right now," Kybil nodded.

"This decoy stuff might work for us." She grabbed a thick bushy branch that was hung to look like an Evoos standing guard.

"There are more of those things over there," the Elven scout pointed to another batch of Evoos' looking hair draped over a clump of bushes.

Kybil shrugged. "Yes, I see. Hmm, well, it's worth a try." He turned to Kess, "I don't want you going into the building with us. If we get in trouble you will be the only one who can help us." He spoke to the Ankhourian warrior. "When we get to the hut, I want you to stay close to Kess. I see a thick grouping of bushes over there." He pointed to bushes on the outskirts of the village. "You two will be able to see us enter and exit the building at a safe distance. She may need your help as well as us."

The tall Ankhourian warrior nodded. "Yes, we will stay back and watch in case we are needed." Her black face broke into a grin as they began to put on the fake-like hair of the Evoos. "This fits me like a vest."

"Yeh, I am afraid we are all going to have to squat and walk," Kybil grimaced with a slight smile.

"And the smell is not too good either," Kess whispered and wrinkled up her nose.

"Okay, that's settled. Now it is my turn for the distraction. Wait here a moment. I think I have enough of a potion to give us the distraction we will need." Rakmor said.

"Go with him." Kybil motioned for the Elven scout to accompany Rakmor.

Keeping low they moved swiftly through the bushes to the other side of the village. After a few moments, hunched over, they ran back to the awaiting group. "Okay, let's get moving." Rakmor smiled broadly.

No one spoke as they quickly helped Rakmor, and the Elven scout to finish putting the hairy branches around them.

The group waddled out of the forest and to the back door of the building. Their swords were unsheathed and held in front of them, but easily concealed by the hairy branches draped over them. They crept around the mud-hut buildings until they were close to the one with the potions.

They moved cautiously toward the building and peered inside. None of the Evoos' inside paid any attention to them. They were too busy drinking and prancing around.

Suddenly, there was a loud explosion on the other side of the village. The Evoos' dropped their drinks, stopped prancing, and raced out the door emptying the building.

Kybil and the others hurried inside and were just about to stand up and take off the branches when an Evoos ran back into the building. He did not seem to be surprised at their presence. He rushed over to the table and picked up a bottle that had been sitting there. He went to the front door to leave, stopped, turned around, and looked at the three of them. Grunted something and then left.

Rakmor threw off his hairy branches and pulled on the side of the fireplace. It opened smoothly revealing a hidden room filled with magical potions of every kind.

Rakmor picked his disguise off the floor and motioned for everyone to quickly follow. Once inside, the door swung shut, and the candles in the room flared up brightly lighting the room.

Kybil and the Elven warrior quickly threw off their hairy branches. They stared at the shelves lined with jars of stones, pebbles, liquids, and powders. "Tells us what we need to grab," Kybil said.

"Anything red, white, and that entire shelf," he pointed to a shelf filled with stones and sand. "Here," he thrust large burlap bags into their hands and began filling his bag.

Before they had finished stuffing their bags, they heard the guttural sounds of the Evoos coming back into the building. Rakmor hurried to a small hole in the wall that was covered by a piece of wood. He carefully moved it and saw three of the Evoos' had returned, but he couldn't see if the dragon had returned with them.

Meanwhile, Kess waited anxiously in a small cluster of bushes and trees. Her attention was diverted when she heard twigs and branches snapping; someone was walking toward her. She tugged on the sleeve of the Ankhourian warrior, but the warrior had already heard. She moved around Kess, pushing her deeper into a thick cluster of bushes.

There was a sound of scuffling, and then nothing. Kess waited anxiously until she heard the voice of the Ankhourian scout whisper to her. "Stay where you are until I come back for you." The warrior crept low and close to the buildings as she hurried toward Kybil and the others.

Inside the secret room, Kybil and the others waited, each holding onto their burlap sack filled with potions. "Get your swords ready," Rakmor whispered. "I think there are only three of them. We can take them by surprise. Ready?" Rakmor said pushing the door open.

They rushed out with their weapons drawn and were surprised to find the three Evoos' lying on the floor. They watched in amazement as the Ankhourian scout wiped the black blood of the Evoos off her knife on their lifeless bodies. "Do not want their poisonous blood on my knife," she said matter of fact.

Rakmor smiled at the tall warrior, "Well done." He quickly uttered an incantation to seal the hidden room.

They started walking out the back door, just as an Evoos entered from the front door. Before the Evoos could react, the Elven scout threw his knife killing it instantly. He ran over, reached down, and pulled the knife from the Evoos, and wiped its blood off on it. "Me, either." He said and sheaved his knife with a big grin.

Everyone raced out the back door and as they ran they began pulling off their hairy disguises.

"Let's move," Kybil said to Kess, who was already on her feet and ready to go.

They ran as fast as they could deeper into the forest and toward their horses.

It only took the Evoos a moment to find out that the four Evoos inside had been killed. The sound of drums and the guttural war cries reverberated through the trees.

Kess and the others never looked back as they ran through the trees. Suddenly, the sound of a dragon's wings could be heard coming toward them. She knew they would never make it to their horses, and even if they did their horses could not outrun a flying dragon.

"Anything in these bags to help us out, Rakky," Kybil asked, running with a couple of burlap bags over his shoulders.

"Plenty of stuff," he said panting. "But I haven't a clue which bags they're in."

"We're not going to make it," Kybil winced as the heavy bag began to slip from his hands.

"The dragon hasn't spotted us yet," Kess said. "Maybe we'll get lucky, and it won't find us."

"It won't give up until it finds us," Rakmor said.

The sound of the dragon's wings was getting closer with each step they took.

"Our horses should be right around here," Kybil said visually scanning the area. "They must have smelled the dragon and bolted."

"No! I have found tracks," the Ankhourian scout whispered. The brows on her black face furrowed. "The horses have been led away. It looks like two people came and took them. We can trace their footsteps."

"Do it," Kybil ordered.

"Listen," Rakmor spoke quietly. "I think the dragon is going in another direction. The sound of its beating wings is getting fainter."

"Good," Kybil said. "Let's get whoever took our horses."

The ground began to slope as they followed the path their horses had been taken. They picked up speed when the Ankhourian scout said the prints were becoming fresher. They went down a steep embankment and heard the sounds of their horses nearby. Everyone carefully put their bags filled with potions on the ground and drew their swords.

A sharp incline brought them around to an overhang under the hill. All their horses, plus two more, were tethered to a tree root that was suspended down from the ceiling of the overhang. But no one was around.

Kybil did not speak but gestured a command to the scouts to comb the area. The two warriors nodded and started to go in different directions when there was a large screeching sound behind them.

Weapons drawn, they whirled around to see Jhondar and Etheria running toward them.

"What are you doing here?" Kybil demanded.

"Just taking care of a little dragon problem," Etheria gave a stunned Kess a quick hug and walked to her horse. "I don't think we should stay around here any longer."

Jhondar swung up onto his horse. "We followed you, just in case you might need some extra help." He looked down at their stunned faces. "Ah, she's right. We have to get out of here fast."

Everyone hurried to their horse and threw the knapsacks over the saddle horn.

"Why did you move our horses?" Rakmor asked.

"Because we saw a small group of Evoos headed their way. We knew you had two scouts with you, and they could easily follow our trail."

"What was that screeching sound?" Kess moved her horse next to her mother's.

"One less dragon to worry about." She smiled at Kess. "We borrowed some potions from the wagon just in case they were needed. It was only a small amount, so it would in no way affect the safety of the others. The Skull of Semetter amplified its power greatly."

"Amplified?" Rakmor scratched his head. "I have never heard of that word before."

"It means making something louder or more powerful. Something along those lines." Kess laughed. "I haven't heard that word in a long time myself."

"I am seriously considering coming over to the Land Between and learning some of this tech . . . what is that word?" He asked.

"Technology," Jhondar said. "And you would be most welcome. However, I must admit we were rather nervous using our magic here. It has been a long time since we have done that."

They rode until they came to a small stream, stopping just long enough for their horses to drink.

"We have to turn here and head back to the wagons," the Ankhourian scout said.

"Oh, that is wonderful," Etheria replied with relief. "I was so lost."

The sounds of the Evoos drums were heard in the distance.

"I'm afraid our 'friends' are not too happy with us. They are going to come after us and the fact that we have excellent scouts, well, so do they." Kybil waited a bit more while his horse drank its fill. "We are going to have to get back and warn the others as fast as possible."

Quickly, they mounted their steeds and rode fast and hard down the road toward the wagons. Scouts riding along the perimeter of the wagons saw them approaching fast.

"Get the wagons moving," Kybil yelled followed by a loud chirping sound.

The scouts turned their horses and raced into the woods to warn the wagons. Shortly, all the wagons pulled out of the woods onto the dirt road.

Other scouts were riding in from their assigned areas. "We have Evoos and demons coming in from the west and the east."

"How far away are they?' Kybil asked.

"They are coming pretty fast. We'll be lucky if we clear the forest before they reach us." She responded.

"Get the potions to the witches. Rakmor, please help them. We are going to need it." Kybil moved alongside Jhondar and Chief Wolf-claw. "We are going to have to make a run for it."

"Yes," Chief Wolfclaw agreed. "My brother and I will see to it that the children are put in the center of the wagons, so there is no chance for one of them falling out."

Kybil interrupted him, "Did you say, brother?"

"Yes," a smile went wide on his face. "Bear Stalker is my brother. What a great day this is for us. But for now, I must give orders for the safety of everyone." He moved toward the warriors and gave them their instructions.

Kess watched as warriors went to each wagon and gave them the information. She got off her mount and crawled back up on the wagon, next to Naomi, who was laying on the seat. She gently nudged her. "Better wake up sweetie, it's gonna get really bumpy pretty soon."

Naomi rubbed her eyes and sat up. "Want me to drive now Jainy?" She looked over at Kess. "Where'd you come from? Where's Jainy?"

She went back to drive the first wagon with her folks. So, I'm gonna be driving these here horses, partner." She said in her worst cowboy impression.

Say, how'd we get here?" She looked down at the path leading through the woods.

"You are a sound little sleeper," Kess laughed. "Okay, Naomi, you had better look for something to grab onto."

"I would, but he's riding a horse right now." She glanced back at the handsome Elven warrior riding behind their wagon.

Kybil signaled for all the wagons to move. The sounds of dragon wings could be heard coming toward them. "Maaleah? Rakmor?"

Rakmor's voice came from the back of the wagon. "We can hear it. We're working on it." Soon a mist poured out of the wagon and began to swirl over all the other wagons. "That'll give us some time," he shouted.

The dragon flew overhead, looking directly down at the wagons, but because of the magic spell, saw nothing. It disappeared from their view.

Another scout rode up to Kybil. Her horse was fidgeting and prancing about. She reached down and patted the horse's neck. "There are a couple hundred Evoos and demons headed our way. If we don't move quickly they will attack us from all sides."

The Evoos drums could be heard all around them, and they were getting closer. The sound of hundreds of Evoos droning mixed with the shrill scream of the demons became louder the nearer they got to the edge of the woods.

"Rakmor? Maaleah?" Kess called back to her. "They're going to cut us off before we clear the forest. Can't you guys do something about the Evoos, and demons headed for us?"

"Yeah," Naomi said nervously. "Now would be a good time."

Rakmor yelled to her. "Whatever we do we have to be careful not to destroy the mist overhead, or we will have dragons to deal with as well as the Evoos and demons."

"How about making the horses go faster? Got any magic for that? Just sending out suggestions here." Naomi piped up, holding tightly to the wooden seat she was sitting on.

"Now, I have to admit I never thought about that," Maaleah laughed.

"Me neither," Rakmor took a pouch from one of the many on the floor of the wagon. "Worth a try. We can't make it last for long, but it may be enough to get us past the demons and Evoos and out of the forest." He leaned out of the wagon and yelled to Kybil. "Kybil, tell all the warriors to pull in close to the wagons and warn the others in the wagons to hold on tight to something."

"This is going to take a little bit longer, but I think we can do it." The other witches began working feverously pulling out stones. Soon the sound of the witches chanting could be heard.

The Evoos' was getting closer now and the sound of their drums was pounding in everyone's ears.

"Anytime soon," Kess muttered to herself as she spotted the Evoos and demons coming through the woods. She looked back in the wagon and saw white smoke pouring out of it.

The smoke moved along the ground encompassing all the horses. Suddenly, the wagon jerked, causing Kess to fall backward. She grabbed onto the bench seat and held on. The horses almost seemed to be flying, she thought. She looked at the wagon wheels in front of her and realized the wheels were not touching the ground. "This is incredible," she gasped.

The Evoos and demons spotted the wagons and began running at full speed. They reached the road just as the last wagon passed them by. They screamed in anger and started running after the wagons and their riders.

The magic did not last long. But it was just enough for the wagons to clear the woods.

To everyone's relief, the Ankhourian fort loomed straight ahead. The horse's feet gently hit the ground and they never lost their stride as they raced toward the safety of the fort.

Arrows from the fort, shot over their heads spraying dust over them. Kess had no idea what was in the sparkling dust, but it did not seem to slow them down or hurt anyone.

The gates were already open as they rode in and closed immediately after the last wagon.

"We've got a couple of hundred Evoos and demons behind us," Kybil yelled to Sirel standing above them on the wall-walk.

"Welcome to Fort Ankhouri, everyone. Glad to see all of you," Sirel shouted out to the warriors. "Most of our warriors are in the city. We are shorthanded."

Sirel yelled down to the people in the wagons. "Get the women and children to the Center Structure." Quickly, she addressed the warriors as she descended toward them, "Be prepared to fight."

Two Spree dragons flew to the fringe of the forest; their green and purple scales glistened in the setting sun. They crept low across the grassy, shrub-covered landscape, almost completely invisible to the human eye. The ground cover was a perfect camouflage in the dusky part of the day as they crept closer.

CHAPTER EIGHTEEN

$\mathcal{T}$he wagons were pulled up beside the stables. Everyone climbed down from the wagons as the horses were unhitched. Most of them stood in awe staring at the inside of the fort. No one, other than an Ankhourian warrior, ever was allowed inside.

"This is huge," Kess said looking around. You could put two football fields inside here." Each of the four walls had three levels, with a walkway for each tier.

Sirel greeted Kess and the others. "We are proud of our compound. Along those two walls are the living quarters for the warriors. On that wall are the stables, a blacksmith area, and supply rooms where food and weapons are stored. There are only two gates into the fort; one is to the city below and the other is the gate leading to the Rils forest.

"Wow," was all Naomi could say.

Kess eyed the four large array of weapons that were artfully arranged on each side of the compound. There were bows, arrows, swords, spears, and shields, all readied for immediate use.

Kess and Kybil walked over to a pile of strange-looking metal shields that looked way too big to carry into battle. They were long and curved with slots cut in them. Next to them were arrows that looked thinner than the warrior's normal arrows, and the arrow tips glistened. She was so busy looking at everything she did not see Mac and Sirel walking toward her. "These arrows are spectacular. What are they for?"

"What took you guys so long?" Mac chided.

"We stopped for a picnic in the forest," Kess smirked. "Good to see you, too," she laughed.

"Everybody here?" Mac looked around at all the people milling about.

"All safe and accounted for," Kybil said.

"Everybody here with you?" Kess asked. Her voice filled with concern.

"All safe and accounted for, too. The boys, I mean, young men are deeply enthralled with the Ankhourian warriors. Drago and Xen flew off a while ago to do a reconnaissance, and I think to grab something to eat. Baalizar is checking everything out and complaining as usual." Mac smiled down at Kess. "Now, where were you before I rudely interrupted you? Oh, yes, back to the "spectacular" arrows."

Sirel picked up one of the arrows and pointed to the sharp and glittering point. "These arrows have been designed by our blacksmith, and a little help with some magic to sharpen them. They have found a use for these bright stones." She touched the sparkling tip of the arrow. "They are very hard and can pierce through armor; a dragon's armor."

Mac took the arrow from her and turned it over in his hand. "Kess, doesn't that look like a diamond on the end of it?"

Kess took the arrow and let out a small whistle, "It sure does." She placed the arrow back on top of the neatly stacked arrows.

"Let me show you our Center Structure." Sirel led them into the center of the compound where poles about twelve inches in diameter, and about eight feet high, stuck out from the ground. The poles ran the entire length of a forty-by-thirty-foot structure. On top of the poles lay a thick sod and mud roof. Sirel took Mac and the others to the center of the structure.

"We use this as protection from the dragon's fiery breath. We call it the Center Structure." She laughed and shrugged. "Not very original. The poles have been magically constructed so that the dragons cannot pull them out, nor can they remove the sod panels on top of them. At times, they have tried to land on this to destroy it, but the poles and sod roof has remained standing as you see it." Sirel gestured proudly to the dragon-proof structure.

"But most interesting is the escape tunnel. This fort was built centuries ago. We have no idea who built the fort, or how they built the tunnels beneath us." Sirel motioned for a couple of Ankhourian warriors to lift the false floor of sod to expose two large, wooden doors underneath.

"The ramp you see leads down to a vast chamber with many tunnels that lead away from the fort. We are constantly on a vigil to keep the food and water fresh just in case we might have to use it."

"Captain!" A warrior called out to Sirel. "Our warriors are coming back with the town's people. They are fighting the demons and are greatly outnumbered."

"Open the gate to the city. Sentries stay your posts. Ready the demon spray." Sirel's orders were obeyed without question. "Have the families brought to the Center. Pull up the sides for protection."

The Ankhourian warriors quickly grabbed the rope handles of the sod lying outside of the Center structure. It was pulled up to protect the group inside from arrows and a dragon's fire.

Sirel pointed to the warriors who had come over from the Land Between. "Start getting the women, children, and elderly into the underground chamber. You other warriors come with me." Sirel ran toward the gate that led to the city.

Outside the fort, the Ankhourian warriors were fighting for their lives. They were cutting and hacking into the demons with a ferocity Kess had never seen before.

Naomi, Danny, Brody, Jainy, and a few others were ordered to stay by the gate to protect it if any demons broke loose and tried to get into the gate. Brody was grabbed by Mac. "Listen to me. You must resist the urge to join the warriors fighting the demons, because if you go into this battle, your friends will follow you and surely be killed."

Brody nodded and gave a half-smile.

Kess, Mac, and Rakmor raced through the open gate and into the midst of a raging battle. Maaleah and the witches hurried to the battlement walkway and began using their magic to destroy the mass of demons.

Jhondar, Etheria, Doc, and Baalizar rushed to the battlement. They stationed themselves overlooking the field located between the fort and the forest. Etheria caught the glimmer of something moving in the tall grasses surrounding the fort when silently two dark figures rose into the sky. "Maaleah!" Etheria screamed. "Dragons!"

Maaleah and another witch drew out a magic potion and hurled it at the dragons. But only one dragon fell from the sky. "Lookout! One has escaped." Maaleah yelled back.

The remaining dragon flew overhead, out of reach of the new arrows, and headed for the warriors fighting outside the fort. Suddenly, Drago and Xen appeared and flew toward the lone, deadly Spree dragon. The green dragon was twice their size, but not as quick. Drago and Xen darted and attacked the dragon, drawing it away from the battle raging below.

The large Spree dragon homed in on Xen, thinking to destroy one and then get the other. But Drago came in from behind striking it on the back of the neck. The huge dragon wavered a moment and then turned toward Drago. Xen seized the opportunity to create a diversion. She sent a mental image of Drago being twice the size of the Spree dragon.

The attacking dragon stopped and looked at the now enormous Drago and quickly retreated.

"We are not safe, Drago," Xen said. *"He has gone to get help."*

"Let's help where we can now," Drago began to descend on the demons below.

Xen sent a message to Maaleah who was sending down bolts of destruction into the demon horde below. Quickly, Maaleah pulled a pouch from her cape pocket and withdrew a silver glowing stone. She put it in her hand, said a few words, and instantly a silver streak flew out into the sky. Then, she turned her attention back to the war raging below.

The Ankhourian warriors had kept the townspeople moving toward the fort as they fought off the demon advances. The Indian and Elven warriors reached the badly outnumbered and tired Ankhourian warriors and began fighting alongside them. They kept moving toward the entrance to the gate as the demons kept coming. The fighting was intense, as the warriors tried to fight off the mass of demons pushing toward them.

Several demons formed a wedge and attempted to break the circle of warriors to get inside. But Drago and Xen cut a fiery path of death, causing them to scatter.

Doc saw that Evoos were advancing straight for the demons to help them in their fight. He raced down the steps and spotted Rakmor in the middle of the fighting. Doc hurried to his side. A few arrows almost struck Rakmor, who was using his shield and magic effectively to protect the warriors from arrows being shot at them. Doc grabbed his arm. "The Evoos' are almost here. There must be several hundred of them."

"Thanks. Now get back through the gate. I'll cover your back. I'll get Kess and Mac." Rakmor looked down at Doc and yelled. "Move."

A couple of Evoos lunged toward Doc, and Rakmor took them down with a burst of light. Doc made it to the gate and was grabbed by Brody and pulled to safety.

Rakmor pushed through the center of the townspeople and spotted both Kess and Mac fighting side-by-side. "Cover them," he yelled to a couple of Indian warriors, who quickly took out the demons fighting Kess and Mac in one fast movement.

"There are too many for us to fight, and the Evoos are just about here," Rakmor said. "You must get up on the wall and use your amulets."

Kybil heard Rakmor and yelled to a couple of Ankhourian warriors, "Protect Kess and Mac at all costs."

Rakmor stayed in the fight trying to use his magic to deflect the arrows of the demons from hitting any of the warriors.

Kess and Mac made it back through the gate and rushed up the steps to the fort walkway.

They ran down the wall-walk until they were directly in line with the demon horde. Demon arrows were flying all around them as they moved along the wall to position themselves.

"If we take out the demons the Evoos will run," Mac yelled over to Kess.

"Right," she shouted back.

Baalizar stood between Kess and Mac's position throwing up a protective shield for both to deflect the arrows from the demons and now the Evoos.

Several demons managed to use ladders to scale the wall. Three Ankhourian warriors immediately charged toward them and were joined by Jhondar and Etheria. The demons were quickly dispatched but more were climbing over the wall.

Mac and Kess held their talismans high in the air and called forth the power in them.

They stood there with their thoughts aimed at destroying the demons. Suddenly, a great light exploded from their talismans. A powerful wind, filled with shards of lightning, surged down the outside wall and into the mass of demons below. The wind worked its way around the warriors destroying every demon it touched. Those that had escaped its deadly surge turned and ran away. And just as Mac had predicted they were followed close behind by the cowardly Evoos.

Kess and Mac both fell to their knees with exhaustion. But it took them only a few moments to regain their strength and get to their feet.

Kybil had assisted a wounded warrior into the compound, and when the warrior was led away by a Sabbot, he began looking for Kess. He spotted her kneeling on the walkway and was up the stairs next to her before she could even take a step. He grabbed her arm and gently helped her down the stone steps to the main compound.

Sirel came through the gate, helping a wounded warrior. "Close the gates. Everyone is in." Sirel ordered. "Get these townspeople down to the chambers with the others,"

The doors to the underground chamber were opened and the townspeople quietly filed down a dirt ramp that led to a vast open area. The area beneath the great walls extended out to create a place for the warriors to sleep and eat. There was also ample room for all their horses if needed.

Mac watched as the wounded were being led underground. He estimated there would be over three hundred people in the underground facility. The only ones left above were those who were physically fit to fight or help in the fight some other way.

Sirel walked to Jhondar and Etheria. "I think it would be wise for you two, and Jainy to go down into the shelter with the rest."

"No," Jhondar said emphatically. "We will stay and help fight. You will need all the help you can get, especially if the Zetche appears with the Skull of Semetter."

"We're not going either," said Brody.

"We're not?" Marcus asked surprised. "You mean we're gonna stay and fight dragons?" His voice cracked.

"Yeah," Brody said. "Stay by me, you'll be okay."

Etheria and Sirel went down into the chamber and surveyed the people milling around.

Sirel looked sharply around the cavern and all the people who were ushered down there. "This is not a good place for them. If we fall they would only have a couple of day's rations." She turned to the warriors who had come from the Land Between. "I want you to take them down this passageway to Castle Remat."

They started to object when she raised her hand. "I am in

command here. You have long been away, and I will not have you perish before you have had a chance to see your families and loved ones. But I must warn you. This may be a dangerous journey. If the demons have found these tunnels, they may need your expertise in fighting to protect them."

Some of the Land Between warriors were about to protest again when Etheria moved in front of them. "She is in command. You will do as she bids." She smiled warmly at her warriors. "Guard these people well and be safe."

"It will take you close to the Castle of Remat. They will have better resources in protecting them. Baalizar, I am commanding you to escort them as well. They may have need of a great sorcerer." Sirel's voice was firm as she addressed the wizard.

"Do I have to walk again?" He asked with great disdain.

Sirel smiled. "No, I think we can provide horses for the children, and for those who are tired and weak."

Etheria looked at the wounded warriors. "Sirel, these warriors are going to need immediate help. Will it take them long to get to the castle?"

"With all the women and children, plus the elderly it will take them a couple of hours longer," she replied.

"These warriors won't make it. They need to get there faster than that." Etheria said adjusting the bandage on a warrior's deep wound.

Sirel ordered one of her warriors to count the seriously wounded. "After your count get enough horses and gurneys for them. Hurry." She pointed to several Indian, Elven, and Ankhourian warriors who were all from the Land Between. "Go with her, she will need help with all the horses."

The warriors quickly counted the wounded and hurried out of the shelter. They returned within minutes with gurneys attached behind each horse. The wounded were strapped onto the gurneys and helped to be made as comfortable as possible.

Sirel turned to some of the warriors from the Land Between.

REVENGE OF THE DEMON

"You will ride with my warriors and help them take the wounded to Castle Remat. My warriors are familiar with the false turns in the tunnels, so follow their lead. May your journey be safe." Sirel saluted them as they headed swiftly down the tunnel.

Doc made one last adjustment to a wounded warrior and nodded to the lead Ankhourian that it was now okay to start their trip to the Remat Castle.

Sirel watched solemnly for a moment and then turned to speak to the much larger group heading to the castle. "Listen up." She waited until the people quieted down. "My warriors are in command. They will lead you safely through. Stay as quiet as possible as you weave through the tunnels. I leave you now." She hesitated for a second. "For those of you that have made the journey to us from the Land Between I am sorry your return into Mystovia has been one of war. Welcome home and be safe." She gave the warriors a salute and left.

Etheria and Sirel hurried up to the Center Structure. "Close this up," Sirel ordered to the warriors waiting at the top of the ramp. The doors were closed, and the sod was replaced to hide the entrance.

"The green dragon that escaped has gone back for reinforcements." Drago let everyone read his thoughts.

"They will send many dragons, plus the Drakluf dragons will be among them." Xen sent her thoughts as well.

"We must be prepared for aerial attacks, as well as from the ground," Sirel said to a warrior standing near her. "Give the warning to prepare for a dragon and ground attack."

The Ankhourian warrior grabbed a large, twisted horn and raced out of the Central Structure to the center of the courtyard. She blew into the horn causing deep, resonant sounds to burst forth and repeated the signal a few times.

Kess, the teens, and Mac watched with amazement as the warriors immediately responded to the horns signal. They ran to one of the piles of weapons that were placed on all four sides of the fort. The Ankhourian warriors grabbed a large bow and put slender, diamond-tipped arrows in their quivers. Each grabbed one of the larger, strange, shaped shields. They motioned for the Indian and Elven warriors to do the same.

After everyone was fully equipped they hurried back to the fort walkway. There the Ankhourian warriors showed the Elven and Indian warriors how to affix the large shields to the battlement walls.

The battlement walls had slots in them with metal knobs sticking out. They pulled on the knobs and a couple of long, thin metal pieces came out to create metal legs on either side. The warriors attached the large metal shield to it giving them protection from a direct assault from the front. There was a three-foot opening on each shield for them to see and effectively fire their arrows.

Soon, all the shields were in place. There was room enough for two warriors in each encasement, with plenty of room to maneuver with their bows and arrows.

Naomi, Marcus, and Brody were told to stay under the Center Structure because they were not familiar with using bows and arrows. Reluctantly, Brody moved under the sheltered area and stood with the other people that were there to help but could not shoot bows and arrows either.

"This is more like it," Marcus smiled and sat on the ground. "No dragons can get in here. Yep, I'm liking this."

"I do not like being ordered to stay out of the fighting," Brody fumed.

Drago and Xen flew under the protective covering. "*We heard you Brody. Xen and I were ordered to stay here to protect you when you have to bring the warriors what they will need.*"

"Bring what to the warriors? Marcus asked.

"*You must bring weapons to them if they run out of them,*" Xen replied.

"Okay," Brody said, almost smiling. "I feel a little better about that."

"I don't," Marcus groaned.

The loud booming sound of a gong rang down to the teens under the Center Structure.

"What was that?" Naomi asked.

"*It was a warning,*" Drago said solemnly. "*The dragons have been sighted and are headed our way.*"

CHAPTER NINETEEN

*T*he thin line of gold light, made by the setting sun, was broken by a dark moving mass. The green and purple scales of the Spree dragons twinkled sporadically against the last light of day as it inched its way into darkness.

"Oh, boy," Kess quipped. "There sure are a lot of them."

"They're concentrating all of their strength coming from the west," Sirel looked puzzled. "Something is not right."

"Kess," Mac grabbed her arm. "I don't think we should wait until they attack. We can use our powers to stop them before they get here."

"Wait, until they get a little closer," Sirel touched his arm. "I'll tell you when."

They waited for a few moments until Sirel gave the signaled.

Quickly, they brought their talismans up and aimed them at the approaching dragons. A powerful blast burst out aimed directly at them. But only a couple of dragons were caught in its deadly ray. The other dragons separated, and the blast went past them hurling harmlessly into the air.

"This isn't good," Kess was stunned and saddened by their failed attempt.

"It's like they knew it was coming," Mac shook his head.

"It is not a possibility," Sirel shrugged and took up her place under the metal shield. "They do not have the ability to read other minds. There is something else behind this. You two must get down to the shelter area. You're no good to us up here."

Mac and Kess hurried down the steps and raced under the shelter.

"What happened?" Doc asked.

Kess explained to him what had happened.

"Oh, great," Marcus sighed. "Their powers aren't working against those really, really big dragons. What's wrong with this picture?"

"You're going to be fine, Marcus." Mac patted his shoulder.

Jhondar had followed Mac and Kess into the Center Structure. "I know what has happened. They are under the spell of the Zetche, and he has to be very near in order to have warned them."

"*Mac!*" Drago's mental scream was heard by all before he even reached the Central Structure. "*The Draklufs are coming in behind the warriors from the east wall. They're coming in low.*"

The warriors were deliberately distracted to fight on the west wall and unprepared for the attack behind them.

"Drago send a message. Warn the warriors," Mac yelled.

"*Already done,*" Drago replied.

Kess and Mac raced to the east wall and up the steps. Fear gripped them at the sight of a mass of Drakluf dragons and their demon riders advancing on the warriors who were busy fighting the Spree dragons on the other side of the fort.

One quick look at each other and Kess and Mac turned facing the advancing Drakluf dragons. They called forth the power of their amulets and this time it worked. A large group of Drakluf dragons burst into flames and fell like fiery globs behind the wall, and out of sight. The others were blown backward, spinning, and whirling into the distance.

"At least we did a little good," Kess sighed.

"I think we should stay up here on this side of the fort and keep an eye on the Draklufs approaching again," Mac said.

"One of us should go to the other side," Kess looked across the wide expanse of the fort.

"*Wait*," Drago and Xen yelled. "*Look.*"

Evoos and demons were crawling over the fort's walls.

Now, the warriors were fighting the dragons in the air, plus the Evoos and demons in hand-to-hand combat.

"Now!" Brody yelled racing for the battlement. "Now we can help!" He took three steps at a time to help a warrior fighting off the demons and Evoos.

Danny, Marcus, Naomi, and Jainy followed him as they ran out of the Center Structure sprinting up the stairs.

The Center Structure was emptied as everyone grabbed a sword and headed to the fort walls to help in the fight, leaving only a few of the women and men who stayed behind to help with the wounded when needed.

Mac ran across the fort grounds, and up the steps next to Sirel, taking out any Evoos or demons who tried to attack her from behind. He was out in the open fighting with no protection from the dragons overhead.

Kess and Kybil stayed on the east wall fighting alongside the other warriors as the Evoos and demons kept advancing over the walls.

Drago and Xen flew down to the Center Structure and gathered arrows for the warriors. They also kept a vigil over those fighting in the open, warning them to duck periodically under the protection of the metal shields.

A dragon managed to break through the defenses and with its sharp talons reached down and grabbed for Danny. Brody, who was fighting next to him, roared with anger and brought his sword down on one of the extended talons, shearing it off. The dragon screeched in pain and flew backward, knocking into another dragon, causing them both to fall clumsily to the ground. Sirel swiftly aimed at the fallen dragons, piercing their armor platelets, and killing them instantly.

The witches stationed themselves along the walls. The sight of the dragon almost breaching the fort compound startled them. Instantly, they communicated with each other and created a protective barrier that prevented the dragons from getting beyond the walls and into the compound.

"*We are almost out of arrows,*" Drago said, depositing several arrows in front of Sirel.

"I know," she aimed and struck another dragon. "We are going to have to fall back to the Center. Its magic is powerful enough to protect us for a while. The warriors are getting weak from all of this fighting."

"*These arrows are only wounding most of the dragons,*" Drago stated as he looked up into the sky.

Sirel aimed at another dragon in the distance. "Only a couple of the dragons came close enough to the wall to get a good shot. They seem to be waiting for something."

"Maybe the witches' spell has kept them from attacking," Mac took out another Evoos climbing over the wall.

"The demons and Evoos are constantly attacking from the ground, and pulling our strength, and the dragons are pulling our resources. I don't like it." Sirel shook her head. "Look at the warriors, they're exhausted."

"What we need is a little rest period, and they don't seem to be wanting us to do that," Mac struck down a couple of demons with his sword.

"I have come to know how that Zetche thinks," Jhondar said killing a couple of Evoos. "That is exactly what he is thinking. He wants to wear us down, and then he will strike himself." He pushed an Evoo back over the ledge of the wall.

"What can we do?" Mac asked.

An Evoos charged him and was slain before he got close enough to use his sword. Another Evoos did not stand a chance against Mac's long arms. Mac picked up the dead Evoos and threw him at another Evoos trying to climb over the wall. Both Evoos fell to the ground below.

"Something's not right," Sirel moved to Mac and Jhondar. "Our warriors are having no problem taking out these demons or the Evoos."

"Exactly," Jhondar rested for a moment on the hilt of his sword. "I think he enjoys this part. He lets us think we are winning. It is like a cat and mouse game to him. Us being the mouse. Then he brings a big surprise to destroy us."

"I think the dragons are pretty big," Mac said.

"Yes, but they haven't attacked us yet. They are out there flying around almost as if teasing us. Once in a while, a couple will come in close, but the rest stay back. The Zetche has something else planned for us, trust me on that." Jhondar picked up his sword and knocked another Evoo back over the wall.

"Then, we have to regroup. What if we pulled everyone off the wall and went to the Center Structure?" Mac asked.

"He would have us trapped in there," Jhondar said.

"But he doesn't know about the underground tunnels." Mac pushed a demon over the ledge with his sword.

"Yes, but he is a very intelligent creature: He would find it." Jhondar shook his head.

Just then Maaleah and another witch came running up to them. "Quickly, drink this. Don't ask questions, just drink the stuff." Maaleah handed them a flask. "We're giving this to everybody." She laughed, and after everyone had a sip, she grabbed the flask and went to the next group of warriors on the fort wall-walk.

All the witches were running from person-to-person making sure everyone drank some of the liquid. Then, the witches spaced themselves all along the length of the wall-walks.

"What are they up to?" Mac asked unaware that he kept licking his lips from the bitter liquid he was forced to drink.

Rakmor joined Mac on the walkway. "We have created a potion that may give us a little break for a while." He stepped back and closed his eyes. "We begin."

A mist began to rise around Rakmor and the witches until it became a dense thick cloud of smoke. The smoke traveled down the walls and encompassed all the demons and Evoos that were attacking. They fell to the ground looking like a large hairy carpet. Then the smoke rose into the sky. The giant dragons flew into the thick mist and slowly began falling. But the Drakluf dragons and their riders fell like rocks to the ground.

"It is done," Rakmor slumped forward a little. Mac caught him and steadied him.

"Did you kill them?" Sirel asked.

"No, our magic is not that powerful. But we managed to put them to sleep for a while. We can only rest for an hour or more. Etheria warned us of the Zetche's fighting habits. This was the quickest spell we could think of."

"We can go out and kill them while they sleep," Marcus said bent over from exhaustion.

"No, it would break the spell," Rakmor spoke sadly. "Everyone in here was given a potion to keep them from falling under the Sleeping Mist spell. If someone were to break out of the protective barrier, it would cancel the spell immediately. I am sorry, that was the best we could do."

"Rakky," Mac slapped his shoulder. "That is a wonderful spell. Let's get down off this wall, get something to eat, and rest before they begin to wake up."

"I will stay as one of the lookouts," Sirel motioned for the others to leave.

"Sirel," Rakmor took her arm. "You need to rest and eat something. They are going to need you as their leader. Put only a couple of sentries to stay the watch and have them brought food and drink. They can rest at their posts."

"I will have them brought food and drink. After I have eaten I will rejoin my warriors." Sirel gave the order to her Lieutenants who passed the orders on.

Sirel moved quickly down the steps. Her first actions were to have food and drink taken to the warriors left on the wall. The wounded warriors were brought to the Center Structure where Doc, the Sabbots, and the civilians began caring for them.

Everyone welcomed the quiet respite. Sirel had her food and drink and then stood up to return to her post. "I want the sod removed from the doors leading to the chamber below. We may have to use it in a hurry. I want the gate to the chamber guarded at all times just in case they have found the tunnels. We don't need any surprises."

"I will place a couple of the most powerful witches to guard the gate to the chamber below. If anything, other than a friend tries to come up, they will not make it into the compound," Maaleah nodded to Sirel.

The sod was removed, and the gate unlocked. Sirel returned a nod of approval and began walking to her post on the battlement. Mac was close behind her.

"Is that where your quarters are?" He asked curiously pointing to the long row of three-story buildings up against one of the fort walls.

"My quarters are not there. That is where our regular, non-officer, warriors are billeted. The officers' quarters are on the other side by the war room on the ground floor. "I'll show you."

They passed a long row of stables for the horses and storerooms for food, weapons, and carts. At the far end of the wall were several doorways. "Commander Fraanel's quarters are next to mine." She pulled a lit torch from the wall and opened the unlocked door to her quarters.

It was a sparsely furnished room, with a small dresser, a bed covered with a coarse-looking blanket, and a table with a couple of chairs. The walls had no decorations, and the small window to her room had shutters instead of curtains. A door in the room opened into a small bathroom. A mirror hung over the stone sink. Mac was surprised to see a toilet and what looked like a shower. He walked back out into the small room and opened the doors to an armoire sitting against the wall.

"I don't see any dresses in here," he scratched his head.

"I have no need for them," she said watching him inspect her room.

"There are no nightgowns. What do you wear to sleep in again?"

"Nothing," she smiled. "Let me show you something."

Mac's face lit up.

Sirel moved Mac away from the armoire. "We never want to be trapped in our quarters." She pushed a hidden lever inside of the armoire, and the back of it opened up. "Come look."

Disappointed she was not going to show him what she didn't sleep in, Mac shrugged and peered inside the secret door of the armoire. There was a long hall running the entire length of the fort. "Wow, that's impressive."

"The warriors have the same thing on their side. If the fort were overrun while we were sleeping, we would be able to escape through here. It leads to the main gate and underneath the gate is a tunnel that leads us back to the chamber below the Center Structure."

"How do you deal with the constant threat of being attacked?"

"It is our way of life. Do you not have warriors who are constantly on guard in your world?"

"Yes. Yes, we do," Mac said. "I guess I just never thought about the vigilance that a soldier must have. Being a police officer you're constantly on guard when you're on duty, but when you're through with your shift you go home and relax."

"Oh, but we relax as well." She looked at him and smiled. "We are given time away from the fort to visit our families and friends. We have many things we do to relax and enjoy ourselves."

"Like what?" He asked looking around at her sparse furnishings.

"We travel, play games, fish, and hunt, play music, and enjoy our friendships."

"You mentioned visiting your family and friends. Where is your family?"

"My mother was an Ankhourian warrior. She has since passed to the Fields of Diophanies. I was raised here at the fort."

"I didn't see any young girls in the fort."

"A couple of them have remained, but most of them were moved to the Castle Remat earlier for their safety. But they will be brought back when this is done."

"How many years does it take to become an Ankhourian warrior?"

"It takes many years of training and is an ongoing process. But not all girl-children want to be an Ankhourian warrior, and when that happens, we send them to homes where they will be loved and cared for. Those that are brave and can take the grueling training are given a permanent home here."

"When a warrior wants to leave is she given a hard time? I mean you put a lot of training into them."

"Mercy, no!" Sirel laughed. "This is not a prison. Any warrior is free to go whenever she wishes with no recriminations."

"Then how do you keep these warriors here? I mean your lives are so . . . so sparse here."

"How do you keep your warriors, or police officers doing what they do? We give our women food, shelter, friendship, but most importantly we are more family than anything else."

"Okay," Mac rolled his eyes. "I've got to ask this. Why don't you have men in here?"

Sirel laughed. "We are asked that all the time."

"Um. . . do the . . . do your warriors hate men?" He smiled as he looked at her beautiful face.

Sirel laughed. "No. We do not hate men, nor do we fear them. Let me explain as best I can. Centuries ago, our men would be sent out to fight a war and would leave their village of women, children, and the elderly unprotected. The men would be killed in battle, and then the enemy would sweep in and kill everyone in the village. So, the women were taught to fight and fight well. It has evolved into what you see today."

"But what happens when a warrior is killed? What happens to her offspring?"

"If the child is here in the fort they are well cared for. If a warrior leaves and then dies before the child reaches adulthood, we step in and help support the child until they are old enough to take care of themselves."

"What becomes of the male-children of an Ankhourian warrior? I mean are they warriors, too."

"Male-children are allowed to go into any profession they so choose."

"I am so relieved that you're not a bunch of man-hating, warmongers that our world has so ignorantly said you were."

"Man-haters, absolutely not. The other thing, believe it or not, is that we hate war. If only this world and the world you came from could live in peace."

"I know what you mean."

"But we must accept the demons, Evoos, and other creatures that roam our world and be prepared for battles that will most certainly come our way." She walked over to Mac, leaned over, and gave him a quick kiss on the lips.

She turned and headed toward the door. "I have to get back to my post. We will have to continue this at a later time."

Mac was so startled he could not even talk. Sirel grabbed the torch from the wall and opened the door. He finally managed to get a few words out. "What . . . when . . . later? I mean, later what? When?"

"Trust me, you will know when." She left the room, putting the torch back into its holder outside her room.

They walked out of her room to find Rakmor and Kybil standing there looking at the two of them. Rakmor and Kybil gave Mac a huge smile and a nod.

Mac returned the smiles and winked. "She's got a really nice room."

"Oh, yes," Kybil said playfully. "They're such comfortable, regal rooms."

Mac shrugged, laughed, and followed Sirel up the stairs to the parapet.

"Well, I had better check with Maaleah and see what's going on," Rakmor said and headed over to Maaleah who was in a huddle with the other Sabbots outside of the Center Structure.

Kybil walked past them and inside the Center Structure. He spotted Kess helping Doc take care of a wounded warrior. He leaned against the pole and watched her until Kess looked up and saw him standing there. She finished helping with the wounded warrior, excused herself, and went over to Kybil.

"Everything still quiet?" She asked.

"So far," Kybil smiled down at her. "Why don't you take a little break? Come on, there are a couple of benches over there against the wall."

"Um. . . Kybil? Can I ask you a couple of, well, personal questions?"

"Sure, go ahead," he said as they walked away from the Center Structure.

"Are you involved with someone? I mean married, promised to be married? I mean are you in love with an Elven princess? Do care about someone dearly? You have never talked about your private life."

He laughed softly. "I am . . ." He never got to finish his sentence.

"Ahem," Rakmor cleared his throat. "I think our 'friends' are starting to wake up." He reached over and gave a quick pat to Kybil's arm." And, when there's time you two do need to talk." He laughed and walked away.

"Come on, we have to get to our posts," Kybil released his hold on her arm. "I really would prefer it if you stayed in the Center Structure."

"No, I am going to cover your back, like before," she ran to keep up to his long strides.

The battle raged for another hour as the weary warriors continued their fight against the demons, dragons, and Evoos.

Suddenly, the sound of screeching filled the air. The two moons in the sky shone brightly that night, and a glimpse of red wings could be seen in the distance. The Arega dragons had arrived. They burst on the scene with a vengeance. The air battles between the dragons were fast and deadly.

On the ground, bursting through the Center Structure gates came hundreds of Indian, Man, and Elven warriors; male and female, led by Commander Fraanel. They raced to the battlements and began fighting the stunned demons and Evoos. The fight continued, as the demons kept advancing on the fort.

Mac and Kess, both exhausted from fighting, were catching their breath when they looked over the wall of the fort and froze in place.

CHAPTER TWENTY

A Spree dragon slowly rose from behind the wall in front of them. It was low enough to spray its deadly flame, but what made it more terrifying was what was riding on the dragon's back. It was the Zetche. A black grin crossed its face as if studying its prey before him.

The Zetche never took his eyes off Kess and Mac as his smile grew bigger. Behind him were hundreds of Drakluf dragons and their demon riders. He raised the Skull of Semetter and pushed it forward toward Kess and Mac. He threw back his head and laughed. But when he looked back at Kess and Mac they were not alone: Jhondar and Etheria stood next to them.

The Zetche was stunned for a moment and then smiled again. "This is more than I had hoped. I shall destroy all of you at once," he bellowed. He smiled as Mac held his amulet toward him; just as Kess was raising her ring.

"I fear not your power. I have mastered the Skull of Semetter. Now feel its power," he screamed and smiled. Suddenly, the smile on his face was replaced by shock. His two mortal enemies from the

Land Between were standing before him with a skull. "No," he screamed. "This is a trick. There is only one Skull. This is a trick."

He regained his composure and aimed the skull at them again. He called upon the dragon to breathe its deadly fire on them, and for the demon riders to send their poisoned arrows. "Along with my demons and my powers, those standing before me shall be destroyed. I wanted you all to die separately, but to watch you all be destroyed together is much better," he said.

The four of them stood there facing the Zetche riding on the Spree dragon and the mass of Drakluf dragons and their riders. They knew what they had to do.

Instantly, the Zetche's power merged with the skull, the dragon's fiery breath, and the poisoned arrows of the demon riders.

But none of it reached the wall. It was met with a force greater than anything ever felt in Mystovia before. At first, the two powers met and seemed to hang in mid-air for a second, and then there was an explosion that shook the foundation of the fort.

The explosion of the two forces meeting burst forward engulfing the Zetche in a brilliant light that had formed around him. He screamed for a moment and then disappeared. The Drakluf dragons and their riders burst into flames and fell sizzling to the ground. The giant Spree dragon that the Zetche rode was dead at the base of the wall.

Everyone stopped fighting when the explosion ripped through the air. The Evoos, Spree dragons, and the demons were released from the controlling power of the Zetche. They all turned, almost in unison, and fled away from the fort.

A roar went up from the fighting warriors at the sight of their enemy running away from the fort.

Everyone was hugging everyone, although Naomi held onto a handsome young elven warrior a little too long. He caught Brody's eye and motioned to him.

"How's about a hug, Naomi?" Brody winked at the warrior as she reluctantly released him.

Naomi caught the wink, "Guess I got carried away." She walked over to Brody and embraced him.

The Elven warrior took her arm. "No, you didn't." He smiled at her and pointed to his ribs. "I got hit hard in the ribs, and it hurts; that's all. Other than that, I like your hugs."

Naomi blushed, "Okay, umm . . ." She was interrupted by an exuberant Danny hurrying over to them.

"Wow, this was better than a video game," Danny bent over trying to catch his breath. "I would have thought I was a great fighter, but I had two Indian warriors covering me all the time. Man, they were fantastic fighters."

"Yeah," Naomi said. "I had two Ankhourians protecting my butt. I was really glad they were there."

"Look at these warriors," Danny shook his head in amazement. "There are some amazing female warriors like – everywhere. Whoever heard of such a thing? And, boy can these females kick some booty."

"So, what do you think I am? I'm a female, and I can kick some serious booty." Naomi huffed. "Besides, I've lost a few pounds in the couple days we've been in the Land Between. I should be svelte in a couple of months."

"There's nothing wrong with you now," the Elven warrior said and bowed slightly to a now flustered Naomi. He looked down into the courtyard and pointed. "Hey, it's the Commander."

Sirel joined Commander Fraanel, who was conferring with the leader of the Arega dragons. "Were many of your warriors injured?"

"Only slight injuries, Commander, but I am saddened by the death of so many of the Spree dragons. Wars are such a waste of life. I hope we can make peace with them again and end this nonsense. There are many Sprees injured on the ground. They will send their healers and take the dead back to their dwellings. We must be gone to save their honor."

The Commander nodded as she glanced over the field covered with demons, Evoos, and dragons. "I completely agree with you about war being such a waste of life. What possessed them to keep coming like that? Usually, the Evoos retreat when they encounter such fierce resistance. That Zetche must have been enormously powerful indeed."

"It was not just the power of the Zetche. It was the Skull of Semetter that he used to magnify his powers" Jhondar said.

"When we sent forth the power from this skull," Etheria held up a lone skull in her hand. "At the same time, Jhondar and I pulled the other skull from the Zetches hands."

Jhondar held up the second skull. "We knew he wouldn't be prepared for that. Luckily, the skull was not destroyed during the explosion." He wrapped the skull in a thick cloth and put it in a burlap bag.

"But it was very strange." Etheria's lips pursed in thought. "The Zetche's skull seemed to come from a greater distance." She paused in thought for a moment and then continued. "Anyway, the Evoos, demons, and even the Spree dragons were under the mind control of the Zetche." She carefully wrapped her skull in a thick cloth and put it into the burlap bag with the other one. "Once we destroyed him and had the second skull they were released from his control."

Commander Fraanel nodded. "Yes, that would explain their unexpected behavior." She began to look around at the warriors and sighed with relief when she spotted Chief Wolfclaw walking toward her. She drew her attention back to Etheria and the Arega dragon.

"*We would like to offer our services to those that wish to go to Castle Remat*," the Arega dragon's deep booming thoughts were heard by all.

"I am sure that some of the warriors would welcome a ride to the castle. But before you go, we would ask one other favor of you. We will stack the dead Evoos and demons and would have you burn them for us."

"*Done. But my warriors and I will do the stacking as well. Your warriors have been battling long. Let them rest.*" He nodded and flew off to join the other Arega dragons.

The bodies of the dead Evoos and demons were carried and stacked in a pile far away from the fort. The Arega dragons blew their fiery breaths on the pile, and it burst into flames.

"We are ready to assist in getting you to Castle Remat. All of those that you sent through the tunnel arrived safely. I was told there was much celebration on the return of warriors lost years ago."

"We accept your generous offer. I, too, am looking forward to returning with great anticipation." Etheria said.

"Yes, it is safe to return now. We thank you for all that you contributed, and I look forward to meeting up with all of you when we are done here." Fraanel pointed to the activity at the edge of the woods. "Sirel, I need you to stay and make a report. You can go to Castle Remat when we are done repairing and cleaning up the fort." She scanned the fort again and nodded. "I can see you handled everything well, Captain. Extremely well, but I would expect no less from you. Now, we must get those who are leaving readied and quickly. The Spree dragons are waiting to collect their wounded and dead."

"Wait a minute," Danny said excitedly listening to the two women talking. "Are we going to ride on a dragon? I mean a real dragon. I rode a real Pegasus, and now I'm gonna ride on the back of a dragon? No way."

"Yes, way," Sirel laughed. "Let's get everyone who is going to Castle Remat readied now."

Kybil stood next to Kess. His face was solemn. "I have heard some unsettling news. I must return to Elhaven immediately."

"Nothing serious, I hope," Kess said touching his arm.

Kybil reached over and patted the top of her hand. "I don't know how long I will be gone. Stay safe."

Kess watched him fly off with the other Elven warriors on the backs of a few Arega dragons. She wished he were coming back to the castle with her. She sighed and started to look for Etheria and Jhondar. She found them conversing with Rakmor and the witches.

"We must get back to our village and see what damage the Evoos have done," Maaleah said. "I will come to the castle when I am done."

"Will it be safe for you to travel through the forest back to your village?" Kess asked worriedly.

"Our friends here," Maaleah pointed to the Arega dragons, "are going to fly us back. Just in case we have any dragons or Evoos lurking about."

CHAPTER TWENTY-ONE

aiting in one of the French doors was the figure of a woman. The first dragon landed, and two figures climbed down and hurried toward her. The Imperial Sorceress Cedwynna let out a gasp and sank to the ground. Cedwynna's fall was broken by the two sorcerer apprentices behind her. They grabbed her by the arms and gently pulled her back up. Etheria and Jhondar were the first ones to reach her.

Cedwynna and Etheria just stared at each other for a moment, and then Etheria threw her arms around her mother and held her tightly. Both women began crying and rocking each other. No one tried to pull them apart or interfere with their reunion.

After a while, Cedwynna pulled away and brought her hands up to cup Etheria's face. "I thought I would never see you again. I thought I would never see you again," Cedwynna repeated. She pulled Etheria back in her arms and held her tightly.

Cedwynna finally pulled away again and stepped back to look at Etheria. She took her hands in hers and kept shaking her head. "You are here. It is really you."

"Yes, mother," Etheria smiled through her tears. "I am really here."

"Oh, my," Cedwynna cried. She dropped one of Etheria's hands but held the other one firmly in her grasp. "Where is Jhondar?"

Jhondar stepped forward and leaned down to hug and kiss his sister. "It is wonderful to see you, Cedwynna. I would like you to meet your niece."

Jainy moved forward, tears running down her face. "How do you do Aunt Cedwynna?"

Cedwynna reached her arms out. "Oh, Jhondar she is beautiful. Come here so I may hug you as well." She embraced him and Jainy. Cedwynna looked around and spotted Kess, who was crying just as hard as her mother and grandmother. "Come here, child."

The three women embraced. Cedwynna kissed Etheria and Kess on the cheek and grabbed a couple of handkerchiefs from a pocket in her cape. "Let us get inside. The night air is chilly. Everyone," she yelled. "Please, let us go to the main hall where food and drink have been prepared for you."

Kess, Etheria, and Cedwynna walked arm and arm until they got to the door. Kess fell back and let Etheria and Cedwynna walk, with their arms around each other, through the door.

Jhondar came up and put his arm around Kess's waist. "Come on, niece." His other arm pulled Jainy to his side.

Cedwynna and Etheria never left each other's side. They sat together as they ate, but neither spoke until they were finished.

"What happened? How did you exist? What has happened to the others?" Questions poured out of Cedwynna.

Etheria began to tell her mother of all of the strange and some wonderful things that had happened over the twenty-five years of separation. She ended by saying, "Unfortunately, when we were thrust into the Land Between the two Zetches we were fighting entered with us. They managed to kill some of us, Xdalt, my dear husband, was killed during the fight." She stopped talking and looked over at Kess. "I have taken another mate. His name is Saaz, and he is a wonderful man."

"I have met him, grandmother, and he is a wonderful man."

"Where is he?" Cedwynna asked.

"He had to stay behind. We could not leave the city completely void of leadership. He wishes to meet with you the next time we come to visit."

"I would love to meet him. But my heart is heavy when you say the next time we come to visit." Selfishly, I was hoping you would stay for good."

"I love you, and Mystovia, but my home for the last twenty-five years has been in the Land Between. I have come to love that beautiful, barren, deadly land," she laughed and shrugged. "But I will be coming to see you more often than not. I have served our people well, and now it is time for me to step down in my leadership and let someone else do all the worrying."

"If you say you will be coming often, then I am more than happy with that arrangement." Cedwynna grasped Etheria's hand firmly. "How long are you staying?" Worry etched her face.

"I am going to be here for a long while." She rested her hand on top of her mother's. "I cannot leave you right now, and Saaz will be coming with the next wave."

"I think you are going to be quite pleased," Jhondar motioned for one of his warriors to come forward with a small device. "This device was created by the Plexias with the help of the Stone of Iszel."

He put the metal object on the table. It was a twelve-inch square block with the Stone of Iszel encased in the middle of it. "There are three of these. The Plexias cut the stone in thirds and created this energy booster that can open a door between our worlds anytime, and anywhere we wish. We no longer need to worry about the barrier wall, and where the door will eventually appear."

"Is this so?" Cedwynna asked excitedly.

"Yes, dear mother," Etheria said squeezing her hand gently. "It is so."

"That means we can come and visit one another anytime we want?" Kess was just as excited.

"Yes," Jainy moved closer to Cedwynna. "It means you can now open a door from here and the other stone will bring you inside of the city of Kelador. No one will have to travel through some of the very dangerous places in the Land Between."

"The teens as Mac calls them," Jhondar pointed to Danny, Naomi, Marcus, and Brody, "have used it to even go back to the Out World. They have been able to bring some of their things back over with them and even said their good-byes. They have no desire to leave the Land Between. In fact, Brody's two brothers are now in the Land Between."

"Yeah, and they're liking it," Danny said.

"And if we want to go home at any time, we can. It's a pretty good set up," Brody said.

"The device can be used to travel to different worlds with ease. But it must be protected at all costs. If someone were to steal it. . ." Jhondar was interrupted by Etheria.

"But Jhondar, they would have to know the code to use it, otherwise it is useless to them. Although, I do not know if we could make any more if one were stolen. Cutting the stone into three different sections made the stones perfect to work efficiently. Any smaller and there might be a problem. So, we do have to guard these devices well. And, this one," Etheria pointed to the one on the table, "is to be left here for you or anyone else to use. The magic in Mystovia will keep this one working forever. The two in the Land Between has both technology and magic to keep it working forever."

"This is wonderful news indeed," Cedwynna clapped her hands. "This has been a wonderful day for me." She looked over at Etheria, Kess, and the others. "But you must be exhausted. We shall continue everything in the morning, although, I am afraid to go to sleep for fear of waking up, and this was all but a dream."

"We shall be here in the morning, Mother." Etheria stood to leave, "You have brightened my world again."

Etheria hugged Kess before she left. "I will see you all first thing in the morning." She turned and looked at the teens sitting at the table. "Someone will show you to your room. The others know the way to theirs."

"Well, I may have forgotten after all these years," Etheria said.

"Come, I will show you to your old rooms," Cedwynna grabbed Etheria and Jhondar's arm. "Jainy, please come with us."

Jainy hurried toward them and waved goodbye to everyone in the hall. "See you in the morning."

Slowly, everyone filtered out from the dining hall until only Kess, Doc, and Mac were left. "We can go home anytime we want," Mac said.

"This is my home, Mac." Kess moved toward the large window and looked out into the darkness.

Mac walked over and stood beside her. "Yes, that is true. But I like the idea of being able to go back to what 'used' to be our home and see what is going on."

"Maybe someday. Sometimes I feel like what grandmother said that she was afraid to go to sleep for fear of waking up, and this was all but a dream."

Mac draped his arm around her shoulder. "Yes, that is a scary thought. I would hate that myself."

"Well, it is not," Rakmor said standing at the door.

"It definitely is not a dream," Sirel said walking past Rakmor into the room.

Mac turned around and a huge grin spread across his face at the sight of her. "Glad to see you and hear that."

"Hey, we see Drago and Xen coming here so, Nor and me followed dem," Yaneth said walking behind Rakmor into the room.

"Yep, we did," Nordaal sauntered into the room and to the large wooden table still loaded down with food.

Drago and Xen came in behind them. "*We may need both of your help*," Drago said.

"You have it, little buddy," Mac quipped. "What is it?"

"A strange and powerful force has been blocking the Oracles visions. But Xen has managed to break through the magic. It was only briefly, but it appears that our Chan-Draa is in danger. Xen sensed pirates and the emblem of the Durtsy Ock pirates before her vision ended."

"Dirty Socks pirates?" Doc's eyes widened.

"That is pronounced durt-see-ock," Rakmor ran his hand over his lips to keep from laughing. "Anyway, these pirates live in the harbor city of Durtsy Ock on the peninsula of Hawks Point."

"Well," Doc mumbled to himself. "It could have been a nickname because they have really dirty socks. I didn't know." He stopped. His eyes widened. "Wait a minute. Do you mean real pirates?"

"Oh, yes, real pirates," Sirel spoke up. "The pirates live mostly in cities on the West Coast of the peninsula. They are extremely dangerous indeed and are known to be a very, as you say, a rough crowd. They are treacherous cutthroats."

"Why is this Chan-Draa so vital to the Aregas and what is a Chan-Draa or Dragling?" Kess asked.

"The Chan-Draa is the Aregas High Sorceress and has extremely great powers. She is also a changeling. Her power enables her to transform into a dragon or any other form she chooses. Her magic not only protects the Aregas from any magic that may try to infiltrate their domain, but she can foresee any dangers that may affect them. All dragons have such a sorceress or sorcerer," Rakmor said.

"The Chan-Draa must be protected at all costs," Xen spoke quickly.

"She's right," Rakmor added. "Right now, we must get to the Arega Mountains and the Chan-Draa to protect her."

"The Chan-Draa is in council with the Celestials; the Silver Dragons of the north," Drago said. *"Xen and I will leave first thing in the morning to wait for her return. There is no need for your presence now. She is not expected to return for a couple of days,"* Xen said. *"Take this time to rest and enjoy each other's company."*

Mac strolled beside Sirel, "I like that idea. I like it very much."

Everyone headed out the double doors. "Well," Kess said walking next to Doc. "At least protecting the changeling will be a walk-in-the-park compared to all our other adventures in here."

Xen sent her thoughts to Drago, *"I feel like something is blocking my visions. But they cannot block my sense of foreboding and my overwhelming feeling that there is great peril for everyone."* Xen's chest heaved with a great sigh, *"Let them enjoy the next couple of days because her 'walk-in-the-park' might end up being their most deadly and dangerous mission of all."*

THE END

Dear reader,

We hope you enjoyed reading *Revenge of the Demon*. Please take a moment to leave a review, even if it's a short one. Your opinion is important to us.

Discover more books by S.A. Laughlin at https://www.nextchapter. pub/authors/sally-laughlin

Want to know when one of our books is free or discounted? Join the newsletter at http://eepurl.com/bqqB3H

Best regards,

S.A. Laughlin and the Next Chapter Team